"*Dirtyville Rhapsodies* combines a sharp-eyed satirical verve with pathos and compassion. These richly observed stories navigate the often bewildering terrain of contemporary America, from the hallucinatory reality of breastfeeding clinics to the spandex paradise of membership gyms.

Josh Green has a fine grasp of how to bring the rhythms and idioms of everyday life into the art of storytelling, and the sustained verbal inventiveness of his prose brings a compelling power and authority to this remarkable collection."

Dr. Patrick Hayes
Author of *J. M. Coetzee and the Novel*
St. John's College, Oxford University

"In *Dirtyville Rhapsodies* Josh Green does not shy away from tackling life's big themes head-on, and what he achieves in the space of a single story is remarkable.

The scope is big, the detail heartbreaking; from the husband in 'Missing Athena' who spots his abducted wife's umbrella rolling in the night breeze, 'caught between a bus-stop vestibule and a garbage can,' to the body builder ejected from his gym in 'The Delusional Mister Necessary,' who curls up on a curb and sucks his thumb, while inside, another has-been Hercules 'sits on the Lower Back Extender and rows his invisible boat.'

That tragedy and comedy go hand-in-hand is implicitly understood and used by Mr. Green to maximum effect: when the humor comes—and there is plenty—it is of the caliber to make a reader on a public bench turn to a stranger and grin.

The stories in *Dirtyville Rhapsodies* display an already maturing talent and are a fine credit to the genre."

James Manlow
Author of *Attraction*
Bournemouth, England

"Most of the characters in Josh Green's stories are, to echo Shakespeare's Brutus, 'bound in shallows and in miseries,' but that's not all they are. They're more than the sum of their sorrows, more than by-products of loss and unfulfilled desire.

Green's crackling, true-hearted prose allows us to see behind the sometimes hilariously sorrowful curtains of his heroes' troublesome lives and re-discover for ourselves the potentially redemptive power of empathy."

Tom Noyes
Author of *Spooky Action at a Distance and Other Stories*
and *Behold Faith and Other Stories*

———————

"Josh Green is a wonderful writer, and *Dirtyville Rhapsodies* is a stunning, rollercoaster ride of a book. Sit back and get ready to have the top of your head ripped clean off."

Robert Rebein
Author of *Dragging Wyatt Earp* and *Hicks, Tribes, & Dirty Realists: American Fiction after Postmodernism*

"This collection feels like a modern American neighborhood. Here stands a story with a secret. There stands a story with a missing child. Up the block lives the narcissist weight-lifter and, a few houses over, a couple off on a honeymoon that changes everything. Josh Green reports from the literary homeland with a lion's heart and a steady hand. This fine book belongs on the shelf with any other collection published in recent years."

Charles McNair, *Paste* Magazine

Praise for stories from
Dirtyville Rhapsodies

"Josh Green's sharp, in-the-moment prose captures universal feelings in a situation both mundane and peculiar. 'Blood Allies' is a short, potent study in brotherhood and insanity."

Eastown Fiction review of "Blood Allies"

———

"My favorite piece in [Lake Effect, Volume 13] is 'Twenty-First Century Itch' by Josh Green. The story starts with twangy sort of dialect I feared might weigh down the narrative flow, but I was pleasantly surprised at Green's ability to dial the technique back when appropriate, allowing a charming and sad story to unfold... Any story about this kind of topic runs the risk of being overly sentimental, but Green handles it deftly."

Robbie Dressler, Pacific University

DIRTYVILLE RHAPSODIES

STORIES BY JOSH GREEN

Acknowledgements

Full Book:

Finalist for the 2011 St. Lawrence Book Award

Stories:

The Baltimore Review: "Missing Athena"

Los Angeles Review: "Pinch Points"

The MacGuffin: "Exultation"

The Adirondack Review: "Clarity"

New South: "The Abduction"

Lake Effect: "Twenty-First Century Itch"

The Midway Journal: "The Bushmaster"

Eclipse Literary Journal: "Hanging Abdul"

Eastown Fiction: "Blood Allies"

Hoosier Writers Anthology 2010: "The Delusional Mister Necessary"

Main Street Rag's "Law and Disorder" Anthology: "The Gulch"

Creative Loafing (Atlanta):
"Down and Out at the Breastfeeding School"

For L and L

DIRTYVILLE RHAPSODIES

STORIES BY JOSH GREEN

Publishers Online!

For updates and more resources, visit
Dionysus Books and Parkgate Press online at

www.dionysusbooks.com
www.parkgatepress.com

Page layout by Dionysus Books
Cover design by Andy Kurzen

ISBN-13: 978-1-937056-63-6

Library of Congress Control Number: 2013936231
Library of Congress Subject Headings:

FICTION / Literary.
Short stories.
Short stories, American.
Short stories, American--Georgia.
Short stories, American--Southern States.

First Edition (worldwide) May 2013
[Parkgate Press: Dionysus Books reference number: 015]

DIRTYVILLE RHAPSODIES

STORIES BY JOSH GREEN

CONTENTS

"Every Night and every Morn
Some to Misery are Born
Every Morn and every Night
Some are Born to Sweet Delight
Some are Born to Sweet Delight
Some are Born to Endless Night…"

William Blake
"Auguries of Innocence"
The Pickering Manuscript (c. 1807)

TWENTY-FIRST CENTURY ITCH

———————

On the day my wife died I found myself in a Texas-style barbecue joint, dizzy on mojitos. I'd seen better days. Like those days for instance when the walls of a sorry beaten restaurant didn't bleed with my own misery. An old bluesman was onstage, coaxing crazy sorrow from a weathered Stratocaster. He sang about the sad train and how it comes hard down the midnight line. His voice was a rusty blunted knife, his black throat a piston of bad news. Not to blame him, but the bluesman triggered it all.

Without really thinking about it, I snatched up an empty beer bottle. I felt powerful just by holding it. Something had come over me, a dormant urge strangely boiling. Two booths over sat a blond man with corporate teeth and his Buckhead Betty beside him. I wanted nothing more than to hear a Pilsner bottle thud on the man's glassy forehead. I needed a new calamity, a diversion. So I threw the bottle—a real green laser and then smack. My reasoning was why the hell not. I didn't care. My wife had just died pitifully, the poor pretty girl. She was the victim of a sickness that was strange enough to attract the broadcast news vultures. They had descended on us quickly, picked us to the bone with their inquisitive little beaks. "Dependable. Accurate. To the Point. Atlanta's Only Local News at 11." Fuck those bastards.

The guy got up from the booth, clutching his forehead. That much was hilarious. But he was bigger than expected, a real linebacker, his fists like coiled steel. His face was blotchy and kind of glowing with so much rage. I wanted to say I'm just a skinny Army vet who likes barbecue with his sorrow. I tried to say my wife had been taken by a virus—that despicable, cowardly thing—and she wasn't a teacher anymore but a rotting hospital carcass. I steadied myself on both elbows but couldn't spit the first word. He was in no mood to listen anyhow.

Call me a cynic, but the world was letting me down again. This one could have been my fault—sure—but my generation isn't typically one to accept blame and stuff.

The guy was definitely taking his time, savoring the aroma of certain violence, I guess. His woman pleaded with him to sit down. He kept on coming. At least twenty other folks were in the joint— families devouring Brunswick stew and pulled pork and that jalapeno cornbread that's too dry. I was out of bottles or else I'd have let loose another one, dead-aim at those happy yuppie families. Then I'd have chucked a bottle at the bluesman. He was one of those classic Old South cats with huge pain balled up in him. I wasn't in the mood for his hurting face. And last thing I needed was a song about women spreading their traitorous selves up and down Beale Street.

"Hey, bucko," said the oncoming man. "What's wrong with you? Look at me. I said what's your problem?"

I didn't look at him so much as through him. Even with his bulk he didn't seem consequential, not when my Sue had withered and died. I imagined that his flesh was invisible and the roof of the barbecue shack was like glass and beyond that the smog gave way to bluest heaven and there I could see my girl frolicking in the clouds. But then he got in the way. He was certainly there, leaning over me. I tried to let my anguish boil visibly to my skin. I thought maybe my deepest sorrow could deter a charging man.

"It's been a bad day," I said. "Go back to Buckhead. Live richly, be happy, vote Republican. You're about to make me angry."

My wife and I were married under a deep row of those ghostly shaggy trees they have down in the Lowcountry. This was after the Army, after my lowest emotional ebb. She understood my frustrations with the world, and also my fears. Like me she was a rebel. But she wasn't so wild that she lost touch with the delicacy of womanhood. There was nothing better than Sue.

We had met in a bar. All my nights of planning and searching and twisting the stars so that she might appear came simply to a shot of bad rum and a cab ride home. She danced around my room that night while I brushed sand off the sheets. I lied and said the sheets were silk. I spun ridiculous yarns about upholding the honor of my countrymen overseas. Somehow, my imagination made me appealing to her. We wrapped up around each other but didn't take it too far. Maybe it was the rum, but I said on that first night that she was like porcelain, and rushing it would break the sanctity of that. I'm fairly sure that's how I said it. She wrote it down the next day and someone recited the line at our wedding the following year. My drunken line on bad rum made her fat aunt weep.

Like the kids we were, and are, we uprooted from our towns to roll dice in the only metropolis within a half-day's drive. We guessed the energy would do us good.

She took a job outside the city as a teacher's aide and volleyball coach. I couldn't do much with myself but bartend. I wanted to prove all the high school guidance counselors and my drill instructors wrong and take my management degree to great heights, like one of those suited corporate fat cats who laugh up and down Spring Street. But Sue was cool with me slinging drinks. She never lied to her school friends about what I did, bless her. I always wanted to catch her lying about me so that I might be ashamed and find real employment. But that girl was gold and loved me for whatever made me tick.

Things were good until volleyball season. I told her it wasn't healthy to hang around so many sweaty teenagers for so many after-school hours. She only shrugged. Her enthusiasm for my bonehead commentary was starting to wane. One night she rolled up her sleeve and exhibited a scratch she had gotten from brushing a rusty open locker. The tiny incision had deteriorated her flesh something awful, all scabby and brown and rank. She said the itch from it was like poison ivy times ten thousand.

"That's tetanus," I diagnosed. "My cousin had it as a kid. He shut the hell up twenty years ago and he's still mute today."

She only turned her back and went to bed. Her attitude became what I later described to the news reporters as skeptical. Something was pulling her down into a dark sick hole. All night long the bed quaked with her moving. Even in her sleep she dragged her nails across her bleeding skin, like an animal dreaming badly. She whimpered and scratched at her limbs, then scratched more. In the morning there were terrible maroon traces of her sickness on our white sheets. Finally we bit the bullet and went uninsured to see the doctor.

The big bastard had me by the throat. I tried to squeeze out words like end it, end me, you sissy elitist, but damn his grip was nice. The background blues kept going, dirtier than ever. Finally he released my neck and said, "Get outside." I thought he'd surely crushed my trachea and you bet that pissed me off. His wife stood up suddenly— fake chest and a pink jogging suit, a real prosthetic princess. He told her to sit. She obliged.

I kicked open a spray-painted exit door and led my tormentor to the parking lot. The afternoon was warm. It could have been Sunday. I walked behind a row of Dumpsters and he followed. To passersby it probably looked like a daylight drug deal, but I was in no position to sweat those details.

Behind a rank bin with yellow grease spillage I turned around and felt like vomiting again. It had nothing to do with him or the grease but rather with what was behind him—the wicked twenty stories of Peachtree Medical Center. The big hospital sort of framed this guy. He was like its impending messenger of death. I wondered if my Sue was still rotting in that network of concrete. The hospital had been a horrible place to die. My girl deserved a serene mountaintop death with all her dreams realized, her admirers cheering her on to a greater glory. I'll never go down in a hospital bed. Give me parking lot death any day.

He rolled the sleeves of his IZOD shirt. He unclipped his watch and tucked it in the pocket of his pants. He told me I'd screwed up awfully bad, plunking his face with a beer bottle and all.

"Alright, cowboy," I said, hunched over like a grappler. "Let's rodeo."

The first doctor visit was puzzling. Sue was part-time at school, which meant those board-of-education dilweeds didn't pay for things like mystery infections from outer space. None of our friends were insured and they survived fine. The Army and I weren't on good terms, me being a year behind on the necessary paperwork or whatever, so my camouflaged past didn't exactly help. Not to get preachy, but it felt like we were puttering around in a strange social void. We all lived under the illusion that, if tragedy struck, America would have our backs. What dipshits we were.

During that first examination Sue was downright trembling. She climbed across the crinkling paper in her white-pink gown, her smooth legs exposed above the ankle socks. I sat with her in the quiet little room. Those spaces are always so silent, so muted by apprehension. I flipped through a back issue of *Hot Rod*, worried that my tips alone would have to foot the doctor bills. I was naïve at that point. Still thinking about only me.

The doctor stank like coffee and plastic. He took one look at my girl and gasped.

"Have you kept this clean?" he asked us, holding Sue's delicate arm on his fingertips.

"Spotless," I said. "Peroxide, alcohol, gauze. It's not helping."

"And the scratching," said my Sue. "It's not the right thing to do, but God I can't stop."

"This is not good," said the doctor, spectacles hugging a brain. "Your arm is greatly deteriorated. This looks similar in some respects to contagious diseases that were eradicated eighty years ago. Think Small Pox. Think the latter stages of Measles. Sorry to alarm you—certainly it's nothing like that. It was obviously triggered by this outer abrasion but it eats from within. Please make the necessary arrangements because you're going to be hospitalized for some time."

"How much is that?" I said, but Sue had gone off weeping to call her school.

In two weeks she had burned all her vacation and sick days. The sterilized world of bleak hospital winter pulled us both to all shades of hell. I left her only at night to work closing shifts at Club Volcano. A former grunt like me didn't really belong in there—too much glitz and Midtown pretense—but the tips were easy and frequent.

I had stopped drinking because I didn't want to smell like a good time when I nudged against Sue's good arm at daybreak. The most esteemed docs in the hospital network said she wasn't contagious, but I didn't care either way. With all my weight I trapped her hand to restrict the scratching while I slept. Where her nails used to leave marks they now tore flesh, despite the antibiotics. The worst patch webbed over her shoulder and under her right boob. She wouldn't look at it. She hardly spoke. It was the worst thing I'd ever seen.

Then came the vultures.

In January some administrator said loudly at a school board meeting that a Peachbrook Middle School teacher was dying of a mysterious disease. The administrator wanted to start a fund for my

Sue, a pleasant girl with so much future ahead of her, he said. Within earshot that night were three broadcast news reporters, each taking notes. I can imagine how their sorry mouths watered.

Old steel fists grabbed me, reached back, and asked for three good reasons why he shouldn't break my nose. Naturally I said kiss my ass three times. But instead of blasting me he clutched my jaw and rotated my face, as if he'd been sculpting it.

"It's funny," he said calmly. "You look *so* familiar."

The Army had been a blunder in my case, period. Another bonehead idea. I thought somehow the service might award me with fame—or at least its lesser cousin, honor.

When the government started bombing those ancient desert cities I felt left out. I hate to admit that, and I rarely do, but the general state of things had been bothering me for a long time. Everything was too damn easy. South Georgia was no different than North Dakota or Bangor, Maine. People took to bitching about the most trivial little shit. And though I continued to get older I wasn't really going anywhere. I was leaving behind a legacy of nothing, a minor blip on the unending scroll of human history, a guy who stumbled through college, hated his job, and spent his weekends at the outlet mall, buying shit. So in a way I welcomed the war, especially a war that had no bearing on my life unless I chose to let it in.

I joined the Army at age twenty-four. I did it to wake up.

Joining made me nervous, sure. I'd heard of a kid from a few towns away who died in a city I forgot the name of. They said he was blown to quarter-size bits by a landmine built in a kitchen. They drove his hearse through the town and everybody paused for a minute, the courthouse draped in flags, a bugle crying over a karaoke machine on the downtown square. I read the newspaper report and nearly cried. People had good things to say about the kid, John something. In a way I was envious of him. He had found a purpose. In dying he had done something with his life.

They sent me to Fort Brackner, a swampy outpost in lower Mississippi. I was the second oldest guy in my battalion. For a few months I yearned to make it to sergeant and really take charge, to get decorated to the nines. But like usual I got complacent with mediocrity. It was a close-knit community over at Brackner and people just kind of did their duties and hung out. It made the local newspaper when another one got deployed. It happened every six months or so but it didn't happen to me. They usually picked the younger mavericks who worked with bomb-sniffing dogs.

So I stayed clear of the K-9 crowd and was back in college a couple years later. Nothing had really changed. The same sort of spoiled faces with different names. The same ditzy girls puking in the same dive-bar toilets and bitching about the same brand of imported vehicles their daddies weren't buying them. I wanted to appreciate the boredom but it didn't always work. I was free, sure, but free to do what? To mope? I tried to come to terms with knowing I would never have a parade in honor of my death. That didn't work either. I was quickly becoming nobody again.

Sue was a reason to stop dabbling in graduate school and get my act together. Surely I would find purpose with her. For a time she put me at ease, blind and deaf to the rising tide of global lunacy. We entered the sacred gates of matrimony, as they say, and we were proud of that. The outlet mall, as I came to find out, isn't so bad when you're shopping for somebody.

I still don't know how the vultures found my phone number. I was in the hospital lounge eating a Swirl Bun and sipping a vending-machine latte when the first woman called. I get submissive when cornered.

"Mister Sparks? Is this Tommy Sparks?" she asked, very professional.

"Yeah."

"Tommy, this is Angela Worrenstein from Channel 83 Atlanta. I'm so sorry to hear about what you're going through. It must be devastating. I can't imagine. Listen, we'd like to air a piece about Sue and her disease. We understand she's one of the best teachers Peachbrook has ever had. Her colleagues said that. If you could step outside the hospital this evening we'd love to chat with you. It'll be therapeutic. Can we say eight p.m.? Good. The more people know about this disease, the more people will want to help. The public will come to your aid in droves, Tommy. I guarantee it."

I'm usually pretty shy but somehow I agreed to speak on camera to bastards by the millions. For two months I'd been cooped in a room basically talking to myself when Sue's family wasn't around.

In my head I started scripting my first television appearance: I'd begin the story talking about Sue's hardscrabble childhood in Macon, then cut to the scratching in our bed and finish off with this miserable hospital dilemma. I convinced myself FEMA would send its highest brass on the double. I brushed my teeth that night and went down to the street.

Angela Worrenstein wasn't alone. There were four white vans down there with antennas shooting from the roofs like giant spoons. I walked into a wall of tripods and men and bright lights that froze me in my bones. This woman in faux fur and heavy lipstick walked up, faked like she was about to cry, and hugged me. I guess that's how those news whores piss on territory.

"It's such a pleasure, Tommy Sparks," she said. "I'm Angela. Please, when you answer, look to the camera at left."

Then up tramped another one, this time a guy with white hair and a purple suit. "Tommy. A pleasure," he said. He told me his name and it sounded like Leroy Stupendous.

"They're calling your wife's disease a complete mystery," said Leroy. "As wicked as it is unstoppable. We'll get this out there and someone will see it, my friend. Don't worry. Someone will have answers."

Leroy Stupendous and Angela played a sort of tug-o-war with me until the white lights were hot on my face. I got dizzy and

11

frustrated. With very serious facial expressions they both started asking questions.

"All I have to tell you at this point is that I'm the world's saddest man," I said, and the words just came to me without thinking. It felt good, like a purging of demons. "Sue grew up without much. Her daddy was killed on his motorcycle. Let me tell you it wasn't easy. Here's what happened…"

That night at eleven I sat with Sue and told her we would be saved. I held the remote like a pistol, ready to shoot the channels to the next broadcast, on each a different angle of my same heroic face. I tried to nudge Sue awake but she only died a little more. Channel 49 cut to Leroy Stupendous and there, in a little box at the top of the screen, they had me pictured with my mouth open, like a frightened wax figure beneath a horror-movie headline: "Mystery Disease Strikes School!" They cut to a shot of Sue in seventh grade.

"Where the hell did he get that?" I belted out, disturbing the invalids behind neighboring curtains. Then they showed Sue's mom, the Wild Turkey queen, for about five minutes. I switched to Channel 83 and there was mom again, sharing the screen with that wench Angela. Back on 49 it was all Leroy.

"Doctors are up in arms, frantically tracing the young teacher's symptoms to all sorts of diseases not documented here in eighty years," said Leroy. "But this is something new. The young woman is quite literally scratching herself to pieces. Although unresponsive, she uses her free limbs at any given second to tear away her skin, reducing her weight to an alarming sixty-five pounds. Sue's husband, Thomas, an Army veteran, is as distraught as her former colleagues…"

There I was for nine seconds. Beneath my face it said husband. On television I said something about the government letting us down and man did I sound stupid. Then came sports guy Ted Denton with an update on the Braves' latest debacle. The great spotlight of the media machine went cold in seconds.

12

"That's it?" I said to Leroy Stupendous, who was no longer there. "That's all we get? Two minutes before the commercials? Don't call *me* again."

Of course they never called back for the follow-ups they'd promised. Nobody called me. Sue's family couldn't handle the weight of being in the room any longer. Her mom said it spooked her. So I weathered the final week alone. My wife's pale beauty decayed into something skeletal, something gray, her gaunt face stretched tight like plastic. I was out of promises. I was tired of chasing the reasonable explanation. Life is just a miserable test with no answers, and you either die looking or embrace your ignorance and live on.

I stepped out for barbecue as the bastards pulled the plug.

Conversing with a man who wants to crush your face is remarkably difficult. He had my entire head in the grip of his two strong hands—my chin, my lips, my scalp, all his. I let my arms dangle, the quicker to get it over with. If I don't die, I thought, surely I'll reap some pain-and-suffering coin from this shit.

Somehow my senses were keen. He wore spicy cologne, a masculine odor. The teeth were perfect. I could smell that the beer on his breath was imported. He was a handsome guy, really, untainted by working-life fatigue. My mark still graced his forehead, a purple tinge to the little injury. That much made me proud.

Then something changed. He held his breath, studying me deeply. If I didn't know better I'd call his expression...*reverence*. The change started in his face and wormed to his extremities. I can only describe it to say he loosened up, all of him, and the rage in his eyes went dormant, like a flatline.

"That's you," he said, as if my face was something other than me. "It *is* you. I know you."

"Eh?" I said weakly.

"You're him," he said. "You're the husband."

"Come again?" I said.

"Holy shit, man," said the guy. "Like holy shit."

13

He released me and stepped away. He gaped at his open hands. He wiped his fingers on his jeans.

"Nice," I said. "You saw my show?"

He went back two steps more, onto an old drain.

"It's terrible what happened to her," and he rubbed his palms viciously on his hips, probably fast enough to generate heat. "I can't imagine, man. My wife cried."

I was ten shades of happy to see him so vulnerable, so feeble. There must be thousands more like his wife, I thought, a weeping legion of Tommy Sparks sympathizers. I scratched my forearms, my elbows, my neck.

"They have a name for her disease, don't they?" he said.

"*They* tell me it's highly contagious," I said, fighting a bubble of laughter.

"And knowing that you chose to eat in public?" he said. "To eat in there among families? In the *nicest* part of town?" He scrunched his forehead, obviously disgusted. He had a point but his condescension was getting old fast.

"Last night I scratched my face until I bled all over that hospital," I said. "Puddles of blood."

"Stop," he said.

"I lost five teeth on Wednesday," I continued. "I'm growing hair on the roof of my mouth."

"Damn it," he said. "Stop what you're doing."

"You want to make a donation?" I asked. "Send it to my legacy fund. They predict me dead by August."

The poor twit almost fainted.

"I know your name," he said. "I'll pay your tab—just go. Get away from us."

He back-peddled into the restaurant, ensuring himself with each step that at least ten feet remained between us. I felt sorry for him. It was weird. For a minute I was inclined to saunter back in and hug his wife. Or maybe lick her face. But then I let that bad energy go. What had she really done to me? I'd gotten my point across, my meal paid for. Besides, it was too damn sunny outside.

I walked a few blocks to Piedmont and took a left. A hilly tangle of streets I had yet to explore unfurled in front of me. Ironworkers on high beams pieced together a skyscraper. A woman in dreadlocks sold boiled peanuts behind a sign that, for some reason, read: World's Best Ice Cream. I wished Sue could see these things, trivial as they were. Since she couldn't I dedicated them to her.

A boxy, modern school bus belched a group of children onto the sidewalk, a blur of pink and blue backpacks. The children chased each other in circles and played tag on the grass. They were laughing. Nothing could stop them. I crossed Piedmont to distance myself from the children, just in case.

THE BUSHMASTER

Juan Picasso waits at the edge of the Grande Guanacaste resort, near the kayak rentals on the beach, a barrier imposed on him by the tourism board, a stodgy bunch he likes to call pussies. His toes curl in the cool volcanic sand. He shuffles a stack of handwritten business cards and checks his breath for the odor of rum. He will wait beside the mango trees until he hears the tourists' giddy chirps, that telltale exultation, their first glimpses of the Costa Rica for which they'd prepaid—and then he will pounce.

What they first notice about Juan are his skinny pupils, and then his hands, wide and limber like lowland palms. Next to bedazzle are the pistons in his forearms, how distinctly they permeate his tanned skin. His hair hangs strong like helecho gigante, the rainforest ferns. His face is a proportionate sphere of dried leather, though nothing to stop traffic on the avenidas. The voice is his true tool,

17

reliable as a stone-sharpened machete, said to make the female abdomen dance meringue.

"A fresh herd," mumbles Carlos, Juan's competitor, in Spanish.

Carlos points his mangled hand (snakebite atrophy) toward the resort's check-in cabana, some three hundred yards up the mountain.

"Let them trickle to me," Juan says in grubby English. "My turn."

It's low-tide Saturday on Playa Panama, an idle time when even the white-throated magpies seem bored. The Pacific falls back in the bay and the tourist currents also shift. A great sunburned mass of Portland accountants, Texas Marines, and Chicago nurses goes out, as another hustles in. The newcomers are drenched in fragancia, which is what the beach hustlers call disposable income.

Juan and Carlos peek through the foliage to find several beachgoers filtering down to sea, a lily wave of florescent towels, wicker totes, and Frisbees. The resort is typical of the Guanacaste Province—tiki bars, floral walkways, and cabanas with clay roofs, all rising like stairs on a mountain of ancient lava swells. Dance music—Cyndi Lauper meets Paul van Dyk—echoes from the main pool at painful volume, even before noon. A poolboy on the microphone is drunk already. The Papagayo Hilton it is not.

Juan stretches his arms as if paddling surf, his ritualistic warm-up. He has worked the last twenty days, since sometime in late Mayo, and he's only getting started, for ceaseless profiteering is in his blood. It's the high season for American vacationers, and most of them are scared shitless by the ramshackle housing and soiled kids they see around Aeropuerto de Liberia. Having researched nothing of the country, they expect to be abducted by coffee growers with AK-47s and aspirations of toppling some dictator. But they've arrived in the Switzerland of Central America, a neutral and gun-shunning paradise, or as Juan describes it, "One lush hunk of peace."

Juan wriggles off the titanium wedding ring his third wife let him keep (how the tan-line makes the muchachas wonder) and stuffs it in his Hollister backpack. Like most of his attire, the backpack is blatantly floral. Carlos, a towering ignoramus who'd chopped enough cane to buy a jet ski—which he rents at *ninety* American dollars per hour—offers Juan a pull of sugarcane liquor. "No thanks—makes me crazy as a no-nose bat," Juan says, refocusing on the resort. "And my diving board limp." Carlos laughs as Juan digs his bare feet deeper, a step in front of the competition, the angle his.

Summer of last year, Juan guided a Globetrotter Magazine journalist (a redheaded, studious woman from Belfast) on a tour of Laguna Arenal, a massive manmade lake shared by windsurfers and crocodiles. "That would be ironic if they were the boat-eating bastards of Africa and Australia," Juan explained, captaining their skiff. "But they're fish-eating, American Cocodrilos, all easy catches." He then leapt to shore and hogtied a five-foot specimen, which he promptly mimicked making love to.

The writer was taken by Juan, his rustic charm and vast—albeit shaky—mental store of jungle trivia. The more he talked, the more he picked the locks of her lonely, travel-weary hormones. In her piece ("A Week In Central America: Jungle Zipping, Croc' Chasing and Living On the Edge In Earth's Natural Zoo") she described him as follows:

> *Juan Picasso, a hulking and wildly perverted Costa Rican tour guide, makes his living leading bivouacs of married couples into the mountains and rivers of his native country—and bedding the wives. Suave, mid-forties, and deathly superstitious, Juan feels pressured to spread his seed before cancer kills him like it's rapidly doing his family. In the last decade he's lost his mother, a sister and two aunts, due in part, he believes, to the persistent laziness of his youth. He lives each day as if it were his next-to-last. For on his last day, Juan Picasso would devote his every waking hour to erecting a shrine to himself, a bejeweled, mountainous homage to narcissism befitting an Aztec ruler.*

Her last night in the country, the journalist drank a dozen Imperials and wandered up to Juan's cabin, her hair pulled back and spectacles ditched. He came naked to the door and carried her to bed, ran through her 'til she saw Catholic Saints beyond the mosquito netting. Not a word of that appeared in her writing. Nor did she mention it to her husband.

Clark Murphy's long white feet—described by his wife as the gnarly twins—are the first to meet sand. He pulls from a Pilsen beer and catches sight of what looks like a surf-beaten caveman approaching him, the nearing smile pirate-sly.

"You, amigo, look thirsty," Juan says, extending a big hand. "Let me guess—too much screwdrivers on the airplane?"

Clark takes the hand firmly, stares at the sea. For an instant he recalls this morning's plane trip, the first with his new wife, Marianne. The wedding behind them, the couple had stuffed copies of their passports in their socks (Clark's idea) and boarded the 8 a.m. direct to Centro America, land of plentiful abductions, according to Clark's coworkers at the firm. Clark didn't mind flying anymore, not since the lulls of international travel had become billable hours with the advent of onboard Wi-Fi. Making three hundred dollars an hour at thirty thousand feet (mimosa in hand) suited his ego fine; flying, however, did a number on his digestive tract. The first twenty minutes were smooth enough to walk the cabin, so Clark fled to the lavatory. He hoped the remnants of yesterday's paella might find his father's vintage Datsun, parked somewhere in suburban Orlando, but then again Clark's aim was usually off.

Across the bay, Clark sees the Four Seasons entrenched in a hill. In the far gray water fisherman pull nets into motorized boats. He's been shaking Juan's hand a good five seconds, his mind entranced.

"Pelicans!" Clark says, letting loose. "Honey, out there, on the rocks—they've got pelicans. Bigger, uglier than Florida ones. You see them?"

"Yeah." Marianne deflates. "That's fascinating."

Plum hair and flirty Prada sunglasses, Marianne dons a faded Jaguars jersey over her bikini, which peeks through like teal parachutes. She dips a triangle of pineapple in her strawberry daiquiri, and with red teeth smiles to the men. Juan introduces himself in the loud, genuine way his mother used while pushing fruitcarts through the street noise of San José.

"Picasso," Clark says. "Like the painter?"

Juan steps back, feigning insult: "Like the *explorer!*"

Clark offers a dismissive nod and says, "Right on," a courtroom informality that makes superior court judges squirm. He fiddles with the lid to his thirty-SPF, smears a dollop on his high forehead.

"Come, please, over here, to my office," Juan says, walking away. "Both of you."

Clark turns in the opposite direction. Marianne catches his hand and yanks him back.

Juan readies his office: four plastic beach chairs that buttress a sheet of plywood, which holds his brochures, a folder brimming with wildlife pictures, and his full cooler. He throws a victorious wink to Carlos, who is tipsy and more concerned with catching—and inflicting pointless death upon—red crabs.

Juan squeezes his chest pocket to ensure his contracts—Post-It notes with his business name in tiny print—are handy. "I'm el presidente of Outlaw Tours, and you've found the greatest bargains in the country," Juan tells the couple. "I understand you have only just arrived, but you have to know about our very special tour. My family goes back in this country for thirty generations, dating back to the first Spaniard, and this place is what I know."

"This whole island?" Clark says.

"This is no island—but, yes, every mountain, every type of animal."

"That's a lot to know, man," says Clark, sitting on a driftwood palm. "Costa Rica has the greatest density of species in the world."

"Ho, look at this—*a genius!*" Juan laughs and pulls a sandy business card from his shorts. "I offer the quality, independent tours those fools at the hotel can only imagine about. Come, today, I'll show you."

Clark snatches the card. "We were thinking of renting a car and—"

"Then your life, muchacho, is in your hands," Juan says.

"Told you," says Marianne.

Clark reclines on the palm and drains his drink, inconspicuously flexing his biceps. Juan passes him an icy beer from the cooler. "It was last month," Juan says, "a couple from Cleveland went driving, ended up in Nicaragua. Snatched up by the banana cartel ..."

"*Shit*," Marianne says. "What happened?"

"Cut to pieces, fed to spider monkeys," Juan says. "Only their wallets were found—empty."

A skeptical Clark sits up. "Whatever," he says, though he can tell the yarn has unnerved his wife. "Okay, amigo...I'm listening."

Juan exhumes a ballpoint pen from his cargo shorts. "I'll take you to the most beautiful jungle, with views of the greatest volcano— all you came here for," he says. "Now we can drink, and at eleven, we go!" He pretends to make calculations on a spare contract. The accommodations, he tells the couple, will be free, being that they'd paid for lodging already. "In the mountain air—where we'll be—the air-conditioning is not necessary, especially if you sleep naked."

Clark bows up in the perturbed stance he gives supermarket cashiers. "You're starting to weird me out."

"Sorry, amigo," Juan says. "Sorry. Sorry. We'll be back, on this beach, tomorrow evening. Plenty of time left to play. For this I need three hundred each."

Clark wants a second opinion, to somehow wrest control of the situation. He looks beneath the trees. Two local kids, the sons of potters, toss mango bits to green iguanas, marauders of the groves. Clark doesn't speak Spanish, and as such he's dealt an unfamiliar feeling: helplessness.

22

"I think we'll take our chances with renting a car," Clark says. "It'll be fun, babe. You can be my hot little navigator."

"Hell *no,*" she says, tossing her hair. "You're helpless without a GPS, and my head is *not* ending up on some bushman's spear."

Juan howls and slaps his table. He scribbles "$300!" on a contract and pushes it across the table.

"I'm fine with paying whatever," Clark says finally. "But there had better be cold-ass beer."

Marianne springs like a cheerleader. "Let's do it," she says. "I'm in—*we're* in."

Clark stands up and unbuttons his Tommy Bahama shirt, a gift from Marianne on his fortieth. Never said it, but he thinks the shirt a tad predictable, beneath the standard of his retail dalliances in Miami; not to mention it broadcasts his belly. He wants to tell Marianne the shirt—and the many she's bought him like it—is hardly retribution for five years of graduate school tuition. Instead he stares Juan in the face. "How do we know you won't skin us alive in the jungle?"

"Muchacho," Juan says disarmingly, digging into his backpack. "Consider this for proof..." and he hands over the Globetrotter article, careful not to expose too much of the text. In pictures, Juan prods cocodrilos with a walking stick; a crowd of Parque Nacional Palo Verde tourists laughs behind him.

"*They* did a piece on you?" Clark says.

"Oh, friend," Juan says. "They did it so well."

More than the twelve-foot cocodrilos in the rivers of Palo Verde; more than the German shepherd-sized iguanas near Papagayo; even more than tropical rattlesnakes that attack from fallen leaves, the indigenous Costa Ricans fear one anti-human demon above the slithering multitude. They call it the Bushmaster, the largest and downright nastiest pit viper in the world.

The children of Filadelphia hear rumors from their mountain-trekking tios about the dark jungle serpent. How it's indestructible, too swift for machete-swipes, a muscular killing machine with no heart. Its dorsal ridge rises like that of a reef shark, its nose upturns like a pig's, its scales run rough as brick walls, and the whole thick body is the color of dead leaves. Its name wrought from Latin to English is said to mean silent, stalking devil.

Rumor has it a biologist studying the mating patterns of rainforest butterflies stepped on a Bushmaster in the late eighties. Bad move. It struck at him but missed, at least at first. The biologist ran like hell off a path of stones, into a tangle of ferns and monkey vines. The Bushmaster gave chase, caught him as he turned around. A single fang to the index finger and the biologist died—three days later, in the hospital. Atrophy of the arm, the nervous system, the heart. Always the heart.

The final day of his life, the biologist begged his crew for a pistol, pleaded to be shot or to have his throat slit. Deep in diphtheria-like sweats he screamed that el Diablo had lit his soul on fire, that God was a farce.

In the turismo van, leaving Guanacaste and bouncing like rocks in a soda can, Clark turns to his wife and belts, "Have I told you how much I *hate* Orlando?" An awkward pause cripples the conversation, a silence disrupted only by the choking four-cylinder motor. The driver, who speaks only the words "yes" and "party" in English, is perplexed.

"Muchacho, calm down," Juan begs from his co-pilot seat, Ray-Bans masking his eyes. "*Pura Vida*...all is cool."

"Excuse me?" Clark says.

"Orlando is fantastic," Juan says. "Think about the Mickey Mouse and things."

"Have you been?"

"No," says Juan, "but my cousin ran a brothel there."

Clark peels his arm from Marianne's sweaty shoulders and dabs the perspiration from his eyes. "My argument precisely," he says. "I mean, what a God-forsaken, tourist-clogged shithole. All those people at the hotel sort of took me back there for a moment... I'm cool now."

Lowland cane fields and mango farms give way to blue rolling hills that Clark likens to a sweltering Kentucky. He points to cattle led down dirt roads by sabaneros, a scene that harkens for Clark the dusty county fairs of Central Florida. Growing up, he couldn't stand the stagnant pleasantness of Orlando's suburban fringes, that false courteousness reserved for guests. He'd been wired, in his opinion, to lead a Harley gang or Cuban cartel, to buck his too-busy father. But one suspension for pot possession in high school and his dad threatened to pull funding for law school at Miami, and that cooled the kid's deviant urgings. Clark's last trip home, he served his father with a civil lawsuit, a vitriolic document he'd authored himself. The demands: pain and suffering for an adolescence of social depravity and zero baseball outings. Being that thirty years had elapsed, Clark wasn't expecting much from the trip, but to see the old man's flaky lips fall open, his bathrobe unclosed as always, so inspired Clark that he folded his vendetta away, flew back to Jacksonville and proposed marriage to his on-off flame of six years, the perpetual student. "I've bolted an old door shut," Clark had cheesed, supermarket roses in hand. "Let's get *freaking married!*"

"Shit," Marianne said, "let's." She hugged Clark with her eyes literally on his law degree, hanging in a shadowbox in the kitchen.

Back in the airplane lavatory, Clark had remembered the proposal, an episode he thought suave. He savored the memory like butterscotch until the Boeing 757 hit a turbulence minefield. Clark swore he heard two stewardesses outside the door gasp "engine" and "kaput" in close succession, sounds he likened to the grim reaper's first nefarious whispers.

Clark stumbled back to seat 17G, inserted earphones, and tried to focus on the in-flight movie, something putrid starring The Rock. It didn't work. A cloudless day and yet the plane jolted like the King Kong attack at Universal Studios. Clark convinced himself the whole shithouse was going down in flames. The captain's voice cracked over the intercom and said you'll have this sometimes, that he'd try to veer around but the choppy air was Texas-big. Clark ordered a double Johnny Black and tried to recount the prayers of his Baptist youth. None came.

"Honey," said Marianne. "You're sweating."

"Hot in here."

"Think positive," she said. "Happy thoughts."

"I'm too hung-over for turbulence."

"We'll be in paradise before you know it, babe."

"I read there's snakes there—big ones," he said.

"I said happy thoughts, you boob."

"Valium," Clark said. "Did you bring any?"

"That's *just* what I need." Marianne tossed her copy of *Bride* on the tray table and dug into her purse. "A limp pecker on the first day of my honeymoon."

They ascend two thousand feet in the turismo van. Juan points to shanty rows, the chocolaty water of rivers, and lush green mountains like the backs of prehistoric lizards. He has facts, but interspersed within the truth are outlandish tales of personal adventures. "I climbed Irazu Volcano, which you can't quite see in the distance, in 1980," he says. "It earned for me nineteen marriage proposals. All of them were cows." He translates the story for the driver, who nods to the couple, as if to certify it.

"An equatorial salesman," Clark whispers in his wife's ear. "That's what we're stuck with. This was more your idea than mine." She scoots away, her damp, soft thighs catching the vinyl, emitting a sound like rubbing balloons. "Sorry," Clark says aloud, "but it's true."

They travel the Pan American Highway to Canas, where they drink Pilsen and take photographs outside a clapboard bullfighting arena. Next is Angeles, then Tilaran, and lastly Laguna Arenal, the windsurfer playground. Juan points the driver down a long gravel road. The van quakes as it beats up dust, frightening cattle away from a wire fence. Juan hops out to unlock gaudy steel gates, to call to Howler monkeys in the trees. He climbs back in and cracks an

Imperial. "Thought I saw Howlers," he says. "Their nuts sometimes look like fruit." In a moment they arrive at a jungle clearing, a misty plateau in the sky. A crescent of green-painted cabins flanks a visitor's center built of logs. "I call this a fingernail of heaven," Juan says, stepping outside the van, a rucksack and suitcase in tow. "A little piece of God's grace, fallen into the rainforest."

The couple disembarks, their eyes on the dark floral jungle. An affable-looking, gray-bearded man hustles up to the van, chewing an unlit cigar. He hugs Juan and they speak loudly in rapid Spanish. He hands Juan a set of keys.

"This is Erick," Juan says. "Best scientist this side of Mexico City, owner of all this, the Arenal Oasis." They all shake hands. "Take these," Juan says, tossing Clark the keys, "and unpack. Yours is Cabin B. I'm next door tonight. Tour begins in one hour."

Clark and his wife use a walkway crowded with canna lilies and heliconia plants, the latter sharp like sideways spears. Clark knows that Jacksonville hath never dealt such heat, a persistent thermal blast that, unmoved by offshore breezes, cuddles him like wool. He squints to see the horizon: Beyond the trees stand rigid lines of volcanoes, moody titans in the mist.

"Thought he said it'd be cooler up here," Clark says. "Feels like Scotland, with a fever."

"It'll cool off tonight, babe," says Marianne.

"I think he talks out his ass."

In the cabin a fridge is packed with the heavy beer, Bavarian Dark. Clark complains the beer is lukewarm but downs one anyway. They shed their bags, and Marianne dabs her face with a wet cloth. She lets out her ponytail and parts her hair to the left, though she knows it's a style—the one she favors for Christmas galas, boxing matches, and power-attorney brunches—that ignites Clark.

"Can we?" he says, cuffing his hands on her hips.

"The question is—can *you?*"

Clark grins. "Oh, yeah," he says, stepping back.

"Do you have the pill I gave you?"

"Listen," he says. "The flight was intense, but I'm good…especially in a place like this, way up here. We're *adventuring*."

"So you took it?" she says.

"I slept it off."

"Don't waste my goddamn time, Clark." She ducks into the tiny bathroom and locks the door.

At the entrance to Monteverde rainforest, Juan points to a small sign planted by Panamanian scientists who worked ziplines in the area: "Jesucristo es mi senor." He tells them the sign was said to be good luck until a smart man died from snakebite. Farmers in the area are too superstitious to remove it, he says.

"Please, in the rainforest, don't step near plants you can't see under," Juan says. "You never know."

"Never know about what?" Clark says.

"About a viper that prowls this forest," Juan says. He whacks a few vines and kicks them away. "We call him the Bushmaster. Your chances of surviving are nada, amigos."

Clark gives Juan, and then his wife, an incredulous roll of his eyes. "Surely this place has antivenin by the bucket?"

Juan cuts low ferns, spots the path, and motions them in. "The risk is very small." He pushes in deeper, swinging. "I joke."

They follow Juan, tiptoeing on a path of round, flat stones in the mud. Clark turns to his wife and whispers, "They take such pride in their little jobs, don't they?" She slaps his shoulder.

When they come to a Volkswagen-big termite hill, Juan hacks a shoot of bamboo, trims it, and pokes the mound. Nothing happens. He clears away ferns for a view of the canopy. "There," he says, pointing the knife up. "Your lucky day—a three-toed sloth!"

A lethargic, shaggy creature, aloof and gray, clings to a branch, some thirty feet above.

"He's adorable," Marianne says.

Clark eyes the sloth through a telephoto lens. "It looks like a panda, crossbred with a rat."

28

"Stop it," she says.

"A dirty mop, at best." Clark laughs.

Juan jabs the machete in the ground and crosses his arms. "Hey, Orlando," he says. "That guy up there is no rat. They are very rare, and very beautiful."

Clark snaps a picture with his Nikon to appease the agitated guide. He brushes by Juan and takes the lead on the path. "Orlando, eh?" They keep walking.

They come to a ravine walled by high, moss-covered trees. A timid macaw rainbows from one tree to the next. The group shares water, warm as summer street puddles, from a canteen, and Juan plucks a plant from the soil, exhibiting heart-shaped markings under its long leaves. He spins some tale about the blood of Spanish lovers who first settled in these mountains, and Clark issues a loud, wet yawn. Marianne jabs him from behind.

"Tell us another story," Clark says. "Tell us how you got involved with this, how your Outlaw Tours came about. I'll bet there's an astute business model in there somewhere."

Juan drops the plant, packs its roots in loose soil with his boot. "Come, muchacho," he says. "I'll talk for you as we walk."

Juan recounts that his business took shape when he was twenty-two, when he "borrowed" a van while its driver napped on a Playa de Coco bench. A crew of surfers knew what Juan was doing but said nothing. Not a peep to the bodega owners, seashell peddlers, or the drunken French wandering jewelry booths. "Silencio," Juan demanded, twisting wires. He fired up the van and sped off, bound for the Pacific highlands.

He had arranged to store the van at his tio's farm near Curator Bocas. He drove four hours without drawing the attention of police, and he parked the hot ride in a bamboo shed, where it would sit for three months as Juan lay low. His tio, Manuel, met him in the yard, trailed by a loud wave of children, his. The men embraced.

"You call this starting a business?" his uncle laughed.

Juan handed over a shoebox with several thousand Colones in it, cash he'd earned waiting tables and blinding gringos with his

29

signature Buenos Noches Mojito. He was eager to dry out in the jungle for some weeks, while his uncle thought the time with his nephew—albeit harboring a felonious criminal—a service to his cancer-stricken sister, who was anchored in the town of Liberia by her uterine curse.

At dawn, Juan would rid the farm of dangerous snakes and magpies, earning a day's stipend of gallo pinto and tilapia. He played with Manuel's children and learned their temperaments. In the evenings, helping his uncle roll cigars, they discussed the attributes of wealth.

"It's all there is," Juan would say. "There is wealth and there is slavery."

"I have a good life here, on this farm," Manuel said. "But I don't have wealth. Never will."

"Then that is your wealth, that feeling," Juan said. "I cannot feel like you without unlimited money…and unlimited women."

"It's just youth," his uncle said. "It will wear off."

"No, it's more."

All those nights Juan never mentioned his madre, though Manuel knew her best of all, having walked her to school in the gutters of San Jose. "Why do you think good people get sick?" said Manuel one night, chatty and sentimental on sambuca.

Juan pinched a robusto and laid it on a bamboo table. "The best people you know are lessons put here by God," he said. "I know the ones that won't last; there's something in their voice that you can hear."

Ten weeks gone, they spray-painted the van from gray to a gushing-lava orange, a badly inconspicuous choice. Juan promised to repay his tio—along with that napping chauffeur—tenfold when his business had subsidiaries from Nicaragua to Panama.

"Yes, okay," his uncle said. "Pura Vida."

Juan drove to Liberia and shacked with his madre, where he'd treat her with tea and fruit the last two years. He bought a collared shirt and sold a tour his first day. From the couch his mother cheered.

Never book-smart, Juan's street-wits alerted him to something he could feel in the volcanic foundation of Costa Rica: the invasion of privileged gringos. Their presence scarred the hills around his favorite surfing coves but their money sped his heart. With their postmodern condo stacks and shipped-over Land Rovers, this new breed had grown bored with Florida, too sophisticated for Myrtle Beach, too adventurous for south Alabama. Or else they were aging corporate miscreants who liked to fuck brothel slaves.

In two years Juan had five vans, including the Toyota he would eventually repay the driver. For entire seasons he took no days off.

"Do you have any regrets?" Clark says now, on the path.

"Nada," Juan says. "Regret, as the elders say, is God's chief curse for being a pussy."

Clark says right on.

Dinner that night is a bona fide fiesta. A Canadian couple and an irritable factory man from Vermont, the property of another guide, join the group. They dine on ceviche, pollo, and bistec, all swimming in tart Salsa Lizano. They drink beer from glossy, kiln-fired pottery studded with turquoise. They toss streamers into a leafy ceiling fan, which spits strands across the food, but nobody cares. Juan juggles mangoes and papayas, winning applause. He hacks a passion fruit in half with his machete, plunks a spoon in it, and dares Clark to take a bite. Clark, brave on Bavaria Dark, plunges the spoon in his mouth, pulls it out clean. "*Ah*," he coughs, spitting. "It's like seedy phlegm."

Juan carves out the remaining fruit and finishes in two bites. "What's wrong with you, Orlando?" he says. "It's delicious."

Erick, the owner, lights a maduro and tunes a radio in the corner to what sounds like a mariachi band. The room squirms with gringo dancing. Marianne rolls her shoulders, lifts her thin arms, and evaporates in the rhythm of fast guitar. She kicks off her sandals, rises from the dinner table, and pinches the lace of her red skirt, flagging it like a bullfighter's cape.

"You're doing the cumbia," Juan says. "A dance I like so much."

Head wobbling, Clark bursts: "Let's call a cab—ah *yeah!*" He alternates pulling between a bottle and cup, his lips now red with sangria. "We'll all go clubbing…dancing for real."

Juan does a classic salsa number and moves within range of Clark's hearing. "There's none of that for twenty kilometers," he says. "No discotheque, no cabs, no bands. We must entertain each other."

The Vermonter spills outside the cabin to puke in the bushes, leaving the door wide open. Through it, Juan sees something that enthralls him. He stops dancing and tells Erick to cut the music, then the outdoor lights. Juan darts away. The revelers follow into the cool night, stopping at the lip of the porch. The moon is a cracked dish; high clouds creep like ghosts. "Be still," Juan orders. It happens again—a great pyroclastic blast in the distance, red bubbles in space, Arenal Volcano cursing at the stars. Juan slips off the porch, quiet as a coiti, and prays, his knees bent under him and arms outstretched.

"That's *so* cool," Marianne says to her husband. "He's not totally a buffoon." She steps into the grass. "They have so much reverence for nature, for the power of this place." Clark doesn't answer, and his wife turns to find him sleeping, open-mouthed in a wicker chair, an empty Imperial sideways in his lap. "Terrific," she says.

Juan finishes his prayer and claps to make the party resume. Marianne points to her downed husband. "Oh," Juan says, "a little casualty." They hoist Clark to his feet and pull him off the porch, toward Cabin B. "Be careful to stay on the path," Juan says, dragging the lion's share of Clark. "Does this happen often?"

Marianne watches her husband's limp lips. "Only when he takes drugs," she says. "Legal drugs, I mean, of course. Helps him cope with flying, but it shuts him down when he drinks."

"Ah," Juan says. "One of those guys."

They deposit Clark in the cabin and zip mosquito netting around the bed. In a minute his rumbling turns placid, and the snoring rolls.

Juan watches Marianne's face in the moonlight. "Your cheeks," he says. "They drop...why?"

She walks away. He follows. They lock the door and head back to the dining cabin.

"I suppose I should've joined him," Marianne says, keeping close to Juan on the path. "But that's predictable."

"Do you love him?"

She sighs. "He's just so convenient."

"What do you mean?"

"He picks up the check," she says, "for my schooling, my pilates, my indecisiveness in general—everything. Pays for it and always has. I'll be thirty in two years, and I'm still fooling around in nursing school, mostly because I can."

"So you love his money?"

"Hey," she says. "That's not what I said."

"Okay." Juan juts out his lower lip and breathes into his nose.

"Let's be honest," she says. "Marianne Marie Murphy is a horrible name."

"No!" He stomps his foot, but smiles so broadly it somehow indicts him.

"Look," she says. "I hope you understand all that. It's a complicated situation back home. But we're no more neurotic than the next American couple."

"I understand you are a lovely dancer," Juan says.

"Please," she says. "Don't."

A few steps more and Juan brushes her elbow, her hand. He dribbles his fingers down her wrist and puddles them in her palm. "If you would like to dance with me, I can bring some wine to my cabin."

She stops walking and shakes off his hand. Juan's smile penetrates the dark. "If we do this, it ends at the wine—*okay?*" she says. She takes back his hand and leads him to an empty cabin near the jungle. "How do you say 'backstabber' in Spanish?"

"I have no idea."

"A secret," she says. "You know that?"

"Yes," he says. "That I know."

The porch creaks beneath them. Juan cuffs her shoulders, leans into her neck. She pushes away and asks for wine, good wine.

"Inside, near the armoire," he says. "They keep a very good malbec and two glasses."

From the dining cabin music roars again. The Canadians shriek as they whirl around, beer spilling from goblets in their hands. Rainwater drips from a billion unseen leaves. A symphony of heinous insects builds. Juan and Marianne crouch into the dark cabin, blindly looking for some recognizable shape to guide them, some sustainable form, but instead they find the bed, falling together in a soft, silent crash.

A Howler monkey's graveled boom awakens Juan and Marianne. They lie entwined within the spare cabin's netting. For a groggy instant Marianne thinks herself in Jacksonville, in her loft, the mechanical annoyance of a garbage truck outside her open window. The dark arm across her breasts brings a terrible shock.

"*Jesus*," she squeals. She collects garments and frees herself in a hurried escape.

Juan rolls onto his back, his torso blazed in morning light. "It's only Howlers," he says. "Not dangerous."

"No, this—us, *now*," Marianne says, clipping her bra. She bolts to the bathroom mirror and scoops smeared mascara with the nail of her pinkie finger. "I mean, *God*," she says, her voice breaking. "What'd you do to me?"

Juan talks rapidly in Spanish, jolts upright. He finds his cargo shorts in the sheets and dresses himself. Marianne, now crying, tells him to speak to her, to say something. "I don't know," he says. "We were talking in the night and...I don't know. All the beers, I guess."

He wriggles his feet into sandals. "Just stay here, stay quiet." Marianne curls on the bathroom floor. "It's very early," Juan says. "Maybe we are okay." He flings open the door, stomps across the porch, and jumps onto the nearest path.

The morning air is gauzy with dew. The grounds are very still. Juan peeks into the dining room and sees only a cook, the garbage from last night swept into overfull bins. For a reluctant minute, he watches Clark's cabin but sees no movement, no sign the man's awake. He hesitates to approach, at least not by way of the path, so he circles around the dining hall, stepping barely into the rainforest, his eyes to the back window of Cabin B. The window is cracked open but it could have been that way before.

"Quiet," Clark says, standing at the forest's edge, hands at his hips. "Come here."

Juan halts mid-step and holds his breath. Instincts click, and he can't help but size up Clark as an opponent—the saggy shoulders and small hands all inferior weaponry. Juan breathes now, confident in knowing that, should Clark attack him, the aggressor would be pummeled, beaten like cornmeal. The salesman in Juan takes over.

"And where is Misses Murphy today?"

"Oh," Clark says, "around."

Juan swallows. "Not here?" he says. "So strange. She must have taken a walk."

"Listen, amigo, be quiet," Clark says. "Come here, right here. Tell me what this is."

Juan drops his guard and inches closer. He follows Clark's eyes beneath an overhang of ferns, a dark pocket of jungle not three feet away. Clark points his finger and Juan squats, tilts his head to distinguish the shape among the leaves.

"Do not move," Juan says. "Do not breathe."

Clark slowly backs off anyway. "She's pretty," he says. "Biggest thing I've ever seen."

Juan reaches for Clark's wrist to pull himself up, away, but Clark is directly behind him. "My machete," Juan says. "Back away, like a sloth, and we will get it. It's not safe here, so close to the cabins."

"Those black eyes," Clark says, lifting a boot behind Juan's back.

"They are beautiful."

As the boot drops, Clark says, "Give *her* a kiss."

And before Juan can make sense of things—before the physics of this dive spell doom in his brain, before the white flash and the latching of daggers to his neck, before the hemotoxic rush and neurological sizzle—something in his gut tells him dumb luck doesn't last forever, that betrayal is a reciprocating process.

PINCH POINTS

The hollow pop above the factory din was Joanie's ring finger coming apart at the knuckle—a quick severance of tendons and flesh, a snap of her rubber glove. The finger flipped nail over bone into the printing press, the pulverized aftermath clumping in a long brownish mass at the rewind shaft. Joanie jerked away from the press drum, released a pitiful yelp, and reached for a ladder, but she couldn't clutch it. She flipped backwards, shoulder over shoulder, her feet kicking, down ten feet to the concrete floor, a surface hardly cushioned by puddles of ink.

Charlie Goss saw her land, headfirst. He tore across the aisle between them, tossed his safety glasses aside, and bent down to examine. Joanie rolled onto her back and choked, her arm outstretched, a scarlet pool swelling.

"She's pinched," Charlie yelled. "Medics, call medics!"

Six men descended ladders while others charged in from storage aisles. On off days the men were hunters, buck-killers, and they saw that Joanie writhed like a bullet-ridden deer. In her legs and abdomen jumped the eerie tics of possible death.

"Mama," Charlie said, hovering over her. "You stay with us, okay. You're gonna get *so paid*."

Two press assistants shot toward the supervisor's office. The ink blender, Ted, squeezed between the men, his arms full of fresh, white rags. Charlie balled a rag, applied pressure to Joanie's hand, and straightened her flat on her back. She'd always reacted well to Charlie, her predawn confidante on the nightshift. Her breathing stabilized.

"Goddamn quotas," Ted said.

"Goddamn right," said Charlie, his free, ungloved hand on Joanie's forehead, a novice effort to steady her spine. "This should be a supervisor here like this."

Charlie could see frustration, even anger, in Joanie's face. She was a broad, industrious woman with chipper blue eyes, originally from Virginia. She'd ended up at Leemar Plastics in rural Illinois when her husband's military promotion pulled the family six hundred miles from Blue Ridge. She told everybody she'd moved so much that adaptation was second nature. "That damn Army," she'd said. "Shuffles my family around like checkers." She'd bonded with Charlie, another geographic misfit, when he said on break one night he wanted to die because his girl was fucking her dentist.

Emergency alarms wailed. Joanie coughed and flashed her eyelids, then clenched them shut. Two tears cut the mascara like tiny gray rivers.

"Don't try to talk," Charlie said. "Nothing needs said. Hum that gospel shit, if you have to. The medics are coming."

"My ring," Joanie said through grit teeth. "My wedding ring."

"*Jesus*," said Charlie.

She shuffled her heavy boots. "He ain't coming back," she said. "He *ain't*."

"Okay," Charlie said. "It's okay. Last thing you need is to think about that."

Charlie stood up, drew a breath, and rolled his head. Above the commotion he saw the steel beams and high windows that lined the printing department. To Charlie the windows had always shone through the haze of solvent fumes and burned polyethylene, and also through the haze of his failing eyesight. He figured the fumes were burning his eyes away, much like the nightshift was doing to his early twenties. But the windows were incandescent, especially at this hour, daylight rising in a slow purple tide. This time of morning was a benediction for Charlie, a reminder to pray for his meth-addict mother, for his acceptance to Ivy Tech, and now for Joanie.

"We'll get the ring," Charlie told her. "Goddamn it, if I have to tear that machine apart, I'll get it back to you."

A wave of medics in collared shirts poured over a stack of pallets. Charlie trusted them to know their way around the carnage by virtue of the collars.

"Keep beside her, can you?" Charlie asked Ted, the circle around them dispersing. "I'll start digging."

"Go."

Charlie examined Press 23. He passed the dusty knobs and flashing counters and plastic shreds blown by oscillating fans. With his eyes he followed the tight plastic trail, the spider's filament, through the downed printing press. Even when stopped the press growled. He glanced over the hundred rubber rollers, the bulky motors that drove them, the yellows and reds and purples that flecked the great machine. He stumbled on a trash barrel and wondered for a moment if he would vomit. He kept walking.

At the rewind shaft he found Gary Duritz, the white-bearded lifer who served as Joanie's press operator. The two men dropped their hands.

"She ain't good," said Charlie. "You see it?"

"I can't be in here," Gary said. "It's my fault."

"Keep it together," Charlie said. "I'm going to need your help, before they confiscate all this bloody material."

"I heard it," said Gary, his tired eyes vanquished and red. "I heard her scream—and that snap."

39

Charlie peeked down the aisle. The superintendent lunged toward them in a fresh collared shirt and expensive jeans.

"Let it go," said Charlie. "She'll be back on the floor in a month. Don't look, but here comes Dayside Dean. Get your shit together."

Gary caught the kid's sleeve, pulled. "We were running too fast, pushing too hard," he said. "Finnery's Fish Stick bags. They told me to push like that."

"Shut up, man." Charlie shook Gary's hand away. "That big ring of Joanie's," he said, "the one her Army husband paid off…it got sucked in."

"Jesus Christ."

"That's what I said."

"There's no way," Gary said, eyeing the press as if awestruck by its immensity. "Impossible we'll find a thing like that."

"We're finding something," said Charlie. "A stone, a piece… *something.*"

Gary stepped back and kicked his steel-toe against a pallet. Like Charlie, he had a habit of kicking factory materials in frustration. He dug a utility knife from his pocket, extended the blade and checked its sharpness. "What's it been now," Gary said, "about six months since the video?"

"At least," said Charlie.

"That husband's as good as dead."

"Just start cutting."

Charlie turned around. Emergency lights above the supervisor's office flashed like disco strobes, and the haze over far presses slowly fell. The pressroom was shutting down. Charlie hadn't heard the floor so quiet since the company bought Christmas dinner for the crew last year, an awkward feast at three in the morning.

The big-shouldered mass that was Dean Flanders, the superintendent, hobbled up to the press. Dean waved his fat thumbs in downward jabs to the operators, his orders to shut down.

"Where is she?" shouted Dean, his head angled down on Charlie, his neck in folds over the collar. Charlie smelled the oaken scent of coffee on Dean's big breathing, the soap and aftershave of his recent shower.

"She's in the back, sir," said Charlie. "It wasn't her fault."

"The operator?" asked Dean. "Who was over her?"

Charlie stared at a chest-level button on Dean's white shirt. He wouldn't do Gary the injustice of even looking at him.

"I was," Charlie said. "I was teaching her to set registration when it happened. As fast as we were going, it was hard to keep up."

"Don't bitch," said Dean, and he jabbed his pudgy forefinger in Charlie's sternum. "Be in my office at six. Don't leave. You understand?"

"Yeah."

"Six o'clock. Bring your paperwork and toolbox."

"I was trying to help," Charlie said. "I need this job. I'm trying to get back in school."

Dean let out a long, puzzled groan. "What's her name, back there?"

"It's Joanie," said Charlie. "They call her Mama. She's a single mom, four kids."

"The one whose husband..."

"Yeah, that's her."

"When it rains..."

"Yes, sir," Charlie said.

"Six o'clock."

"Okay."

Dean lumbered off behind the press, shifty and bulbous like a circus bear.

Charlie hadn't spoken to a superintendent since his first nightshift, eleven months prior. The night he snuck to the neighboring press around midnight and made small talk with Joanie.

Charlie found her twang absorbing, her motherliness warm, a soothing alternative to the cold mechanical wilderness of plastics production. He told her about his imprisoned Oklahoma mother, about his long-vanished dad, the oilrig deadbeat who existed only in unsavory rumors. His aunt and uncle had raised him; for cash they grew pot in a backyard treehouse, cooked speed in the basement. He tried speed once with his neighbor, Oliver, and they ended up breaking schoolyard windows with lug-nuts and stealing a motorcycle. He told Joanie he was better than drug-runners and general fuck-brains.

"One day I'll fix funny cars on the Midwest regional circuit," Charlie said. "Raising money for tech school as we speak. I'm good with engines."

Joanie pulled her gloves off and roped her hair in a tight ponytail. "Baby," she said, "you know anything about the nightshift?"

Charlie laughed. "*Nada.*"

She covered her head in a fresh hairnet and put a hand on his shoulder. "Prepare yourself to go upside down, and inside out," she said. "Any little problem you got, well, get it taken care of, because in here, at night, there's nothing but thinking time. Nothing—I mean *nothing*—goes away on nightshift. It'll eat your mind up. It'll distract you. And this here's a dangerous place to be distracted."

Charlie said whatever and walked back to his press.

They cut into a roll of wound plastic, big as a barrel, Gary heaving at Charlie's side, their blades quickly dulling. They dabbed off the blood and mush.

"She'll get paid," Gary wheezed. "Rocky, the plate prep guy, got five grand. And that was his pinkie."

"She's all busted up," Charlie said. "Like a hundred-grand busted up."

Charlie's eyes wandered the press. It was too organized for his taste, too cognizant of time, the archrival of factory men. Electronic timers, stop watches, and traditional clocks with hands. Everywhere clocks, clocks, clocks.

"Dean wants to can me for this," said Charlie. "He doesn't know who I am. He won't think twice."

Gary stopped cutting. "You know how many people I got counting on me, on my pension when it comes?" he said.

"Somebody's getting the boot for a recordable injury like this. If not you, the guys will push for me, or Joanie. Her ring being on don't help matters."

"We all need this damn place," Charlie said.

Gary ran his shirtsleeve across his forehead. "These jobs are a dime a dozen," he said. "You're an ox. I'm a busted old man."

A huge overhead duct breathed in fresh, cool air. Charlie stood in place a moment and enjoyed the cascade. It swept the sweaty pools from his eye sockets and ears, from the unkempt blond hair that poked in strands from his hairnet.

"Fine," Charlie said. "But when the time comes, you'll help with my tuition. I can count on you for that, right?"

"The books," Gary smiled. "I'll buy all the books you'll need. Swear to God I will."

Charlie dug on.

When word had come down from Army brass, Joanie used enough disability time to keep her at home for two weeks. Nobody knew why.

"Funny," Charlie told a lifer, over a urinal divide in the bathroom, "she just called me a pussy for calling off sick last week. And that was *one* day."

Then the *Carl City Gazette* ran a front-page story that stunned the pressroom: "Staff Sgt., Stationed In Baghdad, Feared Kidnapped" and below that, in a subhead, "Grim video shows violent captors beating father of four."

That night they passed a lunchbox for collections around the cafeteria, then a second when the first was full. Outside, near the factory entrance, the crab-apples were beginning to blossom.

Joanie returned to work on a Tuesday. No one could find the right way to approach her. A dour pace instead of her bounding walk, silence for that crazy laugh, Joanie's demeanor only served to deter them further. They left her alone the entire first night. At third break on her second shift Charlie couldn't hold back.

"If it helps, I know where you are right now," he said, taking the empty seat next to her in the cafeteria. She drew her eyes up from scripture. "I know, to an extent, with my mom and all, what it feels like."

"Baby," she said. "It's all too fresh right now."

"I wouldn't say I'm exactly *used* to it," Charlie continued, "or that anybody can be. I'd say you kind of get used to the idea of things over time, but never quite used to the thing itself."

Joanie lowered her voice. "What I'm feeling is no idea," she said. "It's real as the blood in my veins."

Charlie pushed a coffee he had poured for her across the table. "It helps, I guess, to try to talk," he said. "Don't be afraid to sound stupid."

She laughed a little, and sighed.

"There you go," Charlie said. "Just keep thinking about funny shit."

Joanie giggled and covered her mouth, as if by laughing she had violated some sacred rule of grief. She pulled off her hairnet and twisted the cap tight on her bottled water. "Can I ask you a favor?"

Charlie said sure.

"I wanna put my head down on my arms and try sleeping, like you used to, when that girlfriend had you eaten up. In the morning, it's gotten so I can't sleep." She pushed over a small, weatherworn songbook. "These words, on this page, I want you to hum them to me. Slow but warm, like nobody's listening."

Charlie tilted up the book, flipped it open to the right page. He couldn't begin to guess the tune, having never warmed a pew in his life. He asked her how it went.

"However you hear it is fine," she said. "Just don't let me sleep in here too long. Gary's out there, expecting me back at half past three."

Charlie cleared his throat and cast eyes to the other guys, each of them feigning indifference. He didn't care if they heard him or

44

what they would think. He let go a shaky baritone that, at first, felt like a cloud of bees escaping him, but in a second he warmed to the words, and what felt like a knot in his chest came loose:

"Oh let nothing keep me from God's love,
Not death nor ill nor pain will drown,
Not fire nor snow nor rain can ground
This love I have for you my Lord;
So let nothing keep me from God's love."

"There's a big bloody mess back there," Dean said to Charlie, appearing suddenly, practically up against him. "Use solvent to clean it, fast solvent. You've got fifteen minutes."

Charlie and Gary hid their utility blades, discretely wiped the sweat from their cheeks.

"And cut all the bloody stuff out of the press," Dean said. "Leave it here for review. I want the back spotless before safety can take pictures."

"Okay," Charlie said. "You got it."

Dean surged down the aisle and hollered at operators to get things rolling again. The dayshift crew was filtering in, their first day on this week. The roar came back.

Gary kicked a heap of cut plastic and the ring spat out. It dinked across the floor and came to rest against the press. Gary thrust his hands up, as if declaring a touchdown. He cursed at Charlie for missing the ring and bent down to pick it up.

The gold was oblong, flat, and jewelless, muddled over with the reflex blues of Jammy Juice packaging. Gary held it between his two gloved fingers. It looked chewed.

"Needle in a freakin' *haystack*," he said.

Charlie handed him a paper towel to conceal the find. "Stay here a minute," he said. "Hit that thing with disinfectant and put it in your pocket." Charlie pushed his toolbox behind a dozen others, confident everything in it belonged to the company. He hurried to the

45

back of the press and shed his gloves. There was truly a mess. Rags like crushed cherries lay in piles, and the scissored ends of bandages dotted the floor. Red footprints led toward the exits, toward the day.

Charlie breathed hard and worked up a big firm wad of spit. He spat into the press and its ten thousand pinch points, those steely connections his trainers had harped about. He hurried back to the rewind shaft and spun Gary around.

"Give me that thing," he said, nodding to Gary's pocket. "Which way did they wheel her?"

Gary dug out the ring and pointed to an exit. "What about your appointment with Dean?" he laughed. "You'll be late, son."

"Books," Charlie said, hustling away. "I know your number, Gary. You owe me those books."

Charlie peeled off his hairnet and bolted toward the swivel doors. He spotted the medics at an emergency station applying fresh bandages. He ran to Joanie, close enough to squeeze her ankle. Her eyes were half-open. She didn't respond.

"Here," Charlie said. "I'm putting this in your pocket," and he did, careful not to upset her with the ring's condition. "You hear me? We found it. You got it."

The medics swarmed Joanie as they wheeled her out. She was strapped onto the stretcher, her head in a brace, the damaged parts immobile. Blue ink had dried in blotches on her arms and shirt, which held down her breasts like cased pillows. Her big chest folded against the gurney straps with the force of her breathing. The pinched hand, hovering at her side, was taped up and softened with gauze, like a massive cotton swab. Charlie watched as she raised her good hand and rubbed her thumb against the tips of her four good fingers.

"That's right—cash," yelled Charlie. "That's *exactly* right."

He watched Joanie roll through the labyrinthine Plant II gates, down the widest aisle, toward the converting department and the click-clack-click-clack machines, then out the swivel doors. Charlie imagined her soaking in the cafeteria air-conditioning, the concern and wonderment of dayside folks washing over her. He walked down a storage aisle he never had before, guessing which parking lot it might lead to. The sun-brightened windows caught his eye one last time.

THE ABDUCTION

The overhead speaker was barking zucchini specials in Aisle 6 when she noticed Nola wasn't behind her. The child was not spinning a plush dinosaur over the frozen turkey in the shopping cart, not issuing her wonderful little annoyances. The child was nowhere, a ghost.

Last time Kathy had felt that way was three years prior, when, as an infant, Nola plunged from her lap, a simple rollover becoming a misshapen skull. The condo floors were hard Brazilian cherry, the head unformed and supple. The dent was barely noticeable once the strawberry locks grew in. The grandmothers called Kathy too hurried, too absent-minded, too self-aware, the epitome of modern motherhood.

In the supermarket Kathy broke a sweat, her woolen pantsuit heavy and confining. Where had Nola bobbed off to? The Laundry Needs section? The Incontinence aisle? Much, much farther?

49

The child had always been a rascal, a product of her father's wildfire spirit. There was recklessness in Carlos that, fed by youth, had landed him briefly in jail. He was a good fighter, too good. Or so he told Kathy through the lunch slot in his cell door, she on the other side like hope itself, an intelligent-looking counselor paid to actually care. When she asked about his life goals he answered a daughter named Nola and son named Marlon. His dark eyes deepened in expressing that, a look she found sincere and exotic. She said the name Nola was beautiful, creative, a window to his artistic side. Through the slot they touched fingertips—a tiny, forbidden handshake.

"Nola Rodriguez," the freckled boy insisted on the microphone. "Please come to Register 5 at the front of the store. Your mother is waiting on you."

Something inside Kathy spoiled—the pang, she thought, that accompanies failure of the lowest order, centuries worth of instincts gone unused. She scanned the aisles from Dairy to Hardware. No Nola. Shoppers milled the aisles, an oblivious herd going about their lives. Her thoughts turned dark and she cried in public. The pang sickened her.

In middle school a boy named Freddy Judson had called Kathy an airhead. She'd suspected an attention deficit problem all her life, but with her intelligence firing on all cylinders, it was never so much a detriment as a nuisance. At lunch she'd gaze at Blue Jays in the leafy school courtyard, dreaming of one day swapping her Indiana surroundings for the south of France. In history class the teacher said workers take six vacations per year, by law, in France. Her parents built toilets at the Delta plant, hardly sneaking one vacation every other year. But those were the highlights of her girlhood, those far-flung weeks, those Florida beaches and Wisconsin Dells. She came to associate vacationing with sound parenting.

"Look, I said I haven't seen her," said the pudgy man near the cart corral, brushing snow off his leather jacket.

"I'm sorry," Kathy said. "This is just a nightmare."

"Call the police."

"They're coming."

The man pushed his shopping cart into the corral, unlocked the doors of his BMW, and slid into the driver's seat. He smelled like pricey cologne, something that would come in dark bottles. "I'll keep my eyes open," he said. "I'm sure she's fine. Probably being a kid, hiding around here somewhere."

"Do you watch the local news much?"

"Look," he said, "that's a pretty scary pattern, but it hasn't happened anywhere near this side of town. Not within twenty miles. Kidnappings are more of a low-income type of problem."

Kathy shrugged the man off and hurried across the parking lot. She looked beneath cars, behind bushes. For the rest of her life she will remember the eyes, but only the eyes. They peeked at her sheepishly from the cracked tinted window of a blue truck, possibly a Ford but maybe a Nissan. They were red and afraid but she wasn't looking for eyes, only for her daughter's hair. In three seconds the eyes were gone, the window fully closed, the truck groaning onto Highway 76, the license plate number anybody's guess.

Five hours before, over breakfast, she'd scolded Nola for chewing the dinosaur's ear. "Little girls don't do that—babies do," she'd said. "That's a good way to catch the Swine Flu."

Kathy called her husband at work, interrupting his rebuilding of a Harley's gearbox. She relayed Nola's reaction to the flu threat, that flash of progress, that miracle.

"You'd have thought she saw the boogeyman," Kathy told her husband. "It was *so* cute."

"Fantastic," said Carlos, washing his hands. "What's for dinner?"

"I was thinking we could go out," she said. "Some place family friendly."

Carlos groaned. "I vote for a couple bottles of wine at home, a cheap Saturday night."

"Then it's turkey," Kathy said, disappointed. "But I'll have to go buy the damn thing."

In six months, she would blame the divorce on mutual repression. A counseling term, she defined it as the inability to sufficiently relive the past together, as a couple, as parents. Blame played second fiddle, but it played well.

Ten years later, Kathy still drives on weekends to towns she's never visited, plops a cut-rate motel room on her Visa, and watches the local news. She uncorks port wine on cold beds and cries. She expects to see Nola in local newscasts—in the backdrop of some accident scene, or in the spectator crowd at a burning building—signaling for her mother to retrieve her, to save her and start over, to take her on vacation.

On Saturday mornings, in these strange towns, Kathy nods and smiles to mothers in supermarkets, savoring glimpses of what was, telling them without words how fortunate they are.

EXULTATION

Maxine had just walked home from the farmer's market when she found him, motionless on the floor next to the fridge. His face was icy blue, a tray of spilled hummus, olives, and cucumbers slathered across his barrel chest. His big powerful hands clutched at his sternum, as if reaching for the one problem those hands would never fix: a heart that had run its course, a diseased coronary artery, the secret he surely felt coming but was too proud to tell.

So ended Maxine's life with Rex, a sixty-four-year séance that felt to her as fresh as the day he'd come home from Okinawa. On his splotchy left wrist he bore a tattooed pineapple; on his right, her name threaded with a long-stem rose. Maxine stood in the kitchen five minutes before calling the ambulance. His head was cocked downward, his right wrist upturned. She knelt to him and wept at the thought: Her name was the last thing her husband ever saw.

"That right there," Maxine would tell her great-grandson at the funeral, "is the finest son-of-a-bitch you'll ever see."

Octogenarians. They had laughed at the word. They thought of themselves as being beyond the confines of age, even eight decades of it. Through science, they could make love, and they did, as ridiculous as it sounded, these two passionate fogies, romping like dolphins under an eternal moon.

The first weeks after Rex felt to Maxine like a thin, chemical daze. She missed her master barber—a status Rex had earned in the fifties—and his crafty hands. She had morbid dreams. In them, an omnipresent voice laughed at her, and she was cut in half, lopped in two at the waist, spinning in pools of blood in search of her wedding ring. When she burst awake, her nightgown would be transparent with sweat, her hands clenching the downy sheets like talons.

Maxine wanted to tell her pastor, the dashing Alexander Schmidt of Marthasville First Baptist Church, about her fractured sleep, her tormented dreams. But she felt shy and ridiculous. She'd never confided in her pastor without holding Rex's hand for spiritual, if not physical, support. She kept quiet.

The congregation knew Maxine as strong-willed and intelligent, a career accountant when her contemporaries tended gardens, prepped meatloaf, and shepherded kids to bus stops. She'd snagged Rex Schuster after all, a feat that had propelled her social standing and left a perpetual pink hue on her cheeks. Everyone could see in Maxine's face that, behind closed doors, she and Rex were enjoying tectonic sexual activities.

A week before Christmas, Maxine sat alone at her desk, upstairs in the craftsman where they had reared their daughter, the grade-school principal. The home ached with silence, the bedroom blue with moonlight. She had left her husband's L.L. Bean moccasins beside the bed, as if he might slip from the covers and fill them. She'd lightly brushed her clothes with Barbicide and handled his oily Oster clippers; that was the scent of barbershops, the musk of him. She turned on the desktop computer her grandson had taught her to operate, from which she liked to cull gardening secrets and comfort-food recipes (she was the queen, for better or worse, of pan-fried catfish and sweet-potato fries). She surfed to Google and watched the pesky cursor flash.

Half-consciously, Maxine typed his name into the search engine: "r...e...x"

Nothing interesting. The mission statement for an architectural design firm and mumbo jumbo about dinosaurs. She yawned. The computer usually did this to her. Overwhelmed her with information, tired her.

She dragged the arrow to the "Sleep" option but stopped before the computer could react. She searched Rex's full name and grimaced when no mention of his obituary appeared, no trace in this technological realm of her old-fashioned man. Most of his diehard customers had died years before; his Army buddies were long vanished around the country, likely dust. When she died would all earthly hints of Rex Schuster die too? She cleared the search box and wished the Internet was a fad, like hula hoops.

In frustration, Maxine pounded the last letter— "x...x...x..."—before smashing down her palms on the keyboard, touching the ENTER key first.

A thumbnail photo flashed atop the screen. Maxine's mouth fell open. Ten naked people in a heart-shaped bed, all of them bronzed and young, writhed together. They were connected at a central location, the source of the feast, their oily bodies stretching outward like an orgy octopus.

Shocked, Maxine scrolled down.

But it didn't go away.

It had her.

It was everywhere.

"It's so...primal," she whispered. "And so...*brazen*."

A portal of infinite, smutty possibility blinked before Maxine's eyes. She fell back in her chair, dropped her hands. She'd wondered a time or two, naturally, but she had no idea it would be this easy. Her church mates would rue her for treading even this far, but she felt like an explorer, a Himalayan trekker, or a brave soul trudging some netherworld her friends at Bingo wouldn't dare. She leaned into the screen and smiled. Her old heart kicked.

"My *good*ness…" she said, her fingertips pensively stalking the keys.

From the pulpit, Pastor Alexander Schmidt extolled the virtues of sinless living, waving his hammy fingers like a maestro. In the pew Maxine had warmed since the seventies, she couldn't help but admire the pastor's zeal—and the cantaloupe-big masses that were his shoulders. His chest was duly thick, the better for building orphanages and Habitat homes on weekends.

"God almighty," Pastor Schmidt beckoned, pointing to a menagerie of stained-glass windows, "give me strength to weather the tempest, show me inspiration amid the dark, dark night…"

"Amen," Maxine said, smiling surreptitiously.

As the pastor snaked the crowd, barking songs from the Hymnal and urging the collection plate along, Maxine nudged her friend, Belle, and pointed to the pastor's ass.

"What's gotten into you?" whispered Belle, a study in polyester and crocheted over-garments.

"Hopefully," Maxine blushed, "some of that."

In two months' time, Maxine had subscribed to three websites—hotfiremen.com, toysrnus.com, and her favorite, bangmejamesbond.com—that required a monthly fee. The free sites were too amateur for her refining tastes. She collected the bills and added them up: One hundred and seventy five dollars in monthly fees signaled to her the beginnings of a problem, if not an addiction. She sought help.

"Thoughts of extremely aged people having intercourse are not something the logical human mind likes to entertain," the professor said, between tokes on his churchwarden pipe, puffs of cherry tobacco wafting. "Thank God I was not stricken with a logical mind."

Maxine wanted to leave, but something in the professor's suave egotism and silver ponytail told her to stay. Besides, he was much cheaper to consult with than a real psychiatrist, being that he made his living reading textbooks to lazy undergrads instead of actually fixing people. And something in the curves of his corduroys hinted at weightlifter thighs and an ass hard as salads bowls.

"I beg your pardon, sir," Maxine said, "but I think you've misunderstood me. It's not elderly people I'm interested in seeing. It's the young. And I can't stop looking."

The professor—was his name Archie?—stroked his dimpled chin. The dimple was so pronounced it looked manufactured, a seductive little chin cave. "Is there any particular, uh, *variety* that you find appealing?"

Maxine blushed. "I don't think I can talk about this—"

"Triple X?"

"Oh," she said, "at least."

The professor adjusted his smart flannel shirt, sucked his pipe. "Can you be more specific? Can you give me some sort of visual to work with?"

"Sir," she said, "I'd rather not. This isn't the type of conversation most people would expect of me. This doesn't feel right."

"Listen, you have to trust me," he said. "If this is going to work, you have to let down your shoulders, you have to *let me in*—"

"Double-penetration."

"Excuse me?" the professor said, nearly choking on the words.

Maxine's face collapsed into her hands, her mauve fingernails caught deep in her wispy, gray-brown hair. "I'm ashamed. I just clicked once, not even knowing the term. But something in the physics of it fascinates me—and appalls me at the same time."

The professor smirked and leaned back in his English leather chair. He crossed his legs in the manner of seasoned academia, ankle over thigh. "Do you think your husband would approve?"

Maxine sat up and stared into his face. Her gut told her to change the subject. "He's moved on."

"I'm sorry," the professor said.

"I mean he's gone for good."

"Again," he said, "sorry."

Maxine deflected his condolences with surprising ease. She felt a pang of guilt for not collapsing at the thought of Rex, for not wheezing with grief's grasp on her lungs, for not acting like a good wife probably should. This proximity to, and talk of intimacy with, another man was surely a major ethical violation, but Maxine yearned to practice the sexual aerobics that had lately consumed her fantasies. She reasoned that, if confronted with a similar scenario, her dead husband would screw a willing and buxom psychiatrist wearing, say, a red business dress. Surely if Rex was privy to this, watching from some high and copacetic perch, he could also see its therapeutic value.

"Your voice," she said. "Have you been trained to speak so hypnotically?"

The professor reached over his head and locked the office door, then inched in closer and fiddled with a button of her blouse. "I don't think hypnosis is necessary," he said. "I think we're on the same wavelength already."

She winked.

"Would you like a glass of burgundy?" he said.

Maxine said absolutely, and she slid her fingertips across his chin.

By the third month, Maxine couldn't hold back. She sold her husband's shop, a dusty relic occupying one-fourth of a former Winn-Dixie, to Italian investors looking to start a café, one that would mutate into a nightclub on weekends. Members of the congregation considered the sale of Rex's shop downright sacrilegious, but like so many widows before her, Maxine ignored sacrilege because profit had blown her a kiss.

The bills accumulated. The professor sent roses. Maxine grew bored and stopped replying. She had only so many years to explore, to conquest, and she couldn't be dragged down by a pompous man-child who wept about being spanked in sixth-grade. She considered writing a letter to the male lead on bangmejamesbond.com, a California thoroughbred with abs like baked muffins. He called himself James Bondage. His stage presence electrified Maxine, but she decided against the letter, fearing her ornate handwriting and concise grammar might turn off a child of the email age.

One day the professor called her in desperation. "I've never had anything like this," he pleaded. "There's so much *fire* in you, Maxine."

"Archie, I don't know."

"You should come over," he said, clearing his throat. "There's a behavioral concept by Erikson that might be applicable in your case. We can discuss, over wine. Plus I have this dynamite new movie that just arrived in the mail."

Though she'd been trying not to, Maxine mentally juxtaposed the professor's bedroom prowess with that of Rex, and again she envisioned a Vespa motor scooter squaring off with a dump truck.

"You're awfully sweet," Maxine said, "but I'm afraid you'll have to do better than that."

She hung up, a true player.

Needing a respite from the drama, Maxine volunteered one weekend to help Pastor Schmidt restore an 1890s shotgun-style home for a single mother subsisting on vouchers. The pastor told Maxine, like the other volunteers, to wear jeans and an old shirt to the job site; she arrived in a billowing sundress and full makeup.

"Dressed like that, maybe we can have you dust the place, but you certainly won't be doing any painting, or any landscaping," the pastor reasoned, examining her. "We can't have you getting dirty in a dress like that."

"Oh," Maxine chirped, "I don't mind."

She pursed her wet cherry lips. The pastor turned away and slapped drywall compound on a nail-dotted wall. She worried he was shaking his head in disgust.

For lunch, the other volunteers went for barbecue at a shack on Memorial Drive. Maxine poured the pastor a Gatorade and urged him to sit next to her on a makeshift plywood bench. He obliged.

They sipped at Styrofoam cups for a couple of minutes in silence, Maxine planning what to say. She decided there was virtue in directness. "It might not be comfortable," Maxine smiled, looking down, "but this plywood contraption could act as a little bed—"

"Stop," the pastor said. "Please stop, Miss Schuster."

"Forgive me." She hung her head.

"I see something brewing in you, and I'm alarmed," he said. "Yours was a good, good man."

"I'm sorry," she said.

"For all those years, you made him feel extremely lucky, and he told me that, in those exact words, at our picnic last summer. He was strong as a bear, but he worried about leaving you behind."

"He liked you," she said.

The pastor shook his head. "I'm not sure he could've predicted this behavior, however."

"I'm acting shamefully," she said. "I absolutely am."

"Listen," the pastor said, "I've seen people pick up coping mechanisms that could kill a horse. Downright toxic stuff—drugs, gambling, reptile fetishes. Whatever's getting to you isn't nearly as severe, but I can see it's leaving a certain residue. Is there something we need to talk about?"

Maxine refastened the three buttons of her dress she'd let down like an invitation. "I married young," she said. "I've given in to curiosity, to instinct. That's all this was. I apologize."

She dropped her cup in the trash and walked out the door.

Maxine got busted on a Wednesday. She hadn't expected her daughter, Samantha, to take the day off school, to schedule a midweek dental procedure, and certainly not to drop by unannounced. Maxine was washing her hands in the restroom when her daughter shrieked in the nearby bedroom.

Maxine knew the sound. Her mind shot back to the day forty years prior when Samantha had fallen off their roof while cleaning gutters, landing in bug-infested kudzu, snapping her left wrist. Now, in her haste, Maxine banged her knee on the vanity and hobbled to her bedroom.

"Mom, what the hell is *that?*" Samantha scolded, pointing to the bed. "Is that a dildo? Yes—yes, it is. Oh, my God. Where the hell did you get *a dildo?*"

Maxine just shrugged.

"What's it doing here? Do you even know what this is, what it does?"

"Please, dear," Maxine said.

"Answer me, mom."

"They call it 'The Rabbit,'" Maxine said. "You see those little ears, coming off the shaft? Those damn things drive me up these walls—"

"*Stop it!*"

Maxine dropped her head, by now a familiar pose. "I had it shipped in from Europe," she said. "The message boards said the Swedes make these things like nobody's business."

"*Mom!*"

"You asked, so I'm telling you," Maxine said. "I'm too damned old to beat around the bush. It's a dildo, honey. Try one."

Samantha plugged her earlobes with her fingertips and looked away. Unfortunately for Maxine, her daughter turned to the desk computer, where James Bondage himself was employing the missionary to slay a hollering brunette.

"*Mother!*" Samantha burst, clutching her face. "I won't let this happen… I'm taking this up with First Baptist." She pointed her index finger, as if tossing a dart, directly at her mother's chest.

Maxine slung a pillow to cover her toy. "You really don't need to do that."

"I need to do something," Samantha said. "Do you realize how hypocritical this is? How this violates everything you and dad taught me?"

"Look," Maxine said, though her daughter was stomping away. "I think you need to relax. This makes me forget how alone I am, how alone we'll all be one day."

"You're *stronger* than this," Samantha said, pounding down the craftsman's hickory stairs. "I'm bringing this up Sunday."

Maxine only sighed, winced at the slamming door, and returned to her desk.

Dear James Bondage:
Hopefully this letter finds you well. I have only the address for your studio, not for your exact room, so hopefully it finds you indeed. I can't describe for you the immense liberation I've found in your work, especially in the earlier episodes, in which you wore a robust mustache. You'll probably never know me, and would likely be appalled at my appearance should we meet, but I wanted to express my gratitude before this séance of ours falls to twilight. I must quit you, James. You are a contradiction, albeit a highly pleasurable one. Best in life and career. Your eldest admirer—M

Maxine walked to church on Sunday, a time to organize her thoughts and refine an excuse. She'd tucked cancellation notices for all three websites in her pocket, proof of her path toward moral cleanliness, though she knew the free stuff was available if weaning was in order. She crested a hill that overlooked the squat brick structure, and she froze. Samantha waited at the church entrance, the pastor standing beside her, tapping his hip as congregants streamed in. It was a trap. Maxine turned around, hung a left on Archibald Lane, and walked home. She loaded up a duffel bag and left again.

She walked two miles under exploding Dogwoods until she came to the wicked iron gates of Marthasville Cemetery. For the first time since the heart attack, Maxine felt relief at seeing the manicured grounds, those green hills freckled with headstones. The groundskeeper, making his rounds in a golf cart, waved.

"Been a while, hasn't it?" the groundskeeper said.

"Too long," she said, walking in. "Place looks pristine, almost cheery."

"Good to see you smiling."

She found Rex's gravesite and its modest stone tablet. She knelt and touched it, but drew her hand away fast, as the tablet was hot with sunlight. Maxine took this to heart. "Don't blame me, okay?" she said. "I don't like you cranky."

She thought for a moment about their first days together. How, before he'd chosen her, Rex had a harem of other girls, these dingy clingers around the high school. Downtown one afternoon, Maxine overheard a fellow cheerleader call Rex a sexual magician, and her mind exploded with possibilities. Rumor was, Rex had gone to barber school the previous summer and came back with his huge hands more nimble than ever. Maxine was uninitiated, and wildly curious. She asked Rex for a ride home from Reckoning High School, then a ride to the grocery. She kept the romance at simple kissing until, impassioned by the smell of his father's cologne, she practically jumped Rex at the movies. He drove her to a grassy, sloping park near the river. "I bet there's buried treasure here," Rex had said, hovering over her, tracing an X below her belt, his hair black and full. "Bet this marks the spot, don't it?"

All the years between, they were never intimate with anyone else. An accountant at a competing firm made an earnest, drunken pass at Maxine in the fifties, but she wasn't curious. Rex had talked dotingly about the mother of a blond boy whose hair he'd cut for years, but Maxine's suspicions never really boiled. They had an unspoken understanding that secrets doom people, that lies erode sacred things, and they were above all that.

Maxine knew she had to come clean.

From within the duffel bag she exhumed a tiny shovel. She dug a hole in the red clay soil about the size of a shoebox and peeked over her shoulders; nobody was there. Quickly, she whipped The

Rabbit from her bag and buried it, patting the earth with her bare hands and sprinkling the spot with grass.

She stood up, face to the tablet. "Happy now?"

Maxine bowed her head a moment and turned to walk home. A few yards down the cemetery's main road, however, she stopped and hustled back to the tablet. "As far as the other stuff, I told you it'd behoove you to learn computers," she said. "And don't give me hell about that professor. A train wreck and you know it."

She found a thin stick and cracked it in half. She smiled so big she worried it was disrespectful, and in the fresh dirt that was the toy's final resting place, she bent down and carved a deep X, just in case. She went back to the road and walked away, perhaps to church, perhaps not.

LOWCOUNTRY

Hans was driving from Charleston to Augusta, leaving the palmetto-studded Lowcountry for the piney swells of eastern Georgia, when he endured the first true country song he'd heard since college, a sappy howler about a one-armed Vietnam vet whose mother was killed by a rattlesnake. The next song, blaring from his Bose sound system, rhymed Pop-Tart with Walmart in the chorus. A total of four people died in the third song, a truly sad manifesto about Hurricane Katrina. But to Hans, still righting his brain after a night of margaritas on Queen Street, that song was also hilarious, being that it took itself so seriously en route to sucking so bad.

Hans set the cruise control to seventy-nine, a speed at which the Cadillac CTS simply absorbed the highway. He asked the prostitute, balled up like dirty laundry in the backseat, if she'd been listening.

"Dude," said the prostitute. "I said no more talking. I can't even think straight."

He smiled, ogling her thighs and orange mini-skirt via the rearview mirror. "Buttercups," said Hans, "you really need to partake. It'll make you feel better. Anyone who listens to this sentimental garbage with a straight face is a bigger moron than the assholes singing it. I'll tell you that much right now."

The prostitute popped her head—a hive of red locks and hairpins, framing pretty young eyes—between the front seats. Her mascara was smeared, her lips flaky as pie. Seeing her, Hans flinched and thought of Medusa, but that made him feel cruel, so he studied the highway. The tall billboards beckoned travelers toward expensive gas, Asian massages, and pole-barns full of pornography, those beacons of Southern interstate commerce. The paranoia that had stricken Hans lately, a byproduct of middle-aged hangovers, came back with vengeance: *Has she been crying? Have I made her cry? Or did her eyes leak while she slept? Is she really eighteen? Because she sure as hell looks fourteen. What was she calling herself at the hotel? Brandi? Bonnie? Bambi?*

The prostitute issued a high-pitched, animalistic whimper. "Why the hell is the air-conditioner broke in a car this nice, Hans? I thought you had, like, *authority* to do stuff about this?"

Hans wondered why every kid under age thirty talked like the bimbos on reality television. "Settle down, sweet plums." He flicked his Parliament cigarette into a furnace of hot August wind. "I'll get you there by five. Promise that on my grandfather."

In the mirror her face relaxed. She inhaled hot wind. "Did you like Charleston?" she asked, so pensive it sounded like an apology. "Leaving seems to have put you in a mood."

Hans craned his blocky head to face her, to blow her a kiss. "She's a beauty," he smiled. "Like Savannah, with table manners."

She leaned in close to his right ear, her sweaty upper chest vampire-pale. A tattoo of plump cherries adorned her neck. Hans noticed the tattoo was pealing, a fraud.

"You saved me," she said. "You know that, right? They won't find me."

"Let me tell you something…" and Hans pushed his t-shirt sleeves over his shoulders, airing his armpits. "In forty-five years, I've never been stabbed for any chick, and I came within twenty centimeters of having that blade in my goddamn femoral artery, of dying in the Roach Motel in Happytown USA. That's not the type of ending that's written for me. I won't die on hotel carpet, I'll tell you that much."

The prostitute slinked into the front seat and gave Hans epic road-head free of charge. But he wasn't into it. He thought about the stitches in his leg, about his absence from the metro Atlanta car dealership with his name on it, about the excuses he'd have to concoct and spoon-feed his wife, herself hospitalized with a vicious scourge of pancreatitis. He would have to paint the void that was the last three days with vivid and viable scenarios; it would be a true feat because, at birth, Hans had been stricken with absolutely no imagination, just the tenacity to sell himself and the products of his many endeavors. This most recent bout of stupidity had begun Friday, when he told his wife's family he was going for a bite, maybe to his brother's to catch the ballgame, to shake off the hospital stench. Instead a time-warp had ensued, his cell phone long tossed into an Interstate 20 ditch, his futuristic Cadillac (now with a cracked windshield, vomit-tinged floor, and an air conditioner ruined by spilled Sweetwater beer) heading wherever it pleased; there was a hotel brawl and police, ten stitches way too close to his jewels, and a teenage hooker entwined in every inglorious minute of it.

Truth was, Hans didn't remember much anymore. He coasted through life in a cool, emotionless fog that some mistook for arrogance. At forty, he'd felt what he described as the "tremors" of a mid-life crisis, and his gusto for sales quotas and pennant races and exotic anniversary vacations started to dissolve. He'd built his dream home, a Cape Cod with strange Southwestern influences, a decade prior; he'd lived in it and parked his car collection in its chasmal garage for so long that every brick and plank seemed tired. "You've gotten sick of having everything," one friend, Joey, had accused him a few years prior. "The luster of having, for having's sake, is beginning to wear off."

Lately, Hans had gotten worse. He couldn't testify with confidence to any detail of his recent life, to why reckless abandon can get the best of a successful man. Charleston to Hans was margaritas in glass globes, a girl hurling she-crab soup in a car fit to sell, a stark bay with an aircraft carrier, and a parade of ghostly human figures on cobblestone streets. His mind scrambled for more clues, more breadcrumbs in the blur. Nothing came. The paranoia snaked up his chest, around his neck, into his jaws, and constricted the muscles of his face. *This can't go on. My children look up to me.*

"Are you laughing at me?" the prostitute said, zipping his pants, finished as she wanted to be.

"No," he said. "Not laughing. I got some sort of face cramps."

She studied his unshaven face, his dilated eyes. "You sure you're okay to drive?"

"Oh, yeah," Hans said. "It's nothing. Could be the blood-sugar thing my doctor warns me about, but he's an idiot."

"You're weird." She retreated to the back and collapsed on the Tuscany leather seat, tucking her fancy pumps under her butt.

"Where the hell are we going again?" Hans said, his voice timid. "I mean, you know, in general?"

The prostitute slapped his arm. "Enough with the random questions, okay? You're starting to freak me out."

To quell her worries, and his, Hans unleashed his famous booming laugh, the highpoint of his car commercials, a trait carried by the entire Schumacher family. The laugh, it was said, dated back to Hans' grandfather, the Swiss go-getter who'd grown up on *Life* magazine and Mark Twain and emigrated for college in New York but instead became a soldier, a corporal in a hardscrabble Army Tank Battalion. Hans' grandfather, Harold, led this battalion into the dangerous hedgerow country of France. They dug ten miles inland, sending coordinates to heavy artillery, until they came to a tiny village; there the Germans fired a charge into the tank's exposed left side, splintering fire through the cabin. The assistant gunner burned to death almost immediately; Harold pushed three others out the escape hatch before bailing himself, his left hand burned and broken. For three hours he sat beneath a hedge and watched the tank burn, his men groaning beside him. Finally some GIs stumbled along and handed out blankets, water, and sulfur tablets. Medics amputated Harold's hand above the wrist by the light of a Coleman lantern, and the Queen Mary took him back to New York. He married a schoolteacher and moved to Virginia.

Throughout his life, Harold, the Purple Heart hero, had spoken freely of his experience, perhaps to shoo it from his nightmares, or to set a very high bar. To Hans his grandfather, felled by prostate cancer in 1987, had always seemed mythic, victorious in everyday life. And so seemed the America his grandfather had returned to, this vintage postcard world of pressed slacks, milkmen, and kitchen aprons, a vast jigsaw puzzle of vitality and success that seemed wholly devoid of vice.

Hans squinted to see the next billboard: "Hong Kong Massage, VERY nice." An eighth mile closer he could see bikini-clad breasts like lassoed cantaloupes. He read the ingenious tagline: "So come on y'all to Exit 143 where you *won't* be disappointed!!!" It was too hysterical.

"What the hell's so funny?" she said from the back. "My head's throbbing, and I got the spins. Wake me up when we're at the Greyhound place, and *please* be quiet."

Hans reached back and stroked her thigh, smooth as a catfish's belly. The softness of her skin abated his bad thoughts. "Tell me," he said, "you too caught up in yourself to see what's really going on here?"

"Shut up, Hans."

"Seriously," he said. "Open your eyes to this shit, sugar. Look at all these silly signs. Listen to this music. This place begs you to make fun of it sometimes."

"*God*," she snapped.

"You'll see what I mean, one of these days."

69

"Who's to say you're any better, Hans?" she said. "I bet you wish you could play music. You can't do shit but sell cars and smile for those cheesy commercials."

Again he unleashed the thunderous laugh. "Go easy," he said, squeezing the wheel, grinding his jaws. "But yeah, you've got a point."

"Just drive…"

Hans ducked behind the dash and lit another Parliament. "My dad was famous," he said, watching the highway again. "You'd know his name, but I won't say it."

"You want me to jump out? I'll fucking jump out."

"You're young, but you'd know him, or at least his story. It was big in the newspapers, and they were talking about movie rights."

"Oh…my…*God*," she huffed. "You are *so annoying*."

Sebastian Schumacher, Harold's only child, was an entirely different man, a total degradation in lineage, as some called him. Too dim to pass college entry exams, he'd set out to sell lumber in metropolitan New York, but instead found work as a strip-club doorman all along the Eastern Seaboard. Hans had seen the photos of his father, taken long before the shooting: a big blond doofus trying to look tough in some Baltimore back-alley, or in a Lowcountry parking lot rimmed in palmettos. In the photos, Sebastian was flanked by bushy haired impresarios in suits and platform shoes, guys who kept him around for no other reason than his brawn. After a couple of decades, Sebastian did finally arrive at some modicum of notoriety, albeit by accident, the night he picked a fight with leaders of a Southeastern motorcycle club called "The Bastards."

Sebastian, as friends would tell police, thought his opponents were a rockabilly band. The bikers beat him bloody but couldn't keep him down, so they carried him to the parking lot and shot him. They dumped the dismembered remains in a huge vat of unmixed concrete, which the next morning became a veranda on the courthouse lawn of Reckoning, Georgia. The feds, it was said, needed Sebastian's death to pin the bikers to drug-trafficking routes along the coastal plains, not to mention the substantial charge of the death itself. So the feds lay in wait and let Sebastian be slain, rumor holds, inadvertently canonizing his death as a testament to the virtues of just saying no.

Hans took a deep breath and lightly slapped his face. The highway dipped through dense hardwood forests and narrow valleys. Ahead lay the roofs of cheap hotels and the blocky spires of more billboards. At the roadside, a family stood angry beside a steam-spewing van. One boy scooped sweat from his eyes and gawked at the Cadillac, zipping by like a red torpedo.

"Look," Hans said, his cigarette nearly finished. "I just want to say I'm sorry. For whatever's happened to this point, for this weekend, for forgetting your name, for everything. I'm just sorry. I'll say that right now."

She sighed so hard Hans could hear it through the wind. "My name's Brandi, remember?" she said. "Like the drink? You've been calling me 'The Drink' like a smart-ass since Saturday afternoon."

"Ah, yeah, it's coming back." Hans flipped the butt out the window and turned off the country music. He put the windows halfway up. "Can I ask you something, Brandi?"

She sat up and rolled her head, cracking her neck. "I suppose."

"How did I meet you?" he said. "I'm sorry for asking, but I really want to know. I can do without the fight details and all that, but other things are important. I slip into these episodes, and sometimes things happen, I mean things like this arrangement here, but the girls are never as pretty as you. I've seen my fair share, unfortunately."

Brandi pulled her bushy hair into pigtails, which she wrangled with rubber bands. Hans could see how beautiful she really was, but something about the pigtails made him nervous. "You were sweet," she said. "You really were. There was a rose, by the water, and you had some wine in a little cup—"

"You mean the chalice?"

"Yeah," she said, "the cup with the turquoise studs. You broke it on that guy's head."

"What else?"

"That's all I'm going to give you, Hans. The rest will be my secret."

He clasped his face in exaggerated pain.

"I guess I deserve not knowing," he said.

"You deserve whatever's coming to you," she said. "Everybody does."

They drove twenty more miles, until the highway fattened and the commercial outskirts of Augusta replaced the white pines and hemlocks. Hans engaged the in-dash GPS system, a major selling point, and punched in the address from the slip of paper Brandi had given him. He watched her in the rearview, trying to calculate her age by the refinement of her manners. Her legs spread wide in a tiny skirt and her knees buckled in, like a baby vulture trying to stand up. She was very young.

"Well," Hans said sheepishly. "I hope you have yourself a good life."

She smacked his arm again. "Don't mess with my head."

"I'm serious. I hope you can keep your nose clean. And keep away from guys like me, wherever you're going."

She crawled into the front seat, the sunlight catching the sloppy mascara and what Hans thought—*hoped*—were the beginnings of crow's feet. He felt a little better about her company, but something in the shape of her knees portended a deep shame to come. He gave her the slick, smile-wink combo that had closed a thousand deals and locked Cadillac greenhorns into monthly payments they could not afford.

She bit her lip; Hans could see she was going to spout a proposition. He exited the highway onto a surface street, turned left at a junkyard, and drove well under the speed limit. "Go on, buttercups," he said. "Get it off your chest."

She clasped his forearm, rubbed his wrist and palm. "Do you want to come with me—to just say fuck it?" she said, now yanking. "Don't call anybody, don't do anything. Just get on the bus. Leave the

72

car behind, like a clue. We'll use your check card until we get to Chicago. You can get a job up there, selling cars, selling snowmobiles, something. We'll never look back. I'll change my name. I swear to God those pimps are way too stupid to snuff me out."

"Chicago?" Hans said. "You must be out of your damn mind."

She laughed until her dry lips cracked. "Don't be such a stiff." She applied sparkly lip-gloss, which appealed so much to Hans he started having second thoughts. The female GPS voice said the destination was three miles ahead on the left.

"Let me tell you something," he said. "You're a firecracker, but I don't know you, and I've got a whole career and family to worry about. They're sure as shit not in Chi-town. As for the car, only a moron leaves behind a *clue* with an MSRP of fifty-four grand!"

She made a frown of sparkly lips.

"Stop it," he said. "You look like a fish, like a large-mouth bass." Her face reddened with either embarrassment or fury, so he backtracked. "I'm sorry," he said. "Don't take this so hard. You'll be fine. You've got a real enterprising spirit about you."

"Just be quiet," she said.

"Oh, now, don't throw a fit—"

"Shut up," she said. "This is almost over. I should've realized you'd bitch out in the end."

Hans slapped the steering wheel and laughed. "You're too much," he said. "Where are your folks, anyway? Have we discussed that yet?"

"They're looking for me," she said. "They're looking hard."

"What does *that* mean?"

"It means they put out one of those alerts, but it was like a month ago."

"What do you mean *alert?*" he said, sitting up straight, pulling his arm away.

She flipped her wrists and smiled. "I don't know," she said. "Like the one they named after that girl."

"You mean a runaway alert?" Hans said. "Is that what you fucking mean? In which state?"

"Your commercials are pure bullshit, by the way." She snatched his arm back.

"Don't change the subject."

"How can you seriously call yourself the king of pleasure—"

"*Luxury,*" Hans said. "Get it straight. They call me the 'King of Luxury.' You know the jingle."

"Whatever," she said.

"Tell me *exactly* what you meant by this damn alert."

She tossed his arm aside and thrust herself into the backseat. "You're a sham," she said. "You told me so last night, and you have no idea what you said."

"Let's just get you there," he said, "and get you gone."

"Fine."

Hans gritted his teeth again, sorting through the last few moments in his head. Brandi's attitude did little to enrage him, but it had some strange, foreboding resonance. She started to cry crocodile tears in the back. The sounds disturbed Hans because he knew them, had experienced them recently, maybe at a birthday party for his spoiled daughter, the teen who'd wanted a dangerous purple Jeep and *not* an economical sedan with nine airbags. Hans thought the car would teach the girl the astuteness of fuel conservation; instead it verified his suspicions that he'd raised a monster, an insatiable prima donna, a Gucci-beast destined for plastic surgery. And now this Brandi sounded just like her, boiling in a tantrum that no adult would throw.

"Please, stop that," he said.

"Fuck you."

He squeezed the wheel. "Look, one day you'll hit the wall—we all do," he said. "You won't be a fashion queen or rock star or the mayor of Augusta. You might have a steady job that you don't hate, and you'll go there because you have to, and you'll think that things could be worse."

"This is wigging me *the fuck out,*" she said. "Stop talking, okay. I want the drunk Hans back."

"You need to lower your expectations," he said. "You need to get off the street."

She forced a prissy laugh and threw up her hands. "You're the biggest damn hypocrite in the world."

Hans turned left into the bus station and parked in a taxi queue. A buxom magnolia shaded the cars and relieved Hans, his first cool shadow of the afternoon. With his thumb and middle finger he massaged his tired jaw, working the muscles like the beef *tartare* his wife prepared when she had the energy. He watched the glass doors of a dated terminal as they spewed new arrivals. Elsewhere, couples hugged.

"Brandi," he said, turning to her. "Let's be honest…that ID you showed me, it's a fake, isn't it? I distinctly remember seeing an ID, but you weren't truthful with me, were you?"

She zipped her only bag, a purple canvas cylinder, and set it in her lap. "You should reconsider," she said. "Come with me, and in two years, nobody can say anything. My cousin will take us in for a while, and she doesn't give a damn what I do. You'll love her, I swear to God you will—"

"How old are you?"

She dropped her fists into the bag. "I'm broke, *goddamn it.*"

"Be straight with me."

"What difference does it make now?"

"A whole hell of a lot," he said. "Be honest with me."

With the rear doors child-proof and locked, Brandi scooted toward the passenger door and tried to squeeze herself around the front seat, out of Hans' reach, but she couldn't fit. She pouted for a second, straightened her back to a respectable posture, and faced Hans. "If you don't come, I'm finding some stud on the bus, some real baller, and I won't even remember who you were by tomorrow."

"Do you know what this could do to me?"

"Hans? Hans who? Who the hell was Hans?"

"Stop it."

75

"Don't try to blame me," she said. "This was your fault. They can't prove anything. All I have to say is that you raped me."

"That's it," he said. "If you want out, I'll come around and kick your ass out..."

Hans started to nudge his door open but halted when he saw the gun, and behind it a t-shirt with rolled sleeves and the GBI logo he knew from true-crime television. His mind danced, trying to recall the acronym's meaning and the show's details, something about Georgia agents swarming a shack filled with interstate drug runners. Two biceps, each cut by surging veins, leapt from the t-shirt's sleeves. The forearms looked lean and clean-shaven, the hands wrapped in tight leather gloves that seemed awfully militant for a public transit station. Hans leaned forward to glimpse the neck and face but was distracted by a woman in a pantsuit. She scurried closer to the Cadillac but kept a safe distance, a barrier of trees between her and the gun. The woman wore heavy make-up and seemed very anxious. She held a microphone linked by a long chord to a camera, and that to a cameraman.

Hans turned off the Cadillac and rested his hands in his lap. A strange solace came over him, but he didn't dare smile. He knew there could be nothing lower, that whatever would become of his children would be a marked improvement, a genealogical pivot, over this, the moment everything publicly caught fire.

Brandi sobbed and held her hands up in the backseat, screaming to the officer that she was sorry, that this wasn't her idea, that Hans was weird and manipulative. Hans' door flung open, a gloved hand shot in, and he offered his arm to the law like sacrificial flesh.

THE GULCH

In the waiting room I worry the legitimately sick people can smell my funk. A boy pops a pacifier from his mouth and cries. A bulbous old woman hacks phlegm into a wadded Kleenex. My palms are sweaty and back tight, my clothes reeking of the street. I want to smash my chair through the receptionist glass and pillage the leftover prescription forms. Instead a nurse appears. The doctor will see me now.

One look at my frantic eyes and he knows I'm hardly injured or ill. I wish the docs were stupid—like the Woodruff Park police, like study hall teachers—and that medical journals hadn't warned them of my kind.

"Out—*out,*" says the meat-fisted Pollack. He can sense the filthy need in me, the thief in my bloodstream.

"Hear me out," I say. "I've got this busted knee, a real bowl of spaghetti. It's an old football injury that haunts me come autumn."

"You should be arrested." He lifts the examining table to an upright position and lumbers toward the door.

So I leave. And that's okay. Rejections are par for the course, the downside of doctor shopping. I exit the downtown clinic with three stragglers, my using buddies, in tow. We plunge The Gulch and dart like military grunts around its dirty underpasses, ghostly trestles, open sewers. We nod to the crackheads and winos huddled on gray mattresses.

My friend Rico, a petty thief from Statesboro, finds a half-deflated football in the hardened muck of a dried puddle. He punts the ball to me and goes deep, his arms outstretched gracefully, like Jerry Rice in his prime. I drop back three steps and fire a high perfect spiral onto his fingertips.

"Hell *yeah,*" Rico booms in the cavernous Gulch, scattering a few pigeons. "Motherfucker's still got that shit."

This isn't where the scholarships were meant to get me. Not where my district attorney father would have liked me. I used to have social grace and a football pedigree. In a regional championship against Brookstone High, I threw for 340 yards and ran for eighty more. Some highfalutin radio man at the city's biggest station called me a wizard at on-field improvisation, the most highly recruited quarterback in the metro. I was grabbing cheerleaders' asses with my left hand and signing glossy programs with my right—the apple of an insulated, suburban town's eye.

Rico says he scored two pills of Oxycodone somewhere on the Westside. I'm a legitimate customer, having hocked a car stereo and baby formula to Honduran immigrants, scabbing together twenty bucks.

"I'm in," I say.

So Rico and I ditch the others. We emerge from an underpass and cut left on Martin Luther King. He drops the dirty football in a garbage can. In an alley near the State Capitol, that upturned golden boob, Rico divvies the pills. They're no bigger than aspirins, but swallowing them would take an hour before we felt anything. We don't have that long. We suck off the protective membranes, crush

78

the pills into powder, add water, load syringes, and plunge the rush of deepest euphoria into scabby ankle veins.

I gush, I rise, and I fly. I evaporate warmly.

Rico falls under a bench, his head on a mound of leaves, his arm in a puddle. That is how I leave him. Fuck Rico.

I wander a couple of miles up Piedmont and come to the park where I'm hassled least. I curl under a magnolia near Lake Clara Meer on this, the first truly cold night. The dazzling lights of Midtown burst beyond the branches. I lay my face in the brittle leaves, sniffing the musk of nature's decomposition, the smell of summer dying.

Rico finds me in the afternoon, still sleeping. He kicks me awake. He has news of Tina.

Tina, turns out, couldn't take the withdrawal diarrhea and the nightmares so she robbed a pharmacy. A tiny little teen no bigger than a prep cheerleader and there she went: the nine millimeter she'd swiped from her policeman father tucked in her low-cut Juicy Jeans, the chunky metal of it protruding up her back, as if startling her tattooed butterflies into flight. Narcotics deprivation makes these bitches think they're Rambo.

"I mean, think of the shit she's in," Rico says. "The FBI don't care who your daddy is. I bet she's halfway to Reckoning by now, driving her ass off."

"She'll be in jail by dinner time."

Rico laughs. "She's going down in a blaze of glory—for a handful of Hydrocodone. That shit is *sexy*."

I push myself into a sitting position, picking free the leaves and sticks from my hipster mop of fiery red hair. We find the bench in the heart of Piedmont Park on which we practice our Latin, the language used by old-school doctors to call in 'scripts. We've both been arrested for fraud twice, and a third time means prison. We're conscious of that but there's no stopping. I can tell by Rico's demeanor his daily crisis is dawning, and mine's not far behind.

"You remember Hope?" he asks out of nowhere. "The girl with the Koi fish tattoo? The one always harping on astrology and good luck and all that shit?"

I try to appear uninterested, calm. "I remember her well," I say.

"I heard she became a nurse or something," he says, "that she's been pinching off Grady Hospital and has this, like, goldmine of meds in her basement."

"I doubt that."

"No, really—that dude they call Sleepy, in Peoplestown, he told me that."

"I'd be interested to see her."

"I guess she lives where she did, back in the day. A couple years in California rehab, and she came back."

"I'll go there," I say. "I'll pop in today."

"You mean pop in, or *home-invade* that shit?" he says, laughing but serious.

With a heave I send Rico off the bench. "I mean knocking politely, asshole. That's what I mean."

He laughs in the grass and climbs back up. "Then I'm counting on you," he says, his patchy goatee arched in smirk. "We'll meet right here, five o' clock. I'll try my luck begging at that drug store in the Highlands."

"Whatever."

I scat the park in search of garbage trucks headed south, not city trucks but ones contracted by intown yuppies. I can usually jump aboard for about a mile before the scumbags kick me off. For now I feel tranquil, purposeful, motivated. The afternoon sun warms the biggest park meadow. A gaggle of kids tossing a football catches my eye. It must be the weekend, these kids everywhere. Mentally I can't help but critique the running back's shifty style, his wasteful jukes and spins. Recruiters can't stand bravado like that.

No garbage trucks anywhere, so I barrel past the MARTA turnstiles on Tenth Street, behind a book-humping librarian who's terrified of me. My eyes, my scent, my subversive aura must petrify her. On the train she watches me all the way to the Five Points station, after which she plants herself near a policeman. I charge up the escalator, around the suits, into the noisy street and on to Castleberry Hill.

On a day like this five years ago I tried to off myself. At least I think I tried. I was taking a shower at a halfway home and couldn't purge my mind of some cryptic line by William Blake: *Every night and every morn, some to misery are born.* I took that way too personal. I felt predestined to fail, to suffer, as if the poem had been scribed with me in mind. I abandoned the home and met the crew down in The Gulch, the city's open dungeon of train tunnels. Thoughts of my sober coins and the Twelve Traditions faded behind. An hour later I swallowed a handful of Xanies and a quart of Dark Eyes.

A deep blur set in. I let go. I shattered all over again.

Then my father was standing over me in the sterile room, his red face and *Hermes* tie hovering, telling the nursing staff I wasn't his, not anymore.

I haven't thought of Hope in probably two years. Her doorframe still looks like driftwood, still bears the dots of cigarettes we'd poked out in guiltless times. I doubt she has stolen meds from a hospital. I know she got clean and that even unclean she wasn't a thief. I ring the bell because there's something else I want, though I don't know what. I ring the bell because I shouldn't. The story of my adult life.

Hope whips open the door. Her face reminds me of the tortured cherub painting that hung at Rico's old apartment, a baby angel caught dead in spider webs. She looks disappointed. She doesn't recognize me. I do my best Charlie Chaplin—the swivel hips and stiff legs, the old stupid skit—and with that her dark face blossoms: a gasping smile, parentheses for hands, and two big blue eyes.

"For the love of Christ, Mike," she says. "Bring yourself in here."

I kind of lunge in her direction but she doesn't touch me. Instead she slinks inside. The industrial vastness of her place surprises

81

me, though I'd slept on these concrete floors for weeks on end, memorizing each pockmark like firebombed cities on a huge map. The loft had been handed down to Hope from her dead mother, a successful curator who'd fought a brain tumor and lost. The chalky smell of it, the coolness captured by its exposed brick, transports me, though it was never so filthy with clothes and bottles before. She offers orange juice but I decline.

"Wine?" she says.

"Okay, sure."

We stand near the kitchen island and say nothing for a moment. It makes me very anxious. The windows wear cracked beige paint, beyond them a small courtyard. Among the golden leaves I see kids warring with green plastic swords. Reminds me of my brothers and me, how I'd refuse to play dead even when heart-gouged, how sometimes they'd beat my ass for cheating.

"Have I caught you at a bad time?"

"Me?" she says, filling a plastic Scooby-Doo cup with boxed merlot. "I've got nowhere to be."

"You're off today?"

"I'm off everyday."

I'm surprised but reticent. She still moves like blown drapes. She wears a necklace of tiny conch shells, her shirt collared, black, and stitched with the logo of a truck stop.

"How was California?"

"Oh, you know," she says. "It's an experience. A confining experience."

"Did it work?"

"Oh, you know."

I wait for her to expound. She doesn't.

"Expensive?" I say.

"It sucked my finances right out of my bones—along with my soul," she laughs, offering me a full cup and raising hers. "A toast," she says: "Be unusual, have fits, go crazy."

We gulp.

82

She sits at a barstool and motions for me to do the same, patting a countertop of speckled granite. I oblige but keep a distance. I wonder if we are alone.

"Let's not sugarcoat it," Hope says. "You look really bad. And you smell like The Gulch."

I choke the cheap wine down. I wish I'd have come at night, in heavier clothes, though she probably wouldn't have accepted me then. I cling tightly to the ends of my sleeves, concealing the ruined veins, the brown crescents of fingernails. As if she couldn't guess.

"A junkie friend said you're back in town, back from the California facility," I say. "Some crackhead told him that. Word's out that you've got a hospital gig, and word travels fast. I wanted you to know that people are talking. You know what people are capable of."

"You see my face," she smiles. "Do I look employable?"

If not for Hope's washer-like earrings, which have bored big holes in her lobules, she looks like any reality show contestant—skinny arms braided with muscle, her chest two ripe fruits, her pretty eyes deep and red, whether from doping or studying you couldn't know. In long sleeves even the red-purple tattoo on her forearm would be a secret, a concealing device itself concealed.

"You're still a fox," I say. "A tired fox, but definitely a fox."

She crosses her arms, plops her elbows on the counter. She's evaluating me, so I evaluate her. I think of her naked breasts, how she'd twist and rub them herself when I was doing it wrong, erotic instructions washed in moonlight.

"Your informant is full of shit," she says. "I had a laundry job at the hospital, but they fired me last summer. You really think, with a background like mine, they'd let me within a half-mile of the meds? That must be the football player in you—Michael Cruz, the meathead golden boy."

"Hey now," I say. "Go easy."

"Bottom line," she says, "I don't have anything to sell you. Sorry."

That knocks me back for a second. "Man, I'm not here for that."

"And there's nothing you can steal."

"Stop it."

"If I thought you would rob me, you wouldn't be in here," she says. "I see the robberies on the news. Mom-and-pop pharmacies—are you *kidding me?* Not that you're stupid enough to go that far."

"I haven't," I say. "I'm just here to—"

"Using is one thing," she says, "but those are high-level felonies—a mandatory ten years. It's all *so* stupid. There's less-risky ways."

"God, just listen," I say. "I haven't gone that far. You should know me better…I'm a pillhead, not a lunatic. We've talked about shit like that, but no, never, not yet."

She spins around once on the stool, a tactical move. She's exhibiting all of herself to me, her clean hair, her persuasive ass. Or maybe I'm thinking too hard. "Do *you* have anything?" she says quietly, dropping her head.

"Damn it," I say. "I was hoping you wouldn't ask that."

She grunts a little and bites her lip. The crow's feet around her eyes relax, and I feel I've passed whatever visual test she's been giving me. "How broke are you?" she says.

"Dry," I say. "Completely. I'm getting pretty frantic, but that's seriously not why—"

"My husband's in prison, and my son's sleeping in the back room," she says. "How do you feel about that?"

I stand up. I pull my dirty palms across my face. Everything about the situation suddenly feels wicked and confining. "Some Twilight Zone shit here."

"Sit down," she says. "Finish your wine. I want you to meet my boy…he'll be awake in about an hour. He just turned four."

I walk toward the door but she catches my fingers with sticky hands, gently persuading me to where she wants me, the stool. "I'm not sure I should get mixed up in this," I say. "And I'm damn sure—with a kid and all that—you don't want a ruined piece of trash like me around here."

84

"You're not ruined," she says. "Your potential is in jeopardy. That's different than ruined."

"Is that the rehab speaking? Is that Clinic Hope talking?"

"Yes, partly," she says. "Rehab is bullshit, but that's coming from my heart."

"Thanks."

She slides around the corner of the island and trickles her pink nails down my neck. Her perfume is a mix of vanilla and something I smelled once on vacation at Barbour Island, a sea breeze with pine. "My husband left a big gun, something in the rafters the APD didn't find," she says. "I'm telling you, it's huge. A three-fifty seven."

"Uh..."

We empty what's left of the first wine box. Hope walks outside to retrieve a second from her cluttered deck, promising a sweeter something she calls Riesling. I look into the rafters, around every steel beam, a dusty realm of exposed ductwork and cobwebs. She gently closes the door, catches me looking up. She rips open the box and positions it between us. She can't take her eyes off my hands, my cheeks. "Has anyone ever said you look like Errol Flynn?" she says. "You know who I'm talking about?"

"I fucking *was* Errol Flynn."

She emits a pitiful laugh. "And now?" she says.

"Now I'm nothing," I say. "*Nada.*"

She slides back onto the stool. "There's a phrase, an acronym, we had," she says. "You're an ASM...another sad marauder. The type of kid who turns everything to nothing and then wallows in it." She tilts back her head, her face consumed with boozy thought and a crooked smile. "I remember when your team played us," she says. "Back in like ninety-eight, a bunch of preppies from the suburbs trouncing the inner-city kids."

"God," I say. "For all the value they put on football around here, it never seemed all that difficult."

"Remind me again what happened," she says. "It's been eons."

I spill my guts to her like a dozen times before. I recount how my quarterback play at Reckoning High was run-heavy, straightforward, and prone to injury: a brakeless bus. Nobody had warned me the style could scramble a knee, could require three surgeries and heaps of pain medication. And nobody stopped to think the pills might toss an addictive personality on the grim reaper's lap.

"God, I love pills," she says. "Xanax, Ritalin, Lortab, Vicodin—even trips on Robitussin, which *I* did in high school. I'd waddle around the hallways between homeroom and some easy shit class, flipping off teachers behind their backs."

"Why are we talking about this?"

"It feels like the 'hab again," she says. "I guess you wouldn't know."

"It makes me feel better."

She pulls a beaten cell phone from her jeans, checks it, and sets it nearby, face up. "I'd just texted Reggie, my guy, before you showed up," she says. "We need something, but I think he's had enough of my bullshit. He knows about my inheritance. Mom's lawyer gives it to me in tiny little bits, like an allowance. I'm indebted to Reggie pretty bad."

I feel the cold, involuntary quakes in my arms, my stomach a toxic stew of wine and what's left of yesterday's soup-house bread. I breathe faster, harder. Distractions don't come easy. "What's the worst thing you've ever done high?" I say.

"Oh, hell," she says, sloshing wine. "A few years ago, on a Friday, I took a handful of Oxy—someone's grandma was dying and the shit was everywhere—at some party; I woke up Monday in a Chattanooga trailer park. There was a naked man beside me, and he was fucking *middle age*. I flipped out and called the police. They didn't file charges. Worse, though, they called my grandparents, explained that I'd been caught on video at gas stations in all these towns, hassling people for rides to Tennessee. Jesus I still don't remember."

I want to latch on to her, to hug her, like two lovers in the climax of a vintage movie. I need her to sustain me, to warm me, one broken promise atop another. For once I want an ally, a purpose. I move one barstool closer. "Do you have dreams anymore?" I say.

"You mean, like, sleep dreams?"

"I mean plans. Something for you and the kid, like moving to a farm, or an island. I heard there's this commune in Wyoming called Acceptance, like one-hundred percent organic everything, tons of ex-junkies and—"

"I go to sleep to forget my dreams," Hope says. "What never panned out doesn't bother me there. I don't shit myself, Mike. I'm a realist."

Another cup in, she says the wine sucks, too slow. "I have vodka," she says. "Have you had this sweet-tea vodka?"

A high-pitched voice pipes up from a back room—" I want sweet tea," it says.

"No," she yells. "Not now."

My panic intensifies, restricts my breathing. I feel despicable, like an interloper in another man's sanctuary, a beggar in a bank. "Do you want me to go?" I say. "I think my business is done, unless you'd like to proceed."

"Proceed with what?"

"I don't know," I say. "With whatever was just happening."

She fidgets on the barstool, peeks out the kitchen window and focuses on the cup of wine. "This is tough, Mike. How you look, it's tough."

"We've established that. I've heard enough. I'm gone."

"Let me introduce you," she says, somewhat peevishly, before calling out that it's okay to come and visit.

Out tromps a frowning boy with mussed blond hair. He wears a shirt with a tiger imprint that glitters in bands of late-afternoon light. He rubs his eyes and yawns, grins as if withholding a secret.

"I need something," I say. "Right now."

The boy pouts. Hope strokes his cheek, his forehead, his chin, a trick to calm. Their eyes almost match. She lifts the child and holds him in a tight hug.

"It redeems me to have him," she says, "to think something like him can come of all this."

"Okay," I say. "It's been nice to see you both, to meet him."

"You want to talk to him?"

"No."

"Please," she says.

"I'm just trying to maintain right now."

"You should talk to him," she says. "I find it therapeutic."

"*No.* I don't know. I mean, I don't know if I know how."

She laughs and eases the boy down. I worry the kid can sense my struggle. He's obviously suspicious, and intelligent. He surveys me like a rookie guard on cell duty.

"Hey," I offer, hunching over on the barstool, scrambling for words. "Do you like football?" He buries his face in his mother's leg, making a peculiar sound like growling and choking combined. "I tried," I say, "and I suck."

She dotes on the boy and cuffs him beside her. "Earplugs, baby, *earplugs.* Cover them all the way." The kid slaps his chubby hands against his ears, inserts index fingers.

"I'm calling Reggie," she says. "He'll hurry. We can stage it to look like we've never met, like you're here to take everything. Just storm in and get loud. Whatever he carries is always in one of those boot holsters. The pills will be in his chest pocket, inside his jacket. Go hide in the stockyard across the street and just run in here…it's not Reggie's money, and it's not his stuff."

"*What?*" I say. "The kid, first of all, he's right here. No way. I'd rather do a pharmacy. Let's drive out to the sticks and do that."

"You don't even have to load it," she says. "We'll be set for a month. You can hole up here, once we get Reggie out." She holds the cell phone over the boy's head. "I got a text," she says. "He's coming."

I step away from them and button my shirt to my throat. I want to run, to curl up in some warm, forgiving bed, but no viable destination comes to mind.

"I don't like football," the boy suddenly says. "It comes on TV on Sundays, when church gets done. It's boring."

"Church?" I say. "Since when the hell…"

"Murray," she scolds. "Be nice."

Hope kneels and squares the imprint on the boy's shirt between his shoulders, locks her eyes with his and pulls down his arms. "Our friend Mike played football, so amazing he was like a legend," she says. "I'd even heard of him, growing up here when he was out where the rich people are. He could probably teach you some things."

The boy eyes me, still suspicious, but not so long as to be impolite. "You look dirty," he says. "I think you need a bath."

Together we walk to the loft's biggest window, the boy dangling like a marsupial from Hope. She nods to what looks like a rundown barnyard behind gates of sheet metal. I can see down Elliot Street, over the bridge toward Centennial Park, where the tourists are. Night falls over the city like a purple sheet, coming, as it does, too soon this time of year. She points out the stony heights of First Baptist Church, a sort of beacon among towering stacks of corporate glass.

"You should go in there, sometime," she says. "They're not like the clinics. No methadone, no bull. They help you for the long term. Just stop in whenever, but don't drop my name. They're not exactly fond of me."

I shrug. "That's not my scene."

"Talk to the church," she says. "It'll do you good."

She carries the boy to the cellar, where a spread of toy soldiers and a hopscotch carpet reminds me of kindergarten. She turns on a plastic record player that whines with hokey sing-along music. The boy sits Indian-style and gallops a plastic horse. She promises to bring him a snack and sweet tea in a little while. She pushes me out and quietly bolts the cellar door.

In the living room she sets a chair atop a table, climbs it and reaches over a beam, finding a wadded black cloth. She comes down and exhumes an incredible barrel nearly the length of her forearm, a wooden grip branded with S&W. She tells me her husband once killed a caribou with it. She tells me it's loaded.

"Should we take the bullets out?" I say.

"Your call."

She hands me the revolver. It's heavy as a fire-poker. "Do you have some sort of mask, at least?" She thinks for a second and darts to her bedroom. I can hear her digging around, maybe in a closet. She returns with all she can find, a werewolf mask.

"Screw it," I say. "I'll take it."

I cram the big gun in my jeans. The cold steel stretches halfway down my thigh.

"You'd better get moving," she says. "Just hide behind the gates and be patient. I'll crack the window and...I don't know, cough real loud. When you hear that, just come and kick the door—I'll keep it cracked—and run in, pointing that thing."

"What if he points something at me?"

"Reggie's a pussycat," she says. "Tell him to dump everything on the table, tell him to run. Rough me up a bit, if you have to."

"Can I ask you something?" I say, sounding more timid than I meant to. She nods. "How long is your husband gone for?"

She unscrews a brown-tinted bottle of vodka and pours a glass. "Long enough, but it's none of your business," she says. "We need to get going. It's a school night. I'm calling him back now. Listen for my coughing." She takes a sip while I walk outside, the mask balled in my hand.

The stockyard is miserable, a spread of rusted machinery and decaying foreign cars. Little paths snake through the trash to former bum encampments, all sleeping options I've never heard of. I climb atop an old bus and watch Hope through the big window as she readies the loft. She flips off all but the living room lights. She's

90

consumed with need as badly as me, running those pink nails down her arms. I'm nothing to her but this moment.

The nausea festers. To fight this I'm going to need real help. I think of the halfway home and the admissions I'd have to make, crowded in that scummy garage they use for meetings. I think of Barney, the security guy, and how he'll scold me for vanishing. I think of admitting it all again: *My name is Michael Cruz, and I am too many bad things to list. I run with dopers, fiends, freaks, hounds, junkies, users, and crackheads. They call me a pillhead because I'll die for prescription meds. I was ostracized from my family and everyone who loves me six years ago. I love drugs now. Chemistry completes me. I have no real friends. I will die if this goes on.*

I start walking away from Hope's, around cars, through busted trestles, toward The Gulch and, above it, the city. A CSX freighter crawls down the line, its bins heaped with some kind of grain. I wipe the barrel clean with the mask, wrap my hand in my shirtsleeve, and toss the gun into a bin. It lands with a slight crunch of grain. Wherever the gun goes, I hope it finds a caribou hunter.

I walk to the center of Baker Street and let traffic pass on both sides. Streetlights illuminate the oxidized spires of First Baptist, the sweeping arches of its colonnade. I drop my hands, exhale, and cross the street. I step onto the sidewalk near an under-construction Brazilian steakhouse, where workmen have left a plastic garbage can outside. I lift the lid and drop the monster mask in. It snarls at me as I close the lid and walk away.

THE DIRTY DAWN

_____

Eddie keeps the rouge, concealer, and mascara caked on well past quitting time. His bare face is beyond unattractive—it's putrid, like a Van Gogh self-portrait pulled through a garbage disposal. He shifts his eyes from the barroom mirror to the lone window. Outside the bar, the last-call horde is lurching toward Victors Avenue. Eddie wants to join them but he's bashful. His stomach growls. He rolls his wad of tips into a tight little drum and clocks out.

Eggs Benedict and jalapeno grits await Eddie at the Majesty Diner, a distant seven blocks up a steep hill. En route he hopes to burn off last night's Mind Erasers, to repress the sting of Burt's wandering finger. But the barroom mirror has given him pause. The mirror always tells the truth, that at age forty-seven and without makeup he would look pathetic, a tired trick wrung dry of last night's charm. He powders his nose and asks Marty, the bartender, if bumming a smoke would be cool.

"No," says Marty. "You've smoked enough to kill a lab monkey. Take your broke ass home."

Eddie makes a prissy face. "There's a fine line between broke and venerable, asshole." He turns away, toward the graffiti-drenched jukebox and the exit.

"Hey," Marty says, shelving a spotted martini glass. "Everything okay with you? I mean everything *below* the Mason-Dixon?"

"Mind your business," Eddie says, walking out. "I'll see you tonight."

Eddie exits a door beside the bar reserved for employees. Even this early, the heat portends the afternoon swelter of the hottest August on record. Eddie ducks into a grove of pear trees and looks around. The last-call pansies are a good two blocks ahead, so he slinks up a leafy lane, a shortcut to that greasy breakfast. There is no wind, only the swish of his arms over sequins.

Eddie wants to count—even *sniff*—his tips, but at this hour he knows better, though these streets are hardly like his neighborhood, the grimy Boulevard East. In a roundabout manner, the smell of money has informed Eddie's whole life. His mother worked the tubes as a drive-thru bank teller in Chamblee, an occupation that had sharpened her people skills, then his by proximity to her. His threshold for patron complaints is enormous thanks to his mother, who smilingly took shit from all shades of lowlifes. Winded, Eddie turns around to see the Ponce De Leon Tavern down the hill, a squat brick shack with a six-story inn behind it, that tower of lewd activity. He keeps walking and the tips roll tighter in his crotch, solid like a short steel rod. He hopes the tips don't touch the blood.

On Victors Avenue cabs jockey for the last batch of club kids. A waiter wipes dew off lacquered benches of split pine. Eddie sweats. The birds to him sound sullen, a fitting soundtrack for dirty dawns. Across the street and still a block from breakfast stands someone new, someone striking. Someone that to Eddie is

94

handsome, a strapping little misfit on the avenue. "Oh, *sugar*," he says, but nobody hears.

Eddie struts in the young man's direction. The kid—can he be a *teenager*, buffed up with no-flab abs like that?—has something up his sleeve. He's ambitious at a distance. He's not merely waiting on the MARTA bus because he has paperwork, which he clings to while shaping a box from slotted wood. Eddie approaches, the sunshine sharpening his old eyes. The mascara bunches and cracks.

"Excuse me," Eddie says, nearing. "Is there something I can help you with, doll?"

"Sorry?"

"I don't know you from Adam, but to me you look plain lost, working like that on a corner like this."

The young man grins. He has trusting eyes, an angular face framed by curly hair so sun-blond it's white. The rims of his lips bear freckles. Around them the blond goatee is precisely shorn, though farm-boyish. "I'm here to tell the truth," the kid says. "To all these bus riders in the vestibule."

"True *that*."

The young man looks down, to the sidewalk. "I'm here a lot, more usually afternoons," he says. "Great spot for preaching. Great mix of folks. I'll be fine, ma'am, but thanks for the offer."

"Oh, honey, that's hardly an *offer*," Eddie says.

The kid says nothing for few seconds. He tugs a chest-level button of his Bahamian dress shirt to fan himself, channeling air across his body. "I appreciate your help, really," the kid says. "Didn't mean to rub you wrong."

They part to let a rush of churchgoers pass. Two boys staple handbills for punk albums to a street post. A vintage bus proclaiming itself "The Decatur Express" consumes the waiting people and groans down the avenue, sooty fumes its wake. "So, preaching?" Eddie says. "Out here? With all this traffic and noise and dirt? Isn't there a nice cool mall that'll let you in?"

"I'll go wherever they pay attention," the kid says. "That's the thing about open-air gospel—it's portable. The noise and heat can't deter me."

"Lord, child," Eddie says. "Aren't you just a *benediction.*"

They laugh.

"Can I ask your name, ma'am?"

"It's Edith, or it's going to be soon," he says. "But don't tell that to my mother."

"Excuse me?"

"Everyone calls me Eddie."

"Alright," the kid says. "Like the vampire boy on TV, in those black-and-white reruns?"

"Just like that," Eddie says, pulling back his thick, black-dyed hair. "A vampire—*Jesus.* You hit that nail on the head."

"Well, I'm Luke."

They shake hands. The kid's palm startles Eddie, not calloused like the contractor hands he's used to but fleshy and warm, like a skinned peach. A palm tender and clean as his aged mother's, only firm with muscle. Eddie doesn't want to let go.

"Nice to have stumbled upon you," he says.

"Praise God," says Luke.

Eddie steps back and takes stock of his acquaintance, unaware he's outright ogling the kid. "I bet you're one nut that's tough to crack," Eddie says. "A real hot challenge."

"Pardon me?"

"Ah *hell,*" says Eddie. "I get so ahead of myself."

Luke readies his materials, caps his box with a thick piece of maple. "Care to sit in on this sermon?" he says. "It's a cliché, I know, but it's truly better on this soapbox. Makes the echoes bounce more when you're speaking down."

"Hell, I'm talked down to *all* the time," says Eddie, perking his breasts. "I'll sit here all day, so long as you let me buy you breakfast afterwards."

"Sounds great," Luke says. "I'll have you know, though, I eat like a horse."

"I bet you do."

Eddie watches as the kid unearths a pocketful of tracts, glossy like the pornographic ones Latinos slap at passersby in Vegas. He shuffles the little cards and picks one. He holds it to the sun and exhibits it to Eddie, as if to verify the promotional material is no illusion. On the front a close-up headshot of Jesus scowls. The words prophet, healer, and teacher swirl around the imposing visage. Luke hoists himself atop the soapbox, draws a deep breath.

"Jesus lived a sinless life, people," he booms. "Jesus performed countless miracles and at age thirty-three—just twelve years my elder now—the skeptics of his day wrongly accused him, and Jesus died a bloody death by crucifixion. But three days later, Jesus proved he spoke the truth, that he was who he claimed to be. He did not lie. Jesus Christ was God in human flesh. He was who he claimed to be..."

Eddie sits on a ledge of stacked stones. The sun has made him feel clammy and ill. He sweats and the rouge separates, but he is transfixed. All these mornings crawling to breakfast he's never seen anyone so moving as this rooster of a man. He feels the need to jot this in his diary.

The urge to call his mother arises in Eddie, a default reaction when talking to himself won't suffice. He contemplates visiting his mother, Jude, behind the gates of Pearl Garden Homes, a labyrinthine compound in the foothills near Dawsonville. In his condition, however, seventy miles is an insurmountable distance, especially with his Dodge Dart impounded. He hasn't visited his mother in several months and he must formulate an excuse. He last wheeled her around the compound at Easter, after her obligatory scorn had subsided: the usual spiel about wasted family opportunities and the expense of needless surgery. Standing above his mother he knew how easily he could flip her wheelchair, a quick somersault preceding silence, quite possibly eternal silence. He'd show her what a man can do. Months later he still regrets the thought. He decides to send a nice card, hopefully in time for her autumn birthday. At the bottom in calligraphy will dance his full name, Edward Archibald Lovelace. He's proud of the idea, his thoughtfulness. He wonders if he should send one to his father, who resides within higher gates.

Twenty minutes pass. Luke steps down to distribute his tracts. Churchgoers in silk suits waddle near the stone wall. Some hold Luke in high regard; others, Eddie gleans from their facial expressions, think him something of a sideshow. Three men hand the kid cash.

Luke dabs his forearm on his cheeks to dam the sweat. "Hot as Hades," he huffs.

"Come," says Eddie. "Let's get you in some cool air."

Eddie leads the kid across a parking lot to the Majesty Diner, a Fifties-era eatery resembling a long spaceship, chrome upon clean chrome. He tries to keep barely ahead but the kid lags, fiddling with his box.

"You gonna escort me in, or just stare me up from behind?" Eddie says.

"Ah, pardon me," Luke says, hustling up. "I think that sun's done melted off my manners."

A hostess seats them in a booth directly opposite each other. Eddie watches the kid's brawny shoulders shift and pull as he explores the menu. The neck to Eddie looks tanned and healthy, unmet with the creases that plagued him in his early twenties. He'd like to know if the neck requires shaving yet, and if Luke takes the razor lower.

"Do you work outside without a shirt sometimes?" Eddie says.

"Huh?"

"Sorry," Eddie says, "a bizarre question."

"Not at all," Luke says. "But what would make you ask?"

"No lines. Tan lines, I mean. Not on your arms or neck or anywhere."

"Oh, that," Luke says. "Heck no I don't preach shirtless. Nobody would hear a thing coming out of my mouth—not with guns like these," and he pulls up his sleeve enough to exhibit a flexed bicep, a lemon-shaped stone. "No, seriously, in school I'm studying park management. I like the outdoorsy things. With two years under my belt, they pay me pretty good as a lifeguard at park pools."

Eddie giggles. "Got a regular *David Hasselhoff* up in here."

"Whatever."

Luke bites the inside of his cheek, fiddles with a cream canister, smiles. He flips to the entrée section and looks down. A waitress comes over. She's a new hire, a redhead, and she's captivated by Eddie, though obviously perturbed. She runs her quizzical eyes up the length of his legs and torso. He asks for the usual, and she looks appalled, as if startled to know a person like this frequents her booth. Eddie senses that he must distract her, adept at these situations as he is. He asks about the duration of her employment.

"A month," she says. "A month and a week, actually."

"Good," he says. "And the city? You lived here long?"

"A year."

"Good," he says. "Tell me, doll, does this place suit you? You look like a snowbird from Iowa who's taken a liking to these Atlanta climes—*no?*"

With her tongue the waitress shifts a wad of gum between her jaw and cheek. "Like any American city," she says, "it's a juxtaposition of affluence and despair, knocking into itself."

Eddies slams his thick hands on the table. "Look at Miss Philosophy Major!" he says, touching the back of Luke's hands, which in the sun are circuit boards of veins. "Can you explain that in layman's terms?" Eddie says. "We're just a couple simpletons."

"Sure," she says, looking at their hands. "What I mean is there's too many freaks. Place crawls with freaks."

Eddie guffaws, retracts his hands. He points his face to the ceiling and breathes a cloud of rank air. "The eggs and spicy grits, babe," he says, folding his menu, slapping it down. "That's what I'll take. And also a tall wet glass of *lighten the fuck up.*"

The waitress steps back, peeks at other tables, checking them without telegraphing her embarrassment. She turns to Luke. He folds his open hands together, bows a little, and hands over the menu. "I'll have the Santa Fe burrito, with a side of cheese grits, plus toast," he says. "As for my friend, I just met her, but surely she's sorry."

The waitress storms away, puffed up and tippy-toed, as if holding her breath.

Midway through their meal, Eddie asks what day it is. Luke says it doesn't truly matter. Eddie, dipping his pinkie in hollandaise, licking it, asks the kid what does matter.

"Goals," Luke says. "Goals matter."

"I'm too old for goals. I'm holding out for divine intervention."

"That could be misconstrued as laziness," Luke says.

Eddie drops his napkin on the table. "Tell me what *your* goals are."

Luke thinks for a moment. "Simple things, really."

"Like what?" says Eddie. "Preaching the good gospel, forever and always?"

"No. Not just that."

"Staying tan? Keeping celibate? What?"

"I want to write a book," Luke says. "I think I can, if I tell what I see and hear everyday, or at least elements of it. You wouldn't believe the things people share with me, right off the bat."

"A book?" Eddie says, leaning back. "Like a church book?"

"Sure," says Luke. "Variations on those themes, but purely fiction. Professors tell me when I get on a roll with writing, it's like a soliloquy, or poetry."

Eddie drowns the last of his eggs in hot sauce and cracks open his purse for his antacid tablets. He pushes aside the plastic baggie that could land them both in prison. "What's gotten into a park manager to make him want to write a novel?"

"Writing a good book would be easy," says Luke, his voice navigating the egg bits in his mouth. "All you do is sit at a chair, pull up to a desk. Then you type thousands of sentences that are inescapable little pleasures to everyone."

100

Eddie heaves a loud, deep laugh. Diners at nearby tables stare. "Sarcasm," he says. "I didn't see that in a babydoll like you."

"There's a lot you probably don't see in me."

"Okay, well," says Eddie, "I like the parts that *are* visible."

"You'd like the parts that aren't even more."

Eddie drops his fork. His eyes bulge out. The check arrives. Her again.

The waitress impatiently taps her feet. Sunlight heats the table and Eddie takes a deep breath. He winks to the waitress, but she's looking out the window, to the street. Two patrons from the Ponce are trying to wave down a cab, wheezing and groaning in the heat like city dogs. Eddie slips his hand up his skirt and exhumes two twenties, hands them over. The waitress doesn't ask if they'll need change.

"I see pain in you," Luke says, cradling his face with open hands, studying.

"So young, yet so profound," Eddie says. "Weren't you just that cornfed stud, over there talking up God on the corner?"

"Come on," Luke says. "Reveal something."

Eddie folds his hands, tucks them between his knees. "Sure I have pain," he says. "Nothing in my life could be mistaken for luck. But don't we all have our little histories, poking at us?"

Luke leans closer. "Sure, but with you it's more of a surface issue," he says. "I can clearly see that. You're in good health, right?"

Eddie clears his throat and tucks his chin over it, so as not to cast the wrong shadow. He's had the Adam's apple shaved once but he thinks a second procedure is needed. Hormonal therapy and voice training go only so far. "There was a guy, some asshole, last night," he says. "Suffice it to say the man got intrusive."

"Your husband?"

"Oh, honey, no."

"Boyfriend?"

"Not even close," Eddie says, hunching his shoulders though trying not to. "Let's just say he got forceful with me, pulled me apart at the stitching."

"You need to be more careful."

101

"I *need* to make rent," Eddie says. "The landlady don't share your concerns."

"The devil frequents these streets at night."

"And he's a cheap-ass."

"Excuse me?"

"Nothing," Eddie says. "That devil ain't got his fork in me yet, that's all."

"Praise God," Luke says.

"Yep."

At the bar, haggard drunks grumble over football prospects and baseball box scores. Dishes everywhere clash. Eddie, worried his conversation has dried up, asks Luke if he's seen the new downtown aquarium. He says it's the largest in the world, touted as the Louvre meets Sea World.

"I bet all that postmodern architecture is great for echoes," Eddie says, smirking. "Your voice would go for miles. If you don't think they'll throw you off the property."

"You just brim with good ideas, don't you," Luke says. "Long as I'm on the sidewalk, they can't touch me."

"Come on, doll, we're *going*," Eddie says, his finger running the tight cables of Luke's forearm. "Cab fare's on me."

"But you just bought breakfast."

Eddie stands. "Last night was traumatizing," he says, "but it was lucrative."

Luke holds the door open for Eddie as they exit the diner, assisting him with a light sweep of the shoulders. A quick eye-to-eye and they turn to the street. They walk to the corner and nod to three homeless men discussing mayoral candidates, the loud hyperbole of wine drunks. Eddie asks if they're in line for cabs, but nobody answers. He rolls his eyes at Luke and dials Day-Night Cab Co. on his cell phone, a number he's had saved since DUI number three.

"Tell me," Eddie says, as they toe the curb. "Why preach in this part of town?"

"I want to make an impression," Luke says.

"No, I don't think that's it," Eddie says. "I think you want to *impress* us, or to shame us into loving you."

"Who is this collective 'us?'"

"Dregs like me."

"Dregs are beyond salvation," Luke says. "And they're certainly not worth hitting on."

Eddie snatches the kid's hand and yanks him closer. "Listen," he says. "I want to suck you off."

"*Hey now,*" Luke says, pulling away. "In due time."

Waves of children rush the aquarium gates. A security guard demands they all spit out their chewing gum, which he says chokes expensive fish. Luke asks the guard how long until the place opens.

"Twenty minutes."

"Perfect."

Luke asks Eddie to pick a good sidewalk location, one with ample sight lines and a concave surface at which to aim his voice. They settle on a space in the shade of a tall pine, near the front gate queue. In a minute, Luke changes his mind, preferring a place in the sun. "I want to try something different here, some cutting-edge gospel," Luke says. "It's a little abstract for a Sunday sermon, but I'm feeling it."

Tourists pour from hotels to sip coffees and squabble over breakfast options, a wandering migration across the Bermuda grass of Centennial Park. Luke builds his box while Eddie ducks into a public restroom, the women's.

"Don't fall in," the kid quips.

"What?" Eddie says, peeking back out.

"I said don't fall in...I'd hate to see you blemish that fine dress."

"Three minutes, sugar."

In a handicap stall Eddie unfurls four more twenties, takes the baggie from his purse, dries his left nostril, and violently coughs. Tiny sneakers squeak the tiles around him, scurrying away. In a room like this at Camp Lilburn, his father would corral Eddie and his cousins to—as the elder Lovelace called it—"dance." His father, vitriolic and grabby at age forty, would bring licorice and his Polaroid camera. When he didn't perform, Eddie would get the basement treatment at home: an old couch and painted-over windows, the smell of moth balls and acetone, their shared name, Edward, embroidered in cursive on his father's janitor uniform. *Don't fall in,* the kid just said. "Don't fall in," Eddie tells himself now. A woman near the sink asks if he's okay. He says nothing until she finally leaves.

Eddie exits the facility to find Luke in full throat, gleaming in sunlight, holding court over a small crowd of conventioneers.

"On television the other day, a morning show guest—this noted psychiatrist—was waxing on America's love of the here and now," Luke says. "Meanwhile, the host was cutting short his sentences and ushering in the next guest via satellite. A man who was urging the nation to slow down was then whisked away by interns. It was ludicrous, people. We think we have so little time to do so much. We're all sprinting to the cemetery. We miss the blessings of today. It makes me think of a sad song from twenty years ago, something my father turned me on to. In the lyrics, a man wanders a cemetery full of dead poets and literary figures. He asks himself how all these lives could ever come to an end, and what really *are* these people now? Really, are these *people* now? Hear me out, because I'll tell you the answer. I have written on this topic, and I know. But it's not just coming from me. It's from the spirit and teachings of our Lord, Jesus Christ…"

Eddie waves his arms, his vision going white. He shakes his hands to get Luke's attention, hardly concerned that he's interrupting. He drops two twenties at the kid's feet, atop his spare Bible, and wobbles on his heels. "Your tip," he says.

Luke's sermon trails off and people turn away, their interest waning. Two men follow Eddie's lead and drop money at Luke's feet.

"Sun's *really* out now," says Eddie, the concealer all but wiped away, his neck and cheeks blotchy. "I'll be in there, with the fish, on my own little whaling expedition. Take that money and join me if you'd like, when you've healed enough."

Luke pockets the cash as Eddie stumbles away, his reflective sequins a thousand drifting stars. "You take care of yourself," Luke says, and he projects his voice again, the Book split open on his palm.

At the aquarium entrance, Eddie is hassled by security, three guys who want him turned over to medics.

"Just water," he says. "I'll be fine with some water in me."

"There's eight million gallons inside, pops," one guy says. "But you'll have to buy a bottle if you're thirsty. I'd suggest you buy a bottle."

Eddie enters, passing gift shops. He absorbs the cool air and wanders the aquarium's grand mezzanine, a neon-lit cavern like the belly of a cosmic whale. From here he sees the entrances to five distinct habitats, each fingering off in different directions. He feels submerged, transported, seasick, though the cool air makes his thirst an afterthought. He enters the habitat to his right, The Coral Kingdom. Jungle drums pound from unseen speakers. All goes black. Eddie can't tell if he's dreaming or not. A mellifluous family of Atlantic Sea Nettles, drifting bulbous and stringy like jellyfish, silhouettes against a deep-blue backdrop. The tank could go for miles or two feet, Eddie doesn't know. *Don't fall in*, he thinks. Deeper in the tunnel he finds a Redspotted Hawkfish, observes it dancing with teams of clownish Anemonefish. One pouty Royal Gamma abstains. That fish is him, he thinks, the outsider, the Royal Loner. He flashes back to playgrounds, to bullies, to his father's trial. *Don't fall in.* Deeper still are the Neon Gobbies, the swarms of Glassy Sweepers, playful creatures all. They're like him: childish, silvery, easily dominated. Beside that tank bursts a menagerie of Cichlids, an aggressive fish. Mean like the defense attorney, the fat one. *Don't fall in.* He remembers himself on the stand, the photographic evidence. With the jury watching he felt suspended in air yet choked by guilt, capable of falling forever.

Eddie exits the tunnel crying. The mezzanine teems with running kids, parents in pursuit. Despite this, he plants his face inside his purse, splits the baggie, and inhales, hacks so loud it echoes. He wipes his face with a tissue and trudges on, searching for anywhere darker, a sanctuary. He finds a cavernous habitat lit faintly in blue.

A crowd gathers to watch the slow flight of Beluga Whales. Like a cinema screen, the clear acrylic wall soars fifty feet, the waterline barely decipherable. The whales are ghosts on a turquoise canvas—effortless, muscular, deep.

"I could watch them roll around all day," says Luke, bluing from the darkness. "Aren't they just beautiful?"

"Oh, lord," Eddie says. "You."

Luke nods toward the animals.

"You're *so* right," Eddie says. "They're so...I don't know...phallic."

Luke leans in, his goatee tickling Eddie's ear. "Come on," he says, "there's more across the way, a bona fide symphony of fish."

Luke leads him by the hand to the biggest tank. They enter a glass tube that traverses the sea floor. The froth of tiny waves laps a hundred feet above. The crowd around them gasps when the first Whale Shark approaches, an economy of muscle and polka-dotted skin. Its counterparts follow, a combined sixty feet of shark, a leviathan pack. Rays and Groupers and Hammerheads drift.

"As a kid, I was more afraid of sharks than monsters," says Luke, quietly, so as not to disturb the tourists. "But these, I feel like I could swim right up and ride them."

"Funny," Eddie says. "I was just thinking how they'd eat me alive."

They laugh under their breath. Eddie wobbles but Luke catches him, hands on his shoulders. Luke pulls him in, runs his fingers up Eddie's thigh, tugs at the panties, slips out the rolled bills, and clenches his fist.

"I have to ask you something," Luke whispers.

"Please, doll," Eddie says, his eyes closed. "I'm in no condition to think."

"A simple question."

"Okay," Eddie says.

"Tell me…are you, I don't know, open?"

"What?" Eddie says, startled. "Say *what?*"

Luke relaxes and pulls away, slips the loot into his pocket. "I mean, I don't much know how this works, but I want to know. Surely, with your experiences, you can make me privy."

Eddie stares at clusters of rocks, just beyond the glass. "You want to know how things fit?" he says. "Is that what you're saying?"

"I know what you are."

"I *don't* know what you are," Eddie says. "I'm beginning to think you're no student, no preacher."

"Hush," Luke says. "I'm your prayers, answered. The best you'll ever get."

Eddie turns to face the kid. "Now isn't *that* a thing to say," he says. "Apologize."

Luke laughs. "I'm sorry, doll," he says. "A thousand times over."

They embrace as tiny flashes burst around them. Eddie worries for some reason that the tube might give in, crushing them all, their bodies mingling with the monsters. In this moment he thinks that would be a travesty.

"Come on," Luke says. "Let's go back out, through that cafeteria. I know a place."

They push through the crowd. They scurry across the mezzanine and a busy dining pavilion. "There," Luke says, pointing. "Beside the men's bathroom. Duck behind that canvas, wait for me in the construction zone."

"Where the hell does it go?" Eddie says. "I thought you've never been here."

"It's a new dolphin exhibit coming in," he says. "There's probably nobody working on Sunday, as Baptist as they are. Just make us a little spot, and I'll follow you, in a few minutes."

"We'll go together."

"Go," Luke says. "Hurry, now. Before those kids see us."

"Whatever," Eddie says. "I want you to know I can't wait."

"*Go.*"

Eddie hurries to the bathroom, slips behind the canvas and enters a vast room. The steel beams of an enormous tank climb like ribs of a warship. He clicks into the construction area and clears a space behind a stack of drywall buckets, a makeshift nest. He pads the floor with canvas, sits Indian-style, and begins to wait. He breathes in the fresh fumes of latex paint, a smell he thinks symbolic of new beginnings.

MISSING ATHENA

"Did you know," asks Joe in seat 17c, "that penguins can swim thirty miles per hour?"

Hank Obelisk doesn't know how to respond. Of course he didn't know that. Or perhaps he could've guessed, having seen that special on Antarctica before dozing off the other night, the half-smoked joint a tarry nub in his fingertips, his Crown Royal drained. On television the penguins seemed awfully stupid. Hank had wondered why some massive, glacier-prowling shark didn't rip them all apart, a chummy stew of penguin meat in the icy abyss. Too quick for sharks, the penguins, he concluded. Then he passed out again on the couch.

Before replying to his son, Hank looks out the cabin window. There's a thick haze over Georgia, a smoggy dome above the black-green carpet of rolling hills and pines—down where his wife must be, somewhere. From twenty thousand feet the topography bears contrast to the checkerboard Midwest, back where the land's cut in

109

sections he could easily search and catalogue. From this altitude he knows the Southern forest is a hopeless expanse.

The kid pulls Hank's sleeve, exhibiting his impatience with a piercing whine. Hank crushes his empty soda can and smiles, his teeth big and white as mini-marshmallows.

"The world record for fast swimming was set by a swordfish," Hank quietly fibs. Joe, a precocious seven-year-old and only child, stores each word as undisputable fact. "One near Cuba went a hundred-fifty."

"When?"

"This one time."

"*Dang*," Joe says, satisfied. "That's like Corvette fast."

It warms Hank's heart to see his son decked out in Chicago Cubs gear. The soft blues and reds are friendly shades in Hank's eyes, the colors of his own childhood bedroom, a cramped space bedecked with aerial shots of Wrigley Field. He'd move his son back to where they'd just left, the Chicago suburb of Glen Ellyn, if it weren't for the apocalyptic winters. His family visits up there never last long enough, and returning to Atlanta has become painful for him, a procession ending in the stark realities of single-parenting. After a few days, the convivial rhythms of the South weave back into Hank, and his longing for home dissolves. In moving to Georgia, he'd spoiled himself with temperate climes, and now his son wears the same thin skin. The boy has never seen the Lake frozen and probably never will. Hank would hate to taint his notion of the northern beach, to paint gray the emerald crescents of Lincoln Park summers. He thinks it best to leave good memories alone.

"Dad," the boy says. "Is this going to be a bad landing like last time?"

"To be honest, that's highly doubtful." Hank suppresses laughter and then guilt for wanting to laugh. "Don't worry so much."

The boy tucks his book of sea-animal pictures in a carry-on backpack. He burns his father with the quizzical stare that tells Hank he'd better be on his game.

"About the landing," Joe says. "How do you know? Did they teach that in the academy?"

"No," Hank says. "Firemen know jack about planes."

"Then *how?*"

"Because our last three landings were bad." Hank opens his hands like airplane wings, yaws them. "The law of averages is in our favor."

"The *what?*"

"Just trust me," Hank says, palming the boy's shoulder. "This'll be like landing in a giant tub of butter."

The fasten seatbelts sign clicks on: *bong.* The middle seat was unoccupied, so between Hank and Joe lay a pile of travel accouterments: bottled water, Skittles, peanuts, taffy, a *Sports Illustrated,* and three twisted action figures. The boy's getting so big his knees bend fully over the airline seat, his calf muscles growing like balloons above his skinny ankles. Hank marvels at the simplest things his son does. The way he turns book pages, smiles back, bumps fists in greeting, laughs at fairly complex jokes. Nothing pleases Hank like seeing the boy learn.

"I'm afraid this time," Joe says. "It's like I don't trust the pilot."

"I told you, there's nothing to—"

"I know, but how would *you* know?" the boy says. "You said you never flew a plane. We're way up in the sky."

"I know how to survive things," Hank says. "I know when we're safe, when there's no need to worry. This is one of those times."

Hank shuffles the magazine around and looks across the aisle to the lone woman in the row. By habit he examines her hands, two sun-bronzed swans, elegant and cappuccino. No ring. He wants to smack himself for looking.

"Look, big man, I've heard of this pilot, heard great things," he says, leaning over Joe to maximize his authority. "He's so good they call him the Air King, or something like that."

111

"*Liar*," the boy snaps. "You lie. You make things up so much."

"Don't talk to me like that."

"I'm worried," Joe says. "I don't know why. I don't know why this time and not other times."

"It's okay," Hank says. "When we get to the condo, we're off to the pool. I'll let you do backflips."

"It's not okay."

"Breathe, buddy," he says. "Put your seat up. Breathe in and out. This is a natural reaction."

"No," Joe says, "not natural."

The boy can be stubborn, pigheaded even, crunching his forehead into little ravines to telegraph his displeasure. Hank knows the attitude isn't from him, and he can't recall Joe's mother acting this way. As a child, Hank was easygoing to fault, borderline indifferent—hardly a budding emergency responder. The last time he saw his own father, Earl was behind the wheel of a Lincoln Continental, the lone passenger a blind neighbor named Scratchy. Southward the men bolted toward Gary, Indiana, the bookie and the blind man. Not exactly cowboys and sunsets.

Joe clenches his armrest, kicks his sandals off. Nearby passengers slyly watch. Hank unclips his seatbelt, clears the middle seat, and hops over. He holds Joe.

"They call this claustrophobic stress," Hank says. "You're reacting to prior experiences, and we all do this in one way or another. Just remember that not all landings are bad."

"Stop it."

"You might not think much of me right now, but I know what I'm doing," Hank says. "Sit still."

"Please," the boy says. "Don't touch me."

Hank met his wife in a barbershop called Johnson's, a few blocks from his firehouse in Glenn Ellyn. She was in town canvassing the area for a marketing firm with aspirations of branching out of the South, and she was lost.

At first she was a curvy silhouette, her cat eyes lost in backlight. Johnson's dirty windows stood behind her, behind that kids running in the street, and beyond it all a picturesque baroque hotel. She asked for directions to Briar Street. The old pervert Johnson asked for her name.

"Athena," she said, pulling the latter half into syrupy drawl. "Like the town in Georgia, or almost."

"No," Johnson smiled. "Like the goddess."

Another barber had just finished Hank's trim and lined up his neckline with a razor. Had Athena walked in twenty minutes prior, with his sideburns and temples like bushy hives, she would have left alone. She would have lived. But Hank could feel his swagger coming on, a hot rush of confidence.

"I'll point her there," he told the guys. "I know Briar Street. Let me pay for this haircut, miss, and I'll get you on your way."

They stepped into the street. A lake breeze pushed clammy air across Chicago's suburbs, gulls whistling overhead. Athena's lipstick was mauve, not red, a dead-on match to the pumps she wore. That impressed Hank. Everything about her was refined, a contrast to the sports-pub floozies he'd been dealing with. Athena's ears were hidden under shimmering, curlicue locks, and Hank worried that the ears were humongous, like his. He worried about his worrying. They walked to Briar Street and chatted, mostly about baseball. He took a chance and asked her to dinner. She blushed like a flattered child and said okay, what the hell.

The next night, over linguini in the Gold Coast, Athena had swept her hair into a ponytail, confirming that her ears were borderline perfect, Hank thought, like tiny conch shells from the Keys. She'd be in town only three days. He felt rushed. Over dessert, he slipped her his business card, proud to have his fire company's emblem in her dainty hand.

"It doesn't turn you off, what I do?" he said.

She poked her tiramisu.

"The long hours?" he said. "The dangerousness?"

She sipped cabernet and swayed to a slow violin. The lights dimmed and the room—quaint, shadowy, and dripping with velvet— took on an underwater quality. Hank worried he was out of his league.

"Tell me," she said, "are all women crazy for big-city firefighters?"

He liked the question, found it easy to deflect. "My only dates lately have been with five-alarm warehouse blazes."

She didn't laugh. He worried she was examining his response, combing it for proof that he was a lothario, perhaps his whole firefighting story a shtick.

"I grew up on the Georgia-Florida line, where dad was a volunteer," she said. "He didn't know a damn thing about fighting fires. I'd imagine you're as professional as they come." She nibbled the dessert, a dusting of cocoa powder on her lips. "I have a question."

"Okay." He filled his mouth with wine and swallowed fast.

"You won't get mad?"

"Shoot."

"With all due respect, what kind of name is Hank *Obelisk?*" she said, napkin to her lips. "I've never heard such a funny last name."

He exhaled without meaning to. "My great-grandfather translated it from something unspeakable," he said. "Not in a bad way, but something not ready for English. He came here from Russia, an engineer fascinated by elevated trains. Believe it or not, 'obelisk' was the first English word he'd learned, other than the essentials. Of all the damn ugly words in the language—"

"But I like it."

At ten thousand feet the stewardesses have vanished. Hank presses the overhead HELP button twice but nobody seems capable of responding, the descent so extreme. He keeps cool for his son's sake.

114

He hopes his composure will shine favorably on the woman in the next row. She wears a pantsuit that from ten feet away looks like seersucker. He shakes his head, expelling thoughts of her at a time like this.

"We'll be laughing about this in an hour," he tells Joe. "You'll see how silly it was, and we'll stuff ourselves with pizza. Think about the pizza."

Joe breathes himself dizzy. He fiddles with an action figure, a grimacing soldier in desert fatigues. He downs the last of his bottled water.

"Did mom ever have this problem?" Joe says.

Hank leans the opposite way, toward the window, watching the plane pull a steep bank around the city, a great bird changing its mind. He sees the canopy and hills. A few carved gaps for shopping centers and major business districts, but otherwise a green abyss, a global cashmere sweater.

"No," says Hank. "Your mother is a cool lady. Wherever she is, she's being cool there."

"Did she like to fly?"

"She *loves* to fly," he says. "What'd I tell you about talking in past-tense?"

"Sorry," Joe says. "It just kind of seems right."

"Right?" Hank says. "You mean appropriate?"

"Yeah," Joe says. "Doesn't two years kind of make it okay?"

Hank crosses his arms in his best authoritative pose, his grade-school principal. "You're not as smart as you think sometimes. You should learn when to bite your tongue."

"Dad," Joe says, "I'm going to puke."

Seven hundred miles, an hour and twenty minutes in the air, the distance between cities was bearable. The first winter, Hank and Athena racked up hundreds in cell-phone overages to compensate. The second, Hank hoisted a white flag on his bunk at the station,

115

declaring himself southward bound. The boys threw him a party befitting his captain rank, and by Christmas he was gone.

The day before he drove down, she called him at home to say her period hadn't come. "Three weeks late," she said. "I have a test stick in my hand that reads positive. It's the third positive since *yesterday.*"

Hank dropped the phone and nearly buckled at the knees, the realities of adulthood draping over him like a plastic sack. He told her issues like pregnancy are best discussed in person, though he knew frighteningly little about what he said. When he hung up, he poured a gin with lime wedges, and well past midnight was still writhing in bed.

At daybreak he gave up on sleep and started the Ryder. He brewed a thermos of black coffee, pushed his keys in the drop box, and roared away. He saluted the Drake Hotel and the soaring Amoco Building as daylight unveiled them, whooping as the truck spun fresh snow down Lake Shore Drive.

Joe heaves in the airline vomit bag as if inflating a raft. Hank runs his nails over the boy's head, taps his fingertips lightly on his back. The passengers who sneak glances are met with disdainful stares from Hank. To think his sick boy is that interesting pisses him off.

"Doing good, buddy," he says, purposefully loud. "Nobody's watching."

Joe got sick like this a few nights after his mother's abduction, in the first frantic days when Hank couldn't bear to stay home. They slept at an extended stay hotel beside the interstate with hookers roaming the garden suites. Oddly, Joe would wear nothing but his father's clothing, and when running to the bathroom his shirt trailed like a parachute. The nausea came from constant microwave pizzas, soda, and Twinkies—a clueless father's specialty.

"All done?" Hank says now. "You've put a hurting on that bag."

"How much longer?"

"We're almost there," he says. "I can see our place now."

116

"What?"

"Okay, that's exaggerating...but we're close."

"Uhhh."

Hank tucks the bag under his seat, hopeful the sandaled feet he saw beneath him earlier aren't still there. The boy cranes his neck to see out the cabin window. Without the babyfat his jawbone is sharp, Hank notices, the cheekbones high, eyebrows straight and persuasive like his mother's. He offers the boy a stick of gum. Joe declines.

Athena liked to put the formula in a bowl in front of the baby, let him dip in his hands and catch the runoff with his mouth, a primitive feeding method that struck her as hilarious, her husband not so much. It made a mess of their 1940s bungalow, filling the kitchen with sour fumes.

"He looks like an animal or something, eating like that," Hank said. "Like a sea otter."

The couple relied on one car, a clunky Toyota Corolla, no small feat in a city of sparse public transit. When people worried aloud that the car was dangerous, Hank shot back: "Our mortgage rate made me do it." He'd been hired at Station 14, though lower on the totem pole than he liked, and his work was five miles away; the MARTA train stop was seven blocks. It went without saying that Athena would do the walking, even when she had to work late, which in winter meant a dark walk home.

"It's my thinking time," she'd say, optimistic even when she hated to be. "Good for clearing the lobes."

When Hank's schedule allowed a weekend off, they'd spend it making love. Long bouts all over the house—often the kitchen, sometimes the hallway, once the screened porch. They broke a barstool and ripped a swag curtain.

"This," Hank said one afternoon, "is the pinnacle of living."

"That," his wife teased, "was cheesy."

117

Athena got promoted to regional manager. They celebrated with champagne, a candlelit dinner of grilled salmon and steamed asparagus on the porch. She was tipsy two sips in. Along with the position came managerial tasks, longer hours editing press material written by her underlings, other menial headaches.

"If it comes down to it," she suggested, "there's no shame in being a stay-at-home dad these days."

"Not in five million years."

The longer Athena worked, the darker her walk home. She walked faster, developing blisters, scabs. She took shortcuts down Boulevard without telling her husband.

The plane rattles through a low patch of clouds, and all eighty passengers gasp. Two genteel ladies in business class demand drinks but the crew politely declines. Joe chews on his fingers.

"Flight crew," the pilot cracks, "prepare for landing."

Joe drains the last of his water and quietly belches. Hank points out rooftops visible between the trees. The nearness to earth eases the boy's tense face.

"Mushrooms," Joe says. "Or barbecue chicken pizza, with pineapple."

"You bet."

The afternoon sun heats the cabin, fills it with a cantaloupe hue. The woman in the next row draws down her plastic blind, and Hank mimics her, trying to catch her attention while avoiding Joe's. He hates to draw comparisons, especially physical ones, but she has wonderful hands.

Joe turned five, entered public school, and Athena got blunt. She asked her husband one morning to leave the fire department, to find something with steady hours. She complained that her feet felt arthritic and she wanted a consistent ride. Hank kicked his feet onto a flea-market ottoman and tossed his newspaper aside.

118

"It's more than a car you'll be buying, and we don't have cash in these walls," he said. "How much is parking downtown, by the month?"

"I have no idea."

"Hundreds," Hank said. "I heard it's hundreds."

"That's exaggerated."

"Listen," he said. "There's going to be overtime in the next few months. I'll work every minute of it. We'll have you a car. In the meantime, if you want to use the Toyota, I'll take the train, end of story."

"That's not sensible," she said. "I can wait."

"You're sure?"

She kept walking.

Two weeks before Thanksgiving, the babysitter rang Hank at the station. The call itself was unusual, but Jackie, the sitter, had troubled him with trivial inquiries at work before. Only this time Jackie was angry, perturbed that Athena had worked late without calling. Nearly eight o'clock and not a text, email, nothing. Hank knew she wasn't working late. His gut told him something was gravely amiss.

Hank entered what families of the missing call a cacophony of negative thinking, an otherworldly knowing that the cosmos is somehow off-kilter. He hung up the phone and told his lieutenant someone would need to cover for him because he felt ill. He left without hearing definite approval.

En route home, he called Athena's cell phone, then her office. A janitor said it was a ghost town, nobody there but him. Hank tried the cell phone again. Straight to voicemail: "Hi, y'all!"

On Freedom Parkway the streetlights hung in gauzy yellow mist. Hank glimpsed his home's clapboard exterior, and it occurred to him his wife might never be there again. The thought struck him as bizarre. He stopped at the Boulevard light, a truck and two taxis preventing the final right turn.

Crossing Boulevard, he saw it, and his mind went ballistic, a thousand directions at once. Athena's ladybug umbrella—caught between a bus-stop vestibule and a garbage can—rolled in the night breeze.

"Drug gangs!" Hank told the responding officer. "They're holding her for ransom. I've heard the stories. They work the Quick-Mart and that pizza shop farther down, work it in shifts. They roll drunks and rob people for groceries. There's no time—"

"Have a seat, sir," said the cop, a thick-wristed Hispanic man with strands of white in his sideburns. "Let's start with a timeline."

"Her cell phone," Hank said. "I'm calling it right now. I know how these things work. Trace the call by how it pings off cell-phone towers. I'm calling her, right now."

"Put the phone down," the cop said. "You don't want to alarm anyone, if something did happen. But I'm sure she's just hung up somewhere, or lost."

Hank walked the officer to his porch, away from Joe, who sat on the couch, awed by his frantic father. Hank thought it strange his son didn't cry.

"Don't ask me how I know this," Hank said on the porch, "but she's in a bad way. I know you handle these cases a lot, but I'm begging you to go after this, with everything you can expend, tonight."

"About that timeline," said the cop.

"*Fuck* the timeline," Hank said.

The cop grabbed him by the wrists. "Shut up," he said. "C'mon, brother, *think*."

"I'm giving you leads," Hank said, shrugging him off, "and you're standing there."

"Think logically," the cop said.

"Watch the boy," Hank said. "I'll walk these blocks myself, you worthless son of a bitch."

The cop radioed for an investigator and watched Hank vanish, a wet vest and two militant arms swallowed by the shadows of Glenn Iris Drive.

Joe bites his lip as the landing gear spreads. He sits on his hands and squirms, tucks his head between his knees. The wheels touch gently, their connection with sunbaked asphalt barely noticeable, a shallow pothole on a country road.

"I told you," Hank smiles. "Hot butter."

They taxi across innumerable lanes. Joe prematurely unbuckles.

"Can we keep the barfing a secret?" Joe asks.

Hank winks and puts his forefinger across puckered lips.

The disappearance made waves with regional media for several weeks. The newspapers grew particularly excited when a team of horseback searchers from Texas descended on the Old Fourth Ward, a band of cowboys on the urban frontier. The umbrella was the eerie touch that editors pine for, and Athena's eventual life-insurance payout lent the story an unfounded layer of mystery.

Hank, once cleared by police, became something of a folk hero, a decorated firefighter whose want of answers outshone his inability to fund a private investigation. His screw-the-police subversion won him favor with hipsters and college kids. The ones Hank took the time to meet would channel him baggies of high-grade weed, which he said aided his sleeping.

"Keep it coming," Hank told one kid with sleeves of skull tattoos. "They don't have the balls to drug-test me."

On local TV broadcasts, and once on the radio, Hank decried the efforts of police—"Quotas! The PD's got one thing on their minds, and that's arrest quotas!"—which, of course, prompted his termination from the fire department. Political science students at the downtown college picketed city hall for three days.

Donations in blank envelopes made their way to Hank's porch, and hardly a street post in the Old Forth Ward was bereft of a reward poster. Neighborhoods came together to cull traces of the career woman who went to work and never came home.

But there was nothing left of Athena.

The investigation stalled and the case was quietly shelved. Hank sold the home to her family, a joint purchase between several sympathizing aunts and uncles. He got fifty thousand over market value and poured forty into newspaper ads. Not a single tipster called.

"People don't care about the vanished after a year," Hank said on the last television broadcast he was invited to. "I take issue with the attention span of police and the city at large. I take issue with the public's forgetfulness in general."

Hank bought a cookie-cutter condo in the sky, a home off the street. In the tiny living room stood a telescope; on the balcony hung expensive binoculars. Hank would invite Joe to the balcony after homework, when the smoke had cleared. Together they watched the day conclude.

"Look at that sunset," Hank said one evening. "It's like red sheets, ripped off the city and pulled out west."

Joe cocked his head, his eyes in philosophical squint. "I bet mom liked sunsets."

"*Likes*," said Hank. "She likes them."

At the gate, a stewardess speeds through her final, uninspired spiel. Businessmen activate cell phones. Hank tilts back his head, enjoys the overhead fan one last time before the heat. He stands up and gathers their bags.

Hank thinks of the progressions they've made. For the first time in a year, he can sleep without too much dope, and Joe can tolerate pitch-dark rooms. It shames Hank to feel any sense of recovery, but a guy has a life to live, two mouths to feed. A self-pity hibernation of booze and smoke is no option.

The woman in the other row pulls a purple snakeskin bag from the overhead compartment. She flashes curious eyes at Hank; he gives her a dismissive nod and turns around to help his son. He pulls the backpack straps over the boy's chest and pats his head, corrects the alignment of his Cubs hat. He knows there will be a time for women with cappuccino hands, but now is not that time.

THE DELUSIONAL MISTER NECESSARY

─────────

Some blond guy is using the Double-Pulley Pulldown when it's my turn. He must be a new member at the gym, because I've never seen his hair before. It seems greatly shampooed, perfect to the point of insult. If my name wasn't Bob Necessary I'd walk up and ask him where he parked his Pegasus. But my name is certainly that. It has power, even in silence, which means I don't have to confront Hercules, and I won't be talking that Pegasus gibe.

It's right about 8:20 now in the p.m. and primetime for the Spandex rush. It occurs to me nightly that Spandex is a gift from Jesus sent down to middle-aged Midwestern males, a species that includes me. The ladies all look so gifted in Spandex, so properly buttressed. The joy of Spandex holds me over through these winter months until I get the swimsuits at Memorial Public Pool. The red-suited lifeguards in particular. In one-pieces they swim on pool breaks like seals. Their hair, usually blond, is milky in the water, their bodies like limber traces of a dream. They pop up for air and chirp about

123

college next year. Hot money I love July.

Spandex on me would be too boastful. On any other man downright flagrant. I prefer gray sweatsuits with high-powered elastic at the ankles. So tastefully accentuating, so perfect for jumping jacks. Nothing says watch-me-perspire like the wetted Rorschach blots that seep out the back of gray sweats. The attire makes its own remarks so that I seldom have to. Bob Necessary doesn't say what's on his mind. He lets the sweat speak for itself. And tonight I'm on a roll.

Hercules is wrapping up. He tufts back his locks and takes a slow cool gander at the Elliptical girls. He is sniffing my turf. In my younger days, this guy might've been in for a grapple, or I might've just kicked him in the plums. But now I take the suave approach, the high ground traveled by us more established and gentlemanly beefcakes. I let Hercules wonder and want and then drown in his own soppy bashfulness. He's too shy to make the approach. Like the rest of us, I bet he's hatched a thousand hypotheses about courting gym women but has acted on none. Nobody talks in these places. They just peek. They keep eyes on the fanning deltoids of the ship-shape crowd around them but never mouth a word.

There goes Hercules. Turning around, retreating from the Ellipticals, not a chance. He shows his back to the cardio crew and hawks another machine, defeat at its puniest. Finally he sits on the Lower Back Extender and rows his invisible boat, his sorry tattoos peeking out from the unwashed white T.

I take his place, triumphantly. In a burst of sheer explosive might I latch onto the Pulldown and enjoy the view: every floppy breast Flecksers Fitness has to offer. The mirrored walls, the hanging plasmas, the rows of joggers, the Spandex princesses on big pink Ab Balls, the meatheads slapping chalk. It's the busiest hour and for twenty two dollars per month and no contractual obligations this place is mine. Beyond the Incline Bench and the Calf Raiser my head looks fantastic in the mirror. Not bald but with wings of hair. I pull down—*herrrmph!* And let back up—*ffffsssooo!* I conquer the Pulldown and everybody takes notice.

A brunette is headed this way, one o' clock. She looks so

124

familiar, and so stern. The insignia on her shirt is authoritative and brassy. It shines under the gym's heavy halogen. She's so close I can read her nametag—Monica. She has forearm veins.

"Mr. Necessary?" says Monica. "Can you hear me? Please take off the Walkman."

"Yes?" I slip off the headset, so padded with orange foam. The sound of early Men At Work fades onto my shoulders, cascades down my chest. "Bob, please. Hello."

"Alright, Bob. Did you check in when you came through? At the front desk?"

"Yes," I say. "Certainly."

"Funny," says Monica. "You're not electronically registered as being in here. And technically you're not allowed back in Flecksers in the first place. Our records still show you haven't paid in three months. We can't auto-draft from your checking because you have no available funding."

"Can you say that more quietly around here?" I put a finger on my lips. "We have reputations to uphold."

Monica huffs, hands on hips. She isn't treading lightly. She's pumped. Must be the creatine kicking in.

"I have committed no incidents of misbehavior here," I say. "As I told you last month, your payments are en route. Have some patience, I'm a very busy man."

"Mr. Necessary, I'm sorry. This is a business, and I manage it at night. It's important to wean your muscles slowly, so I'll let you finish your routine this evening. Go light weight and high reps. After that, you can't come back in here."

"Not even for jumping jacks?"

"No, the gym is for paying members only. You can't come in the door."

"Answer me one question," I say.

"If you come back in," says Monica, getting fussy, "I'll have to call the Broad Ripple Police. You'll technically be trespassing."

"One question?"

"One question."

I stand up and turn halfway around. "My posterior," I say. "How's it coming?"

She takes an admiring glance.

"Lumpy," she says. "Like mashed potatoes."

I feel a burn but not *the* burn. This Monica must be writhing with passion—I can see it in her mandibles. But I can't think of anything to say in return, so I pull my Walkman back on. She juts up her left fingers and circles the right ones for numerical significance: four and zero, I guess. Then she says, loudly, over the didgeridoo in my mind, "Forty minutes, Mr. Necessary. That's it. We close in forty."

Truth be told, I wasn't always such the Necessary type. I was on the football team at Chesapeake High School but otherwise this (specimen that is me) could not have been predicted. Mother had seen it coming but nobody else did. With her red cheeks like gelatin she told me late-bloomers do bloom best. That was a very long time ago, 1981, and bloom I did: 250 pounds now of prime man-beef, a chunk of rippling granite, a walking anatomy lesson. Mother was right on the money.

In my football years I played the offensive line. I brought glamor to the trenches. With me on the field the underclass girls were prone to swooning, which didn't sit well with the rock-brained football lords. One time they whipped me so hard with towels they broke open my back and ass cheeks. I can still see the blood whirlpooling in the locker-room shower drain. That happened late in the football season, so late I couldn't wear jeans or wool sweaters for a family Thanksgiving photo at Willard's Department Store. The last photo before dad choked to death and I couldn't even sit down.

Dad was a winner. And smart beyond his janitorial duties. He told me one time our family name had been translated from the opening stanza of a Norwegian battle cry. He was romantic like that, as most habitual liars are. But his lies were benign and funny, so far beyond the truth they landed feather-soft. The only collateral damage was the hollowness it created in him. He got to the point he couldn't believe himself, and when that happens it's best to keep on lying. In fact I thought he was joking when he turned purple and clutched his throat during Ten Cent Oyster Night at the Wok N' Roll Buffett. It was Thursday, our weekly father-son dinner after football practice, and I just sat there, laughing uproariously, until a waiter got wise and screamed for a doctor.

"What's your problem?" the waiter hissed. "That dumb look on your face at a time like this. Do *something!*"

When they pronounced dad expired and crated him away I finished my plate. Call me sordid but it's the truth. I sucked every husk of edamame empty, devoured each shred of ginger, and scarfed the whole stack of moo shoo pancakes. I ate until my belly popped over my football tights. Eating that much felt like a blanket on my insides. It would be my new defense—caloric impalement.

In order to uphold my sexiness, I needed plenty of sweating, and for continued sanity I required loads of thinking time. The rank fumes of old gymnasiums called to me like sirens' songs. In gyms I was nobody's fool, a coward no longer, anybody I could imagine. Public exercise lent me a new perspective on the world and all its flawed inhabitants. I joined the Broad Ripple YMCA and worked my way up.

A man in my position loves a challenge. Monica has no idea. Bob Necessary fills his lungs with the odor of challenge and expels the fabulous fumes of victory. In forty minutes I can attract flocks of Spandex. But I've never responded well to deadlines. Mother allowed me years to triumph.

Before Monica can strut back to the front desk (where she'll peck through Physical Science 301 material instead of working, as always) I spot several Necessary candidates treading away like hamsters beneath the plasmas. They're watching a brainless game show. They laugh at the blinking numbers and they are transfixed. I disqualify them immediately. Not worthy.

On the Exerbike is what looks to be a deranged Irish midwife. She sifts through underwear ads in a colorful magazine filled with celebrity schlock. She has a hideous pucker-face but a fine, fine posterior. It teeters like a sideways eight on the bike seat, half-expanding and half-contracting with the movement of her hindquarter pleasantries. Next to her is a massive brother drenched in tribal tattoos. They could be together, the midwife and the brother, which isn't worth the chance. It's unsettling to know what'll happen to such a tall man when I make him fall. Plus it could strain my hamies to kick so high.

I'm feeling a change of scenery. I walk across the red carpet to the rubberized floor area, nearly undoing the Velcro on my sneakers. Here I find the Cable Sitdown Bench, which I know comes with many great angles. From here I can see the Dip Assist, the Squat Rack, the Lateral Flex and, should I catch the right combination of mirrored images, up to the panties of a loose-shorted lady on the Decline Bench.

Here, the Spandex glows in the gymnasium's far corners. It takes a while to find it all. I have to peer back and forth through the mirror until the really brilliant stuff pops out, like Easter eggs in the grass.

Nothing is popping tonight, however. No eggs, no grass. Only sweatpants and loose button-ups and too-thick clothing. A gray blur jostles at low speed on the equipment around me. And there are very old women here who actually have men. These pairings only amplify the lurking nervousness behind my abs, so I have to look away.

The tape clicks to an end and the music in my ears stops. Outside, streetlights flicker on a steely yellow streetscape. A big, wet dog chases a tumbling Burger Buddy wrapper down a dark alley. The dog disappears into shadow and I fear that it will never catch up.

And then He enters.

The gym patrons fall silent, the glass doors open. A gust of wind announces the entrance of the man I've named Brutor in my mind, the absolute alpha meathead. He is incredible, this Brutor, all six feet nine of Him, the hulking trunk of Him. He rips off His trench coat and shoves the bundle of it in a locker. Even Monica stares. On His big feet are white and red high-tops, untied. Across the wide waves of His chest is always a t-shirt, usually red, brandishing the old Music Television logo. Tonight He's dressed as usual, like a Russian pitfighter in basketball gear.

Brutor walks in huge impressive steps, and without exception He walks toward me. Everything that comprises Him is superior to the composition of me. Among this Flecksers tribe He has no rival, only silent admirers. Other patrons sigh.

"Is this bench free, jumping-jack?" Brutor says.

I pretend to not hear because looking up to Brutor makes me feel so small.

"You on here or not?" he asks, to which I do not reply. I sense mirrored eyeballs on us. "Then get up and spot me," he says. "Do you *want* me to get pissed?"

I stand up for Him but I step backwards, nearly tripping on a Triceps Rope with fat rubber handles. I have never understood how one man can spot another on a machine with cables, yet He always demands it of me. It makes Him appear even bigger with me nearby, and I don't want that comparison to ruin my last night. He hovers over me, pokes my back, quips about my sweatpants, and there is nothing I can do. I want to call Brutor a chest-pounding, veined-out megalomaniac with nothing better to do at 8:50 in the p.m. on a Wednesday night. But I wouldn't do that. I don't need to say that. Then again I need to say something at some point. It's just that my bones don't feel secure enough within me to say anything at all.

Brutor rips into the exercise and I dissipate into the squirm. In His every heave and grunt I see an awesomeness that can never be mine. His routine is gaining fury and He hasn't noticed my leaving. He is the only one allowed to keep pumping after close. Rumor has it He stays and rips away in the dark.

In my only year at Elizabeth State College, the kids in my dorm dubbed me "Megadork," and "Dorkosaurus," and "Dorky Dorkerton." It was too much to handle, being cooped in classrooms with jealous nincompoops of that caliber. One night in my room, they pushed a drunk girl in and held the door closed behind her. She had money in her hand and red lipstick on, so thick it nearly dripped. She bent over my comic book and crammed her tongue in my mouth. I had drunk a lot of Muscle Milk before bed and so I peed myself. She screamed, pulled a tiny camera from her pocket, and immortalized me with a flash-bulb picture, the wetness looking like an aerial shot of Australia.

I dropped out and never officially got certified in applied electronics.

Mother didn't care. She wanted me around as much as possible. It didn't feel right being away from her anyhow. By leaving the dorm I could snuggle with mother during the evening news and bake the snickerdoodles she can't live without.

We continue the news-and-cookies ritual to this day. She's becoming somewhat brittle, so I have to mind the placement of my hands, strong as they are. I can tell it's her favorite time, our evenings together, just her and me and the anchormen with great hair. On the couch with her only child, my mother kind of blossoms. She even talks sometimes between gulps of sorbet and cookie dough. Mother clammed up like me in the wake of dad's sudden passing, but the way I see it, that doesn't mar her qualities. She embodies every single thing I could desire in a woman, with the exception of fitness, personality, and intelligence.

Sometimes at night I take a flashlight under the covers and explore old family photo albums. I can tell that, as a baby, I was a blessing to mother and dad. Those sepia photos with curved corners tell me so. I flip the pages and voyage to places I've already been but don't recall. The vacation pictures stick with me the most. I lie awake and imagine myself in Myrtle Beach, building sand forts with dad. I see us pulling balloons together through Battery Park in New York City. I watch him carry me like his own personal Medicine Ball, a dying Miami sunset over our shoulders.

Monica guards the entrance desk with her heels propped on a Formica countertop. Come to think of it, her legs aren't shabby. She chews a thick wad of bubble gum in voracious, churning bites. She flips into her book as if she doesn't know I'm leaving. I approach the exit with eight minutes to spare.

"What should I do with the towel?" I ask, and she looks up, bedazzled. I watch the pupils of her eyes adjust from the tiny print of her reading material to the stunning visage of me. Maybe she's vexed by the question. "The towel. It was issued to me when I became a member. Now I'm not one. Should I take it? I'm very sweaty. Well, usually I am."

"It's yours," says Monica, and she slips back into her reading.

"If I want to come back, do I have to pay for all the months at once?"

"Yep," she says.

Cold silence. She isn't even looking at me. The overhead racket of heavy metal guitars is not what I want to hear. I toss the towel over my shoulder and pull my house key from the clothespin to which I hook it in my pocket. I don't drive here; I walk it. The house where mother waits is just up the street.

"I run a small business, and times are slow right now," I say. "I also take care of my mother. For rent mostly, but it's a big job. She went all catatonic after dad died."

"I'm sorry about your father," Monica says. "Cancer?"

"Not even close," I say. "He was setting a world record for the largest oyster ever consumed. We come from a seafaring people. Anyhow, he choked."

"He choked on an oyster?"

"Yes, sadly."

"I thought that was impossible."

"It was the size of my fist."

"Huh," she says. "That's tragic."

"As I was saying, mother needs plenty of looking after. It's good for me to come here during breaks with her."

Monica perks. "So you still live with your mom?"

131

I have to gather myself a second, wipe my palms across my thighs.

"My skill is to fix video game machines," I say. "I'm good at it. I've practiced for over twenty years. It's just that the kind I fix are the ones nobody plays anymore."

More silence.

"It's hard to believe you're not married, Mr. Necessary," says Monica. "The ladies in here are missing out on a real prince."

"How'd you know that?"

"You're listed as single in our records."

"You checked?" I ask with considerable pep.

Monica sits up slowly. "I was searching for an alternate source of income in your family," she says, flipping her eyelashes in a final rejection. "You're so full of the wrong ideas."

I slip the silent headphones back over my ears and exit Flecksers Fitness. Harsh, wet winds bite at my hands. I turn around to walk backwards, now halfway across the parking lot, and I expect to see the entire gym clamoring at the windows to know where I'm going. Of course they're not doing that. The silly activities are going on without me. The gymnasium squirms and squirms. Nobody in there is perfect enough, not even Brutor. In and out, up and down, the futile pursuit of absolutely nothing. I wish the windows would suddenly fog over and stay that way.

Hovering in a huge illuminated rectangle above the fitness center is the billboard that first got me to join. It was glowing in the night, like now, with its low monthly figures scribbled in cursive red. On the billboard is a shirtless man with a superbly white smile and huge hands that I could just crawl into. The underline of his pectoral muscles is glorious and cut, the same with his outer delts. I take a seat on a curb in the parking lot and sit half-covered by a bush. Blanketing myself with the gym towel, I pull my knees into my chest, give a little cough, and then I push my right thumb behind my teeth and onto my tongue, biting down. In my suckling I feel the folds of thumb-skin with my curious tongue. The thumbnail itself is smooth. I watch the billboard as its lights flicker. Up there, the teeth and hair and

132

manicured nails are really booming. I can see the serendipity between the letters and the skin. And yes the twinkle of eternal galaxies goes on behind the man forever.

IN THE PREDAWN

Tania Boley's flailing limbs had rubbed an angel pattern in the schoolyard mud. Like a snow angel in red clay. Like a game, only not.

I saw the angel left by Tania as the techs took photos. The fanning arms, the dress of legs, the skull dent. I saw the plastic butterflies in Tania's thick, licorice braids. I will always see that when I hear children laugh. I cannot take it out of me.

"There," says the captain, catching my wandering mind, "stand your ass *right there.*"

"Got it," I say, stiffening. "Ain't my first rodeo."

In a scorching autumn drought like the city's never seen—the Bermuda grass dead, the red dust swirling—a rainstorm has hit hard enough to prune a little girl. She's bad evidence now, a soggy riddle. The lone witness says the man was Hispanic, six feet tall, age thirty to forty. That's all we have. I hold a perimeter and the mother comes at me. She senses I'm about to stop her, so she screams—a banshee's wail across the playground.

"Goddamn it, she needs me!" the woman says. "Let me up in there."

"She needs you to stay here," I say, holding the cordoning tape behind me. "She needs you to be strong. We'll work nonstop if need be. We *will* find them."

I tell the mother I'm a sergeant, a seasoned tracker, but she's not hearing it. She shuns the gold badge clipped to my belt, my authoritative necktie, the silver splotches in my goatee. She screams into my face as if my hands wrenched the life from Tania. Should this woman break free and dart thirty feet closer to the twirl slide, to where the girl's pink shirt is ripped up to her clavicle, to where her chest is washed in moonlight and coagulating blood, this woman will die angry. I've seen this enough to know.

"You didn't know her," the mother says. "Fuck y'all pigs."

"She's in good hands."

"No, *fuck* y'all pigs."

Her face wilts in strobes of red and blue. She cries without trying to and, in a way, I'm jealous.

In the gray hour before dawn, when I am home alone, which is pretty much always without Sheila, these voices will pipe up again. They will hiss and growl and call me ignorant. When the victims are children I see sleep, like cotton in a wind, but I cannot catch it. The adage is that police officers are never really off duty. That's truer than anyone knows. Because when I am off duty, when I have time to sleep or work side jobs, I am emotionally on the street, working bodies, working leads. I physically have left the gutters of Bankhead and Vine City but my thinking has not—not when business is unfinished. There is no reprieve then. With every down hour I'm paying penance to the families I have failed.

"Get me some water," the mother says, clasping her hands in prayer. "I'm liable to pass out."

"I'd be glad to…just as soon as you step back."

"God's seen this," she says. "His eyes don't forget."

136

"Nor do ours, believe me."

"Please. Water."

"Yes, right. You have a seat on the curb. I'll fix you up."

In the final minutes before daybreak, I resurrect the children. I imagine that life and vitality have filled their bodies. I see them laugh again, climb trees again. Though I have never heard them speak I know the cadence of their voices, the words they would say. Their hands, which I've seen only as the claws of first-stage rigor mortis, hold basketballs and cellos. In my unit we see ghosts. That's just how it is.

"I swear to God these wetbacks are giving our city a black eye," says Felix Montez, a detective with aspirations of sergeant.

"You're not supposed to think that way," I say. "Keep cool. Less coffee."

I wait with Felix tonight in the cafeteria at eastside precinct. At three-fifteen on the microwave clock we are only beginning. Despite the rain our techs lifted two complete fingerprints from the victim's plastic purse, both too large to be hers. It's up to forensics to provide us with a name. Otherwise we are hamstrung. This could take hours, days. Or any second we could bolt out the doors, the address in hand.

"Of all nights," Felix says, "it had to piss rain tonight."

"Complicates things, but it's kind of refreshing," I say.

"Refresh this," Felix says, walking to the vending machines, tugging at his crotch. Classic him.

Felix is my partner, four years now. He bears a scar on his face that I find unavoidable, this red-pink ribbon of gnarled tissue and stitch marks, a souvenir from Baghdad. He's proud of the scar and the story behind it, though his details about the insurgent who popped one lucky round before Felix knifed him to death have many variations. Enough that I suspect Felix has manufactured the story. I roll with what he tells me because I like him. His cocksureness makes him valuable, especially in the deepest drag of night. A case without suspects is an insult to Felix.

"Maybe our river-jumper did some voodoo rain dance?" he says, sitting back down.

"Kind of ironic, you putting it that way." I lean back in my seat, shaking my head, disappointed. "Is that a theory?"

"Yes. It's my primary theory at this point."

"Here's my theory: You're a dumbass."

He sips fresh coffee. "Look at the rain, you old bastard," he says.

"I don't see rain."

"Exactly. It's gone."

"I don't see your point, either."

"Game on. Let's go."

"Sit tight, amigo," I say. "Or go play in the puddles. Makes no difference to me."

I tease Felix, but he's come in handy outside work, especially when Sheila cut me away, back in those desperate first weeks. At forty-nine I was sleeping on Felix's couch, emotionally gutted. His mother would drop by each weekend and ask how I could be his mentor and so pathetic at the same time.

Since the split I've rebuilt myself, for the most part. I tell the guys I hike the foothills near Dahlonega to clear my head. I describe for them the piney air of lower Appalachia and the hairpin turns of mountainous Highway 429, places I haven't been in decades. I don't feel that I'm lying if my lying is descriptive. But these are investigators—they dissect lies for a living. They probably smell the bullshit before it fumbles from my mouth.

Sometimes I want to talk about the real impact, the toll of sleeping pills and predawn sweats. It takes all I have every morning to not drink myself sick. To not unscrew the malted scotch that's gathered dust since I swore off booze. It's especially hard to not drink on my no-call days, Monday and Tuesday. For the most part I spend my downtime working, earning, and occupied. I pick up traffic details at Inman Elementary School, stand guard over the Midtown Bowling Alley by night. More than money, the value of side jobs is that they convince me, if only for a while, that modern society is benign and functional, that every family bowls together and goes home laughing.

"That lady went ape shit tonight," Felix says. "Complete psychosis. I don't know how you handle those things."

"I thought she might slap me."

"Ditto," he says. "It's been a while since I've heard that kind of screaming. That level of…I don't know what."

"It isn't hate," I say. "That sound. Not hate. Remember that."

"Then it's confusion."

"No, it's worse," I say. "I guess you'd call it delusion."

Felix rips the cellophane off a high-cal hunk of carrot cake. He nibbles at first, then pulls back his lips to bite, chasing with a huge swallow of coffee.

"Say you had kids," he says. "Could you still do this?"

I rap my knuckles on the hard-plastic table. The wall clock ticks. He has a way of digging too deep sometimes.

"I think it'd be too much," I say.

"It's situations like this, with the Boley kid, that would get me, you know, if I had a family. It's this shit that makes dads into vigilantes."

"That's what I mean."

Felix skyhooks the coffee cup toward the trashcan and misses. "The rest of their lives, the fathers, they have that purpose," he says. "Whether they tell us or not, they want to kill whoever the motherfucker is, you know?"

"I think I'd more than kill them."

My bluntness startles Felix. We sit quietly for a moment. He fingers his gold necklace, runs his tongue between his teeth and lips. I think about the medallion Sheila wore, the soft dimple between her neck and clavicle, her value as a ghost repellant. That's what I called her, my personal Ghostbuster, which is pretty goddamn cheesy now that I think about it.

Sheila blamed the collapse more on the job than me. It wasn't in my soul to choke a woman. She knew that.

It happened after her company Christmas party three years ago, whiskey everywhere. She was a partner in some highly regarded Sandy Springs consulting firm, a dainty bird high above the stagnant air of police work. She worked in a shining tower of glass while I trolled Section 8 housing for gas-station bandits whose Glocks had gone off. Yet something in the savagery of my occupation had always turned her on. The savage in me did not.

There was this skinny guy at the party from Boston, all pinstripes and checkered cufflinks. He grazed Sheila's midriff with a little too much affection and then waltzed toward me. I told him every New England transplant I'd met in the city was a prick, and that the same probably applied to him. He cowered a little, maybe blushed. Not that I don't like the northeasterners, I remember saying, just that their mouths run so much. He called me Southern and evolutionarily backwards. That's his wording exactly, evolutionarily backwards. We squared our shoulders and spat boozy threats, ice cubes clinking in our glasses. I told him he'd better not stumble—not out in the city, not anywhere—and that wasn't like me. Sheila hurried over in her fancy Vera Wang, her coworkers whispering in the periphery. She tugged on my blazer, put a fingernail in my ribs, and that was that. Really, though, it wasn't.

The car ride home, Sheila drove. I droned about the man from Boston. My memory's patchy but I know his brush with her was gnawing at me. She was crying by the time we pulled up to our townhome.

I smashed a tumbler on the living room wall. She slapped my face.

"You're above this," she said. "This isn't you. This isn't Bill."

"I saw you talking to him."

"Oh, Jesus," she said, tossing aside her handbag. "He's a client. A *client*. That's what I do—I talk to fucking clients."

I rolled off the couch sometime after 3 a.m. I remember thinking I was parched and then stumbling through moonlit murk toward the sink. Earlier that week I'd worked a triple murder in

Tucker, the aftermath of rival Hispanic gangs crossing paths in a bodega parking lot. The kid from *La Raza* ambushed the *18th Street Locos* crew, wasted three teens near the cart corral. I'd spent four hours in that parking lot marking shell casings. Dozens and dozens of little brassy shells spat from nine millimeters. I was on the kitchen floor, hands and knees, apparently feeling for casings, when Sheila, a white apparition in her nightgown, asked too loudly what the hell I was doing.

I pounced. That's the only way to say it. I attacked my wife.

When I came to she was pinned against the hallway mirror. My first instinct was to reach for my holster and demobilize the man doing this to her. But now I was the offender, the despicable factor in this violent equation. I followed my arm with my eyes from her face to the rest of me. Then I was nauseous. In the instant before I let loose, before she fell to her knees and gasped like a fish, I caught a glimpse of myself in that mirror, a lurid snapshot of my face half-lit by the moon. Only it wasn't really me. My face was a snarling wolf, the killer when he's first apprehended, when he realizes a force greater than himself has outdone him and that he must succumb or die.

My wife hacked on the kitchen floor. She asked if I was finished. I curled underneath her and wept.

"If I didn't think it would kill you," she said, "I'd have you fired for this."

Between Felix and I sits the empty coffee pot, brown and scabby. He's on his sixth cup, his teeth starting to grind. I like him more each shift but I don't let on. He'll probably make it to sergeant while weaker recruits from his class will not. They'll end up in administration, wiping coffee circles off the chief's desk, replacing the placard with my name on it. I've seen it happen to hard asses before them, former paratrooper medics and Army Rangers, the whole Special Ops alpha male clan.

Felix scratches his chin. I check the safety on my nine

millimeter. Then I check again—an impulsive, nervous habit. The room smells like a cooking burrito, a blend of cheese, beef, and peppers, probably a late lunch inhaled by some dayside rookie.

"Won't be long before the office stiffs roll in," Felix says.

"What, maybe, an hour?"

"I don't have a good feeling," I say. "I'll call about the prints before seven. If they're snagged, I say we head home, nap a couple hours."

Felix packs a big pinch of snuff and spits in a Coke can. I nibble on barbecue sunflower seeds. My workday began twenty-three hours ago and my eyes are tight and sore, my back in tender knots. Some mornings I rub my back along the doorframes of my apartment to ease the tension, but it doesn't really work. Another miserable alternative. I miss her oily massages.

Sheila's last words to me were warm but not so comforting: "Keep your head up, Bill." I loved her voice. I clung to it. Maybe it was the slow order in her speaking, the Southern cordiality you don't find much anymore. With a voice like that she probably deserved better than me. A man who was there, a husband.

The last of my boxes in hand, I stood in our foyer and swore I'd never drink again. She waved and folded away her red fingernails. She closed the door gently as I walked to my cruiser.

Driving to Felix's apartment, I tried to file away the most vivid memories, the Greek dinners and summertime Braves games, the feel of her skin beneath cool sheets, the massages. But all those things were gaping wounds. I drove fifty aimless miles. I put down the Crown Vic's windows and wept into the wind.

Felix keeps shaking his head, as if answering no to questions I can't hear.

"You okay, amigo?" I ask him.

"Yep, yourself?"

"Hair's gray and I'm getting fat. Otherwise, living the dream."

Felix doesn't react, which is strange. Self-deprecation usually gets him rolling.

"When it gets to this point," he says soberly, "I keep thinking about the deceased. I like to think they're cheering me on. Especially tonight, with the girl, it's like I'm sticking up for someone who couldn't fend off these people, this trash."

"There's brick walls in this business," I say. "You should've realized that by now."

"Yeah, well, this sucks," he says. "Every case like this sucks ass."

"You have to grin and bear it. You'll lose your mind if you don't."

"It's like I owe them something," he says.

"I know the feeling."

"I hate it," he says. "I hate to lose momentum."

"There's none of that now, no momentum," I say, loosening my tie and bending up my collar stays. "It's obvious our guy has no record. The body is fucking waterlogged. It's fun to sit here pretending the call's coming, but it's not. There's a body, a kid with a mother, and nobody else. Everyone else—her daddy, her granddaddy, *everybody*—disappeared years ago, fucking *poof!* Chalk that up to what you will, but there's always a simpler truth beneath these things…no one gives a damn about that kid but you, me, and the mother. And that woman's worthless tonight."

"There were footprints in the mud," Felix perks. "That's something."

"Reeboks, size ten," I say. "Take a ruler, door to door. Or put an ad in the *Journal-Constitution*. Call me next Monday with your findings."

He scoffs and kicks a leg of our table, though lightly enough to not spill the coffees.

"Don't pout on me," I say. "I won't tolerate your rookie tantrums all over again."

"I'm working with a pessimist," he says. "You sound so burned out. You constantly complain about shit. How am I supposed to glean things from you?"

"Well…"

"Well, what?"

"Goddamn it, you little prick," I say, bringing down my fists, coffee splashing. "I'd slap your face if you weren't onto something. You probably deserve better than me, this whole department probably does. I can't concentrate. For what it's worth, here's my mantra: Keep your head up, but not up your ass. You're too optimistic."

"I thought you might say I'm learning," he says.

"Now that would be optimistic of me."

"Fuck you, man."

In an hour I call forensics, the downtown office. Linda, the studious-looking woman there, says she has bad news—which is no news. She's waiting on the clothes and body to fully dry. She says a break for us would be in order, at least until noon. I don't need much persuasion.

"It's nap time," I say, snatching Felix's spit-can and throwing it away. "Call one of your girlfriends. Tell them breakfast is on the way."

"I think I'll stay here," he says.

"Yeah?"

"Yeah."

"Suit yourself, but—"

"Don't tell me it's not healthy and all that," he says. "Just keep your phone on vibrate, in your pocket. Anything breaks, I'll call you."

"Sure thing," I say, as I push open the precinct door, slogging toward my cruiser. "I'll probably answer."

As the door eases shut Felix belts out my name, almost childlike in his pitch. I catch the handle with my fingertips and peek my head back in. He's standing now, the sunlight illuminating his brown eyes, his butterscotch face.

"It wasn't your fault," he says. "I know it and, wherever she is, she knows it. This is what you do, so quit beating yourself up."

"Like I said," I tell Felix, letting go, "I'll probably answer."

144

Chipper office types flock in—pressed suits and coffee thermoses, a heavily perfumed bunch—and for them it's just Wednesday, halfway between professional football and martini Friday at Dante's. At these moments, the sun beating down, I feel infectious and sorrowful. These people must wonder how I've put up with nights so long. At times like these I'm prone to wonder myself.

Some guy in blue suspenders and a pink Oxford nods at me and smiles. I think I met him once at the office copier, hated him from the get-go, but still I smile back.

"Rain last night, did it?" he says.

I look around the wet ground, to the puddles still oozing from potholes, as if to call him stupid. "Yeah," I tell the guy. "It rained so hard you wouldn't understand."

BLOOD ALLIES

The lunatic peeks over the bong, smiles like he shit his pants, and through a curtain of shaggy blond bangs says: "When chimpanzees are in full rage, they want to rip a man's eyeballs out, to pluck the arms away like chicken wings," the lunatic says. "That's just something to think about, should you find yourself in a hostile zoo takeover."

As usual, Freddy has no response. Sitting on a couch within stabbing distance of the lunatic makes him uneasy. He digs into a pocket of his Dockers, exhumes his extraordinary new smart phone, and pretends to receive the text message to end all text messages. Like all of modern humanity, Freddy uses his phone to deflect social obligations.

"That's great, man," Freddy says, poking the ultra-thin device. "No more quotes, okay. Just watch football and try to be—how'd the doctor say it?"

"Placid."

"Yes, exactly," Freddy says. "Be placid over there."

Freddy knew his brother, Lancaster, had gone bat-shit a long time ago, maybe seven months back, when the ramblings started. But he wasn't convinced it was sanitarium-bad until he found the notebook. The tattered thing lay forgotten on a coffee table one day, and Freddy started reading. Scrawled in orange ink on the opening page, this:

"Sometimes you have to curl up in an empty bathtub, repeat the phrase 'Susan Really Likes Me' ad infinitum, and slather Neapolitan ice cream all over your face."

Freddy dropped the notebook that day like it was diseased. Like schizophrenia was contagious. Doing that made him feel weak. He wondered what lay deeper in the notebook but didn't touch it again.

Today, the brothers share a bag of sourdough pretzels and laugh at NFL pregame knuckleheads. Lancaster swipes his brother's new smart phone from the table and dabbles in its touch-screen sorcery. The gusts of bleak November rattle windowpanes behind them.

"The gas company can't be more than five days from cutting off your essentials," Freddy says. "Winter's coming."

"So?" Lancaster says, tossing the phone back to Freddy. It ricochets off a pillow and lands on the couch.

"So scrawling on those notebook pages won't pay the bills," Freddy says. "We have to do something. *You* have to do something."

"Just shut up…"

Freddy throws up his arms, exasperated. "That's typical," he says. "You push the world out the door and sit on your ass."

In the same manner he'd ditched undergrad art studies, Lancaster quit his job at the paint store last summer, having hocked enough Glidden to semi-gloss the Taj Mahal. Last month he donated his spiffy wardrobe to the Salvation Army. He's twenty-five and handsome as early Gregory Peck, only blonder. He liked to smoke weed in sweet vanilla blunts to quiet the chatter in his brain, but he recently switched to more economical bong hits.

Freddy, meanwhile, is a study in stability. Freshly minted in the warm dream of fatherhood, he works for an architecture group that specializes in massive structural implosions. He predicts defective interior collapses, and he's good. On Sundays, he peels himself from familial obligations to camp out at his brother's place, basically guarding him from sharp objects.

"They can't help me," Lancaster says, out of nowhere. "I won't go back. Sooner or later, those bastards won't let me leave."

Freddy's mind jolts back to the doctor's face, the rheumy eyes, the words "Indiana Mental Health Institute" inscribed on his coat. He flinches at the thought. "Don't worry about that now," he says. "Be placid."

"Go home to your family," Lancaster says.

"Not just yet," says Freddy. "The wife knows what I'm up to."

"Lancaster's awfully young to exhibit symptoms this severe," the doctor told Freddy and his mother, the three of them seated around the waiting-room aquarium. "You have to stay on top of this. I've seen it backfire on skeptical families."

"What do you mean?" Freddy said.

"He's capable of making the news," the doctor said. "His delusions will progress unless his medication is regimented. We see this from time to time. A woman in Carmel thought her mother was trying to poison her, so she doused her in gasoline, lit her on fire. Another guy in Greenwood, this military type, swore his neighbor was communicating with aliens on his cell phone, so he shot the poor guy in the face. Mowing the lawn, going about his chores, a bullet in the face—"

"Okay," Freddy said, "enough."

149

Freddy gives his brother a hang-loose gesture and cranks up the television. For several hours they watch the Colts pummel some hapless AFC opponent. Lancaster feverishly scrawls in the notebook, the one-dollar variety with geometric collisions on the cover.

"What're you doing over there?" Freddy finally inquires.

"Can't say."

Freddy cracks his knuckles. "Listen," he says, sounding too much like his father, the college professor whose new wife, the brothers agree, is doable. "We need to devise a monitoring system. I want to be sure you're taking all the meds, at the right times."

Lancaster drops his pen. "Can't you just come here, divvy them out for me, watch me swallow, and leave?"

"I have a family, man."

"So did I."

"Don't be an asshole about it," Freddy says. "I can't be chained here forever."

"Ask me again."

"Ask you what?"

"What I'm drawing."

Freddy tosses the clicker aside and yawns. "Okay, Rembrandt," he says. "What's going on over there?"

Lancaster smiles and holds the notebook at arm's length, exhibiting a dead-on rendering of Freddy's wife—naked.

Freddy can't breathe. It's all there, with mathematical exactitude: her drastic curves and crevasses, the thin pubic trail, even her tiny scorpion tattoo, hidden so well the skimpiest bikini couldn't divulge it. Freddy jumps up, balls his left hand to a fist, and stands over his brother. "Schizo or not, I don't give a shit," he says. "You don't spy on a man's wife."

Lancaster winces but doesn't respond.

"Speak up, bitch," Freddy says.

"I've known some things for a while," Lancaster says. "If I get taken away, there's some things you'll want to know."

Freddy rips the notebook from his brother's hands for closer examination. He tears the page out, folds it, and deposits it in his pleated pants. "Start talking."

Lancaster says his brother's wife, Minnie, used to be a stripper, before either of them knew her, in a town an hour away. He says she dallied at the lowest dive in the Midwest, Seventh Street Dancers, where the talent dons spider-web tattoos as hookers in France wear lace.

Still wincing, Lancaster shrugs. "Listen, there's striptease Barbie dolls, and there's downright pole serpents," he says. "Your wife was the latter."

Freddy cocks his fist, thrusts, and breaks his brother's nose. The cartilage gives way and cracks, twists, the bridge a lightning bolt between the eyes. Blood spills in two heavy streams, but Lancaster smiles.

"You're one sick son-of-a-bitch," Freddy says, backing away. "You think I'll give up another Sunday to be treated like this?"

Lancaster stands, his smile gone and teeth gritted in pain. He lifts a plate with the remnants of his breakfast off the coffee table. A butter-knife slides off the plate, but Lancaster catches it. Freddy charges his brother, kicking him in the stomach and knees, pummeling him to the baby blue carpet that's peppered with stains.

Freddy shifts his weight to his brother's forearm and tugs the knife away.

"Jesus," Lancaster says, clutching his bloody face. "Who's *really* the paranoid one?"

Freddy hustles to the kitchen, kicks open the backdoor, and launches the knife into the yard. "Tomorrow," he yells back into the house, walking away. "Be ready tomorrow, because we're taking you up there."

Freddy blasts the heat in his Volvo, his breath condensing on the frigid windows. He feels the first pangs of remorse but he's glad he acted quickly. He turns left down Broad Ripple Avenue and tiny raindrops dot the windshield. His automatic wipers kick in.

In Freddy's pocket, the smart phone vibrates, a text message from his wife:

"You like?"

Though he fears the statistics and hates doing it, Freddy takes his eyes off the road and plunks a much shorter, simpler message in response: "?????"

Raindrops slap the roof and windshield. Holiday shoppers huddle beneath overhangs. Freddy, at a red light, checks the phone again. Another message from Minnie:

"See your gallery (wink)."

Freddy opens the photos marked "checked" and finds one titled: "Your Big 30th!" He clicks it and there stands his wife, posing before their antique bedroom mirror, her own smart phone in hand. Naked, she smiles, her pelvic scorpion alive in the late-afternoon light.

Wrapped up with his brother, Freddy had forgotten his own birthday. He balls a fist, the knuckles still pink with impact, and lightly punches his jaw, sickened. The traffic light turns green but he's too numb to react. He examines the photo and fights the urge to either laugh or cry. "Bastard's got talent," he says, his foot easing on the gas. He grips the Volvo's steering wheel, readying himself for an illegal U-turn, for all the subsequent shame.

SPAGHETTI JUNCTION

A t high speeds the hills went by like dull waves against the night. Interstate 75 swelled to six lanes and I could sense a new proximity to her. I took a well-lit exit, looking to park the Nissan, stretch my legs, and gather myself. It led me up a hill, around a red-clay embankment. I coasted past the up-drawn arms of a security gate, to the edge of a parking lot that seemed vacant enough. At last I could see the city, beyond the hills and piney ridges, an electric tapestry of orange.

The phone in my pocket started vibrating. The longer I ignored the movement the more my car keys clinked and the Ginseng wrapper crunched. The gas station pills I had taken in Tennessee made each twist and gulley and mountain of the drive like a rushing epiphany. I'd gulped them in a scummy bathroom, tapping my nails on the greenish porcelain sink, wondering if I should keep going.

153

There was a jagged message cut into the wall with a phone number beneath. It made me think of her. I kept going.

I dug the phone out and unfolded it. It was my wife. I didn't answer. She left a long message, according to the next vibration.

I'd bought a six-pack outside Dalton to build courage, an ale but not too hoppy. I cracked the last one. The air was warm for March, a contrast to the northern winds that still whipped and bit. Back home in Illinois, my nostrils froze together on midnight walks around the subdivision, when I'd see the Lancasters fattening in the light of their plasma television, the Bushes in loud domestic fury.

I checked the phone message as I drove into town. The squawk of my wife's recorded voice bothered me, raiding my ear like her tongue when she's drunk. I swept down on the interstate and hugged the HOV lane, rider on a great serpent of asphalt. My wife's message dragged: "The thing at Nick and Shelly's went fine. Everyone was asking about you, so I told them you're still an adolescent, a basketball junkie. I only had one martini. Was expecting a call from you north of Chattanooga."

I clammed the phone shut and squeezed it in my fist.

A mile later I reopened the phone, feeling sort of breathless and guilty. An eye on the freeway, I dug through my console and found the folded paper, an ordinary unlined note. Its possibilities made me nervous. Another beer and I'd be flimsy; there was nothing to do but call. I read the digits from the paper and typed them in my cell, the area code a Southern combination I'd never seen. The phone crackled as it rang. Her voice was magnificent.

"Where are you?" And it was a purr.

"Here. Not far from your place. Driving."

"Lost?"

"No, Smyrna. Way west. I'm heading in now, with your directions. You never wrote about this place at night."

"It's pretty," she said.

"It glows."

"You're very close now."

She asked if I was tired from the drive. Her confident voice warmed me, eased the internal me. I told her I was nervous, not tired, because this was new. She wished it was Friday and not Saturday, she said, but she understood. She asked if I talked as colorfully as the emails had read. I told her she would be disappointed.

On Peachtree Road the city's high geometry shone white and green, curious giants spying through my open sunroof. Hooligans spilled from ultra-lounges to kick and twirl in the streets. I slipped my hat down across my eyebrows, a vintage Cubs hat, nothing threatening. The men barked to each other and danced, pointing at big cars booming up the pale street. Everything wore a midnight gloss. I wanted to join them, the hooligans, if only for the brutality in their movements.

　　She lived off Peachtree but not too far. Her directions had been precise for five hundred and forty miles, and now there was this, her place: a luxurious stack of villas flanked by blossoming white dogwoods. I sat for a moment in neutral and listened to the tick and purr of my engine. I watched the Lenox River Villas in the dark. The thin spray of a pool fountain spat behind an outbuilding. The trees were high and jagged against a full moon. Hers was a shadowy complex on the downslope of a rolling hill, hugged in by manicured ridges. The hill swelled over the place, like a green wave with some white. I called the number on the gate box and she buzzed me in. The black gates spread.

　　I parked where there was no light. Nothing moved. I closed my windows and the sunroof so as to sound-proof me within the vehicle. I called my wife.

　　"Where are you?" she asked. Her voice was hoarse, evidence of cigarettes and more than one martini.

　　"John's. I made it," I said. "Just got the message, sorry. Phone was in my bag, in the trunk."

　　"There you go, not thinking."

　　"Don't harp," I said.

　　"What time's the game?"

155

"Noon. The first one is. Then there could be more. It's a tournament. If they win too much I might call off sick Monday."

"Fine," she offered, yawning. "I missed you at the party. It's worse when people keep asking."

"They ask because of etiquette."

"They're our neighbors, Ben. Our friends."

"Can I call back tomorrow?"

"Tell John and your friends hello from your wife."

"Sleep well," and I clipped it at that.

She lived on the top floor, the sixth. I took the stairs up. Slow ceiling fans lined the hallway and tossed the night air with big leafy blades. The temperature was dropping. The railings that fenced off the tallest pines were ornate like New Orleans porches. I was walking slowly, chewing old peppermints to sweeten my breath. She was standing outside her door in pajamas. She asked me to please come in. Her drawl was lovely in three words.

I stepped in the place with my hard soles clicking on white ceramic tile, easing the door shut behind me. Something was final about the click of that door. She went for a long-stemmed wineglass with red in it and spun nervously back toward me. She looked delicate in her flesh, girlish and susceptible, tall and lithe, her blond hair falling in curls across the pink cotton of her nightshirt, her eyes like deep water. I could hear her breathing. She was nearly within reach. I felt forty years younger, as though my mother's blessing was required to approach her, this sheepish stranger. She looked me over and smirked. This was not the electronic visage of her, but her. She moved first, cutting the void to disarm me in a hug, which was firm. Her spicy perfume clung to me. She welcomed me to Atlanta and called me Benjamin; I retorted with Katherine, the same awkward formalities we'd passed slyly across the wires.

"Kathy, please," she said, letting down her shoulders. Her lips were maroon with wine pigment. "My full name sounds stiff."

"I could listen to you all night."

156

She backed away to study me, then leaned forward. "Your face is sadder in person." She ran her nails across the stubble of my chin. She was cattish. "Did you bring anything?"

"A duffel bag, in the car."

Kathy's face tightened. "I'm worried that things aren't cut clean with you," she said. "Illinois things."

She had freckles and big wet eyes, a fresh face for thirty-three. For five months I had gotten to know her in bursts of secret emails, and now her physicality was nearly too much. I feared what effect her skin might have. Strangely, bewilderingly, I thought of my wife, passed out on our burgundy leather sofa with tangled hair and one exposed breast, a party balloon sadly deflated. I wondered if by standing there with Kathy I was technically breaking the law.

"I'm glad John knew about you," I said. "He knows my wife and how she is. He hates to see me down. I've been down."

"You've known John awhile, then?"

"We got in trouble together in college," I said, and held up a fist. "These scars, on the knuckles. I got them trying to get us out of trouble."

She smiled. "You don't look like a fighter."

"I am," I said. "Or, at least, I was. A boxer."

"You?" she perked. "Professional?"

"Illinois regional circuit," I said. "Technically, it's pro. Gold gloves champ in high school."

"Sounds kind of mean," she said. "Kind of stupid."

I smiled, feigning a gut punch. "Low blow."

Kathy let out a quick, incredulous chortle, which in seconds broke into an outright laugh. It made me want to close her mouth. She leaned closer and insisted I never say my wife's name to her. I was taller than Kathy but barely. Her vast apartment opened around her and I noticed the squared lines of Scandinavian furniture. A sloppy acrylic dangled from a single nail, an abstract piece like a bowl of noodles.

"You should put your emails into something," she said. "A book? You're funnier than you think."

157

I cupped the wineglass from her hand, opened my mouth, and threw back its tart contents. We came against each other and rolled over a couch, onto an area rug patterned in oblong shapes, across cold tile, shedding clothes. I carried Kathy to her room, to her bed with its gaudy medieval canopy. We tangled.

She leaned across me afterwards and asked if I could sleep. I was tired and said so. She told me not to think too deeply about it, that the first time breaks the ice and then the sailing is smooth. She traced the silhouette of me with the tips of her nails.

"I'll take you for a ride tomorrow," she said. "I have a place you'll like."

"Don't you have plans?" I asked. "Clients?"

"You'll be on the meter," she giggled. "But at a discounted rate."

I wrote the first check for how much she told me and slipped it beneath a porcelain ballerina. We slept in shiftless knots at no extra charge.

I awoke to the sound of her peeing. She blushed when I saw her down the hallway, her bent legs. I wondered if she kept tally of her blushes. It pained me to think other men had provoked the same reaction, and probably quite recently. The aroma of coffee hung in the bedroom, while somewhere a water-starved coffee machine gargled. She finished and walked down the hallway to pull me onto my bare feet. The hardwood was cold and light as bamboo. Sharp morning sunlight broke across Kathy, and I swore to myself I would be her best customer. She taunted me with a girlish nudge and I chased her, feet slapping, around the living room, the den, and into the kitchen, where she'd arranged a fruit plate with pears, grapes, and cantaloupe. She poured a coffee while I popped a beer.

"We're going to Stone Mountain," she said. "It's the best way to get oriented with this town."

"Alright, whatever," I said. "I'll have to keep track of the basketball tournament, for good measure. The team plays at noon."

"I can keep score," she said, her confidence robust. "You're winning so far."

She put her finger in my chest and I felt invited. We tangled against her stylish granite countertops and she mentioned nothing afterwards of payment. Like usual I had been sensitive in the morning and prone to quick embarrassment. I prolonged myself with concentrated thoughts of my wife.

We packed two sacks with lunches and went out into the sun. She drove a red Jaguar convertible from the early eighties that suited her, the top down. I jumped in. She eased the car in gear and we held hands over the emergency brake. I didn't care who saw me, or what opinions Kathy's neighbors may have held against her. She dug pink fingernails into the wheel and drove very fast.

She took me the wrong way on purpose to illustrate the interstate clockwork of the city's Perimeter—the nine o' clock, noon, and three o' clock of it all. She pointed to freeways that vanished toward the half-built skeletons of skyscrapers. We passed a solemn white factory and I sympathized for the workers in there making it go, missing all this. I forgot the names of places immediately. I couldn't keep up with it all, with her. Then we swooped into a huge tangled mass of exit ramps, fly-overs, and deceleration lanes that vehicles entered and somehow spat out of. It must have been ten stories high. So much converged there on so many perilous loops, so many people in full routine yet wildly so, this massive yarn-ball of concrete and rebar where everything was synchronized despite the chaos.

"They call this Spaghetti Junction," Kathy said, over the wind. "Isn't the name just right?"

"It looks like a mess," I said, craning my neck to see more of the junction, now behind us. "I like that about it."

We broke east and parked at the foot of an incredible rock. Kathy called it the mountain and gave me facts about its height and age. It looked like the earth was birthing a massive, dirty egg. Giant caricatures of Stonewall Jackson and other Southern mythics stood dynamited in its steep slope. Kathy grabbed the lunch sacks from the

159

backseat while I walked toward a tourist village at the rock's base, entranced by the detailed enormity of the confederates. She caught up and cuffed my arm with her hand and wrist. We boarded a lift that cabled us to the summit. From three hundred feet and rising Stonewall looked awfully pissed off.

We dusted a ledge and sat near the highest point. We ate the sandwiches and braced against a cool wind. A rippled green canopy blanketed the suburbs; the city leapt in distant spires. Kathy pointed to what she swore was Tennessee.

"It's going to be April in a week," she said, tucking what she didn't eat into the paper sack, folding it.

"I know," I said. "In a month I'll be cutting grass."

"Do you have a big yard?"

"Not as big as the other yards. But bigger than I need."

"Tell me about the real estate world."

"I'd rather not," I said, looking away. "I'm not here to think about that."

"They say this place is a goldmine," she said, motioning west with her head. "For selling real estate, I mean."

"Is that something you've considered?"

"I leave my options open," she said. "I'm a freethinking girl. This gig can't last forever."

I ate the last of my roast beef and sipped from a box of apple juice. "I think you'd be good at selling, persuasive as you are," I smiled. "But they say there's a crash coming in the industry, that we're riding a bubble that's bound to break. It's lucrative now, but we're putting people under roofs they can't afford."

"*They* talked about the same sort of shit five years ago, with Y2K," she said. "Goes in cycles."

"I could help you through the classes."

She huffed, dropping her lips. "I don't know," she said. "Look how happy it's made you."

"Ouch," I said, puzzled again by her vitriol. There was wickedness in her that, however inadvertent, was penetrative and raw. "Maybe I'm not as bad off as the emails made me sound. I mean, my parents worked nights down at the meat plant. What do we really have to bitch about?"

"I think you should just leave her," Kathy said. "To hell with the mortgage, the office."

"Not that easy."

"Easier than you think," she said.

"The wife thinks we're getting pregnant, this summer."

"Oops."

"Yeah," I said. "Taking that away would crush her."

Kathy unzipped her windbreaker, spilling out. "Must be wonderful," she said, "life with a homemaker you don't love."

I worked the grit of her comment around in my head and gazed across the mountain. Families speaking some Czech gibberish took pictures of themselves with big-money cameras. A predatory bird kited by. "She's not lame, not in the way you're implying," I said. "She's just submissive. Kind of there, wherever I put her."

"She's dragging you down."

I dropped my fists on my knees. "*Okay*, I'm in a rut," I said. "It's pretty soulless, but it's easy. It's just that it feels like a stasis or something."

"I'm telling you," she said, "break out of it."

"That's just it, a stasis. Everything feels like it was decided ten years ago. I'm the world's least spontaneous man."

"I don't get it," she said. "You're a good guy."

I cocked my head. "You *really* want to hear the truth?"

She said yes.

"It built up for years," I said. "Small stuff, me working too much and her wanting a bigger house, shit like that. It came to a head three years ago, late in the summer, maybe August. I don't know how to say this without alarming you, but there was a domestic thing, a 911 call."

Kathy wrapped her knees in her arms. She leaned away. "Charges?" she said.

"No," I said. "Nothing like that. A broken screen door, that's about it."

"I didn't see that in you."

"Don't exaggerate it," I said. "It woke us up. For a time it kind of healed us. Her parents still won't speak to me, though."

"Why are you here, Ben?"

"Because I'm not there."

"It's not too late for a change."

"It's getting close."

"You talk like you're an old man."

"I talk like I feel," I said. "I've tried for years to leave. I can't find the right way to wreck everything."

Kathy reached over and touched my hand.

"Can we make this work?" I said, cuffing her tiny wrist. "We all have our histories. You can leave this, and I swear to God I'll never bring it up."

Her face suggested a mix of doubt and doting sadness. "I have appointments this week and next that I can't break," she said. "A couple of athletes who get what they want."

I tossed her wrist back into her lap. "It ends with me, or I'm out."

"Baby," she said. "I'll see what I can do."

As we left the park I found the games on the radio and jotted down the scores. My team had lost by twenty-five points. The day took on that sad, moribund slant of a Sunday afternoon, the moment when a weekend's nonchalance crystallizes and surely in no time will break. I asked Kathy if she could keep driving awhile. She joked about gas money but the humor didn't register. I concentrated on the hills. She slipped her fingers from my elbow to my hand in a tickling dance, lifted my hand onto her right leg. Her hair, swept by the wind, painted perfect circles.

That night, over a martini in her kitchen, I decided to stay. Maybe for good. Ten minutes later I thought it best to go home. My routine in Effingham was comfortable, but here there was electricity and risk. I felt whisked up by the experience of Kathy but also jammed into a corner, forced to choose. I would have to feel out the morning for the right indication.

Kathy was tossing olives in the air and catching them with her mouth. She had so much girl left in her.

"I bet you were a cheerleader at some point," I said, "and a good one."

She stopped and sized me up. "Funny, I had you pegged for a cowboy," she said. "A lousy one."

That knocked me back for a moment. Another jab.

"Actually, I'm a renegade now," I said. "I'm an outlaw who's moonlighting as a corporate stiff."

"That's silly," she said. "Your imagination is priceless, I'm telling you."

She laughed and said I didn't know what living really was. Her eyes sharpened when she said it, as if to punctuate the sting. It wasn't something she would have written across the wires, not the same Kathy who'd sent me pages of girlish poetry. The comment made me feel much older than her. I fished the olive from my drink and sucked out the pit.

My cell phone buzzed on her countertop, where I'd been letting it charge. "Do *not* answer that," I said. "It's my wife, hounding me."

Kathy grabbed the phone anyway, pulled it open, and with a grin said: "He's fucking me now, bitch."

She closed the phone and tossed it in a fruit basket, then picked up the olive jar to make another drink, like nothing consequential had happened. She reached for the vermouth and quietly giggled. I set my martini on her counter and slapped her across the cheek. She dropped the olive jar and it shattered on the kitchen tile, little green spheres rolling like marbles. She clenched her reddening face.

"I can have you *killed*," she said in a feverish pitch, nearly crying. I worried about the neighbors. "One phone call."

"Do it," I said, reaching for the last of my drink. "I welcome it. Surely this is nothing new for you."

"You're nothing new, Ben. You're no better than the rest of them. They come whimpering through that door every week. Another one will come in tomorrow night."

"Don't say these things."

"It's true," she said. "This is one big transaction."

"No," I said, somewhat pitifully. "It's more."

"You pay well." She dropped her hands. "Now go."

"What'll you be in ten years? In five?"

"Goddamn it, Ben."

"Let's act like that didn't just happen," I said. "It was a stupid impulse. I'm ashamed already."

"Forget it."

With that she pulled her cell phone from her pocket and made the threat of placing a call. I imagined a team of henchmen with wrenches waiting on standby. I squared my shoulders to face her and she crept back against her stainless steel appliances. The dull sheen of the refrigerator framed the poor girl marvelously. She navigated her phone and pushed several buttons. I heard a deep voice crack hello over the line. It was a henchman. My turn was over.

"Send a full day's fee for today, or I'll call your wife," she said, her thumb over the voice slots of the phone. "I can find her. I'll tell her everything."

"You're really doing this?"

"*Leave.*"

She breathed rapidly and glistened with sweat. I wished her luck with everyone who would pass through. She said nothing else, just stared at the door. Her appeal to me was dying. My boots clicked across the tiles, around the widening puddle of olive juice. I eased the door shut behind me, as I'd done a day prior, and I walked down the hallway, into the night.

Someone had shut down the pool. The fountain was off and the water lapped in tiny waves. I had a long drive ahead of me, dangerous now in a more ordinary way. I wanted to rewind everything, to be back atop the hill in Smyrna, or much further back. I pulled the seatbelt across my chest, started the car, and called my wife.

She answered: "You better damn well explain yourself."

"A friend of John's, screwing around," I said, hardly struggling to sound convincing. "Some drunk chick he's been dating awhile."

"What's going on?" She exaggerated the sniffling sounds of a crying fit that I could tell had just subsided.

I merged into traffic, disoriented and hopelessly far from the freeway. "I have to tell you," I said. "I'm not fit to be a father. I'll never be someone to look up to. I'm a malcontent, and that's all."

She was quiet a few seconds. "Sounds like the loss hit you pretty hard."

"The loss was very big."

"There's always next season."

"I mean it," I said.

"Are you good to drive?" she said. "I can tell you've been drinking, sweetheart."

"*Please* don't call me that."

"Damn it, I'm worried," she said. "It's a late start."

"You can say that again," I said. "You can say that again."

A light rain beaded on the windshield. I pushed hard on the gas, cutting people off, burning toward the inevitable, to everything that would always be, to nowhere at all.

CLARITY

The highway cuts by the Dream Motel in a single eventless curve, jogs this way, snakes that way, and then the highway is gone, sucked down by an unending flatness. Distant silo clusters rise from soybean fields like bad teeth, flanked by leaning barns and farmhouses too gone with distance to really see. Little surrounds the Dream Motel but wind and a haunting openness. The low structure itself is a jagged box, a disruption but no oasis.

During harvest, motel patrons watch combines bite the brittle cornfields. The husk leaves sway and there is the illusion in high winds of a golden sea. But here, standing in the gravel parking lot, pondering what must certainly be the end of an old winter, Charles Newburg can sense that the combines are missing, the corn torn from the fields and stored, and for miles instead there is this hard cold void.

Charles grunts. The sun, he sees, is rising to a noontime perch.

167

I've never seen so much nothing, thinks Charles, no traffic, no toll roads, no L trains screeching, no larceny, no hustle, nothing.

I like this, he thinks.

Charles buttons his seersucker blazer against the cold, walks across the little parking lot and toes up to Highway 41. He pulls tight his soft black leather gloves and enjoys the cashmere within. He squints to make out the color of a farmhouse but his vision won't reach, not without his prescriptions. It doesn't bother him, this weakness, his eyesight. Charles accepts the simple fault of nearsightedness. The elements of his aging can amuse him, enough so now that he breaks a smile across the yellowed teeth he consistently hides. He breathes in the cold air. He wishes he'd been here forty years earlier, after the Army and Korea but before the city got its ropes around him. Charles knows he could have done a number on the farm girls.

I like nothing, Charles determines, because it is pure.

A truck breaks the horizon on Highway 41 and Charles turns away, back toward the motel and his long Lincoln. His car is one of three vehicles in the lot, comprising what appears a sparse motel crowd for Saturday morning. Charles watches his wife, Jean, exit Room 135 in a sundress. Jean doesn't bother to push back the door so it would retract shut on its own. She stands at the passenger door, shivering, as Charles approaches in his calculated steps, around puddles that were snow. He is in no hurry to leave. She is.

"Hold on," says Charles. "I have a right to be pokey on vacation."

In the wisps of her hair, or the gaunt trappings of her cheeks, Charles notices something about his wife—that she is flawed by her impatience, stricken by her hurry. She is beginning to look elderly, thinks Charles, and especially in the sun.

"I feel filthy," says Jean, exhibiting her hands. "Haven't you packed everything? Have you returned the key? This is a late start, Charles."

"We'll be at the casino in an hour," he says. "No harm done."

"I don't see the need to stop there."

168

"I see the need," says Charles. "I feel lucky, babe."

Jean scoffs, as she does. "Your fascination with child-play is obscene," she says. "You're an academic, not a high-roller."

Charles pulls his roadster cap lower. Under the cap, at the helm of his big car, he guesses women as young as forty might find him appealing. The truck he'd seen earlier roars onto the lot, chewing gravel as it goes. "I don't suppose you'd settle for breakfast here," Charles says. "There's a little kitchen around back. This looks to be our last option for a long while."

"Fine," says Jean, pouting, "order me something without grease. I'm going to use our restroom again. Make it to go if you can."

Jean darts in the room and is gone. Charles listens to hear the door lock but his wife neglects to do that. He has the room key with its green plastic danglings in his hand but this, he assures himself, is the middle of nowhere. She's fine, he thinks.

Charles walks through a shoddy corridor to the kitchen, stuffing the room key in his trouser pocket. He whistles something jazz, a loop from Bitches Brew, rhythms that served him well while grading biology exams. He whistles when he's hungry.

In the kitchen Charles finds that the desk watchman doubles as the Dream Motel cook. The cook, sitting, calls Charles friend, motions with his head to an illuminated menu board.

"Shitty out there, eh?" says this cook. "That wind'll take your face with it."

"Yes," Charles answers, observing the menu. "Are we south enough yet to order grits? Or okra?"

"Not yet," says the cook, a wobbling brute, "but we get asked all the time. Everybody's always headed south. Up here we just serve eggs, bacon, and coyote."

"In that case," smiles Charles, "I'll have two coyote burgers to go."

The cook stands up from a stool. "Ham and eggs, two orders, right on," and he disappears behind saloon doors.

Charles sits at the lone table and, in his boredom, pits a

169

saltshaker in a race against the pepper, budging the glass containers with his knuckles. Out the window a man in blue is pushing a truck behind a tool shed. No, sees Charles, that's two men, and big men. The wind is warring with a naked walnut tree. Beyond the shed and tree, the winter-stricken land cracks and jags; Charles likens it to the rippled slice of Lake Michigan he can see from his Gold Coast condo. He wonders for a moment if he could find the patience to farm—a city sophisticate turned man of the earth. He could mount a tractor at daybreak and really come alive.

Charles refocuses on the winning pepper. He worries for some reason that laziness will overtake him soon. He's seen it happen—that despicable, listless lull—to retirees before him. He knows there must be a more dignified finale.

"Did you all sleep through the storm last night?" asks the cook, who sounds like he's hovering over a grill. "Knocked out power up the western side of the state. Clear from Carlisle to Cartersville. It's odd, a storm like that in March."

"We drove half the day," Charles says. "We couldn't go any farther than here. I hit the pillow and was incoherent. So, no, it didn't budge us."

The cook pauses, coughs. "A buddy of mine works up at the prison," he says. "Apparently the winds kicked out their emergency generators. Things was in chaos—no lights, no power."

"Sounds like a mess."

"My buddy said the guards had to shoot all these convicts and pick them out of the barbwire this morning."

"Oh," perks Charles. "What a way to go."

The cook returns with a heavy stack of Styrofoam and sets it on a counter. He tells Charles breakfast is on the house. "No," posits Charles, "I insist," and he drops a twenty on the keys of an antiquated register. "Give us a discount next time we stop in."

The cook laughs.

"People only have this dream one time," the cook says, and he licks the skin of a leafy cigar. "You all have a good trip now."

Charles nods and begins to walk out. He turns back to the

kitchen as he leaves, holding the door ajar with his free hand. "We'll send up a postcard from Florida," he tells the cook. "We'll make St. Petersburg eventually," and the door closes.

"We're going the customary route," Charles says to the door, the wall, "because it's warm down there. And we've read it's a great place to die."

From the doorway of Room 135 Charles can see his vacation is over. He drops his breakfast and the eggs spit across the carpet and threshold. His wife is in bed with two young men.

The three of them together are only a series of heads at the end of a brown comforter and blanket. Jean is in the middle, disheveled. Her mascara streaks down her temples and puddles in black-gray blotches at her ears. In forty-nine years Charles has never seen her so helpless.

"Step in," says the left head. He looks like the younger of the two, certainly of the three. His scalp, peeled. The right head is fully Latino. His eyes are severe.

"Shut it," says the right. "Get in."

Charles obliges. He holds his hands above his head though he is not asked to. He feels sweaty and numb. He doesn't see scattered clothing and he is looking everywhere—the lamp, the vanity, the armoire, the hallway sink—for that.

"What do you want from us?" asks Charles. "What do you want from her?"

The right head laughs. Charles sees the vibrations of the laughing in his wife's cheeks, or at least he thinks he sees that. There is commotion at her midsection, instigated, thinks Charles, by the extremities of the right head. Jean closes her eyes, swallows hard. She tightens her face and hardly breathes.

"Fellas," Charles injects, "do what you want with her but keep your hands off my fucking Lincoln." He has the attention of both heads now. "I'll be right back." Charles exits the room and barely hears the objecting men behind him as he squints into the sunlight. He thinks he hears some talk about a knife.

The Lincoln is the last car in the lot. It's an obese vehicle, a Lake Shore Drive cruiser, and disproportionate, Charles realizes, in the tiny parking lot. The passenger side is spacious as a walk-in closet but was never suitable in Jean's eyes. Charles looks away from the car. It pains him to see it, to think of its purpose as a vessel for romantic travel. He notices the empty fields again but the allure in them is gone. He focuses on the ground, circumnavigating the vehicle by instinct. The motel sign near the highway casts a short crooked shadow.

Charles pulls his keys from his pocket and flips open the trunk. In it he shuffles beach chairs and his easel and the beauty case until he comes across a brown paper bag. He lifts to check its weight; it is the bag. He reaches in and snares a full handle of Kentucky bourbon. Equipped, he walks around his car, up two steps, into the room, and kicks shut the door behind him.

"You really don't want any of that," Charles says to the men, pointing to the lower half of his wife. "Trust me."

Charles sits in a padded chair beside the bed and positions the whiskey atop a worn Bible. He stands without looking at the bed and walks to the hallway sink, where he takes two plastic cups from a stack of five. He returns to the chair, pours a cup half full of liquor and kicks one pennyloafer over the other, exhales as if relaxing. He sips the cup and grimaces against the whiskey's bite. The others watch him but do not move.

"Now, please, boys," says Charles. "Enlighten me as to what I was interrupting here."

No one speaks. The silence frightens Charles. He tips back the cup, takes a deeper pull. "My wife and I have worked our whole lives to do what we started doing yesterday. I'm a professor of science and I'm taking what I call an eternal sabbatical. Which is to say, boys, I ain't going back. She's not either. We were off to Florida to enjoy each other, and to maybe find some real estate to buy. That is until you boys got in the middle of things."

The right head, the sinister face, runs his index finger behind Jean's ear, tucking her hair in a tight twirl around her lobe. Charles sees the man's blue sleeve and is comforted.

"Please," says Charles, struggling with the last of his drink, "there's no need to touch her."

The left head tells Charles to not move. "I have a knife against her," he says. "We don't want to hurt her. We need to leave the state. We need to leave right now."

Jean shoots her husband a warning glance that piques his concern. He asks if she's okay. Through her whimpering she conveys that she is. "Why don't we have a drink first, boys," Charles offers, as he pours the second cup full and refills his. "This is the white label stuff. It's tasty and malted and unpredictably smooth."

"We weren't going to rape her," says the left head. "I know how this looks."

"It doesn't matter," Charles says.

"We were warning her on the bed when you came in. I wanted you to think I had a gun."

"That doesn't matter," says Charles. "Don't even say those things. You should have a drink. It's probably been a while."

The left one peels off the comforter and sits upright, introduces himself as Manny but does not offer his hand. The knife he grips is long and clean. He's barrel-chested with a thick neck, a pair of intelligent brown eyes, his inked arms simultaneously elegant and crude. The blue denim he wears is burned with the markings of Carlisle Penitentiary. As he leans forward, Charles can see that Jean is still wearing her sundress, which relieves him. "Sit up, baby," he tells her. "Have a bourbon."

Manny reaches for the second cup, his knife aimed at Charles' midsection.

"There's really no need," says Charles. "I won't attack because I can't. Maybe forty years ago but not now. I've been a hostage before and I'm pretty good at it."

Jean scurries across the bed, her dress trailing behind. She tucks herself between Charles and the wall. "I'm calling the police,"

173

she says. "I'm calling the hotel people."

The right one swells up and lunges toward the couple. Manny intercepts him, calls him Raul.

"Ah, no, babe," says Charles. "There's no need to call anybody. A little talk is in order, and then we'll all be on our way." He offers his wife a drink, which she declines, crying louder.

"Lady," snarls this Raul, "stop that shit."

"Sit down," Manny says to his cohort, his finger buried in Raul's chest. "Stay down."

Manny turns to the couple and peeks through a crevasse in the flowered motel curtains. "We need to make Tennessee immediately. To Manchester, other side of Nashville. We can't hang around here. I like you but I'll cut you. Your car is the last one."

"Your truck?" says Charles. "I saw you in a truck. What happened?"

The men look at each other. Raul rubs his face and bites the long white nail of his index finger. "I like Lincolns," he says. "That's all you need to know."

Manny edges the curtains open with the knife. He looks at the sky, the highway, beyond, then back. "There's a guy out there," he says. "Big guy, white shirt."

"It's probably that cook," says Charles. "He runs this place. He knows about the prison. You'll want to avoid him."

Manny sets his cup on a dresser and Charles stands to retrieve it. He tosses back the liquor Manny didn't finish, emptying the cup before he sits back down to his own. "Really, babe," he says to Jean. "You should try this stuff. A retirement gift from Steve Brennan in admissions. He has impeccable taste in drink."

Charles winks at his wife. She is adorable to him behind the chair. She once acted like this in cars at the Starlight Drive-In. She would put Charles between herself and the horror pictures and shriek in exaggerated fits, pretending to cry. Then she'd touch her husband's cheek—married, as they were, without permission at eighteen—and call him heroic.

"The prison," says Manny, "it's probably made the Tennessee papers. Everyone who got out will be headed this way. There's nowhere else to hide in this county."

Charles kicks his feet onto the bed, a Floridian pose. "It must have been a riot last night," he says. "In every sense of the word. I can't imagine the feeling. How long had you guys been in?"

Raul stares into a wall mirror and twists the graying crest of his mustache, just beneath his nose. "You ask a lot of questions," he says to the reflected Charles. The old man nods, shrugs. "It was an old jail," says Raul. "It wasn't ready for that kind of a storm. There's nothing around here to stop the wind."

"Shit," says Manny. "He's coming."

Manny pulls shut the curtains and holds them tightly together, so tight the material shakes against a wire-thin slit of incoming sunlight. The cook shadows the window as he passes, a heap of forearms and torso. There are three slow knocks at the motel door. Charles whispers to not react and keep still.

"Yes?" says Charles toward the door. "This is the Newburg's."

"Looks like you made a mess here of the eggs," says the cook. "Was everything alright?"

"Oh," says Charles, "that."

The cook coughs. "Are you going to stay another night? It's getting into the afternoon and I have to ask."

"My wife is under the weather," says Charles. "We'll stay again, sure."

"I'll need you up at the office then. When you can."

"Sure thing," says Charles, emptying another cup. "You bet."

"You sure you're okay?"

Raul stares into the old man's face. "I'll be down in a moment," Charles says. "See you in a minute."

The cook lumbers past the curtains toward the office. Raul walks to the bedtable, pours a cup and taps Charles on his forehead, beneath the brim of his roadster cap. "Since when do they malt Kentucky bourbon?" Raul asks. He peeks over the chair, over

175

Charles, to Jean, who is tucked there, shivering. "You want to know what I did?" Raul asks the couple. "Why I was incarcerated?"

"Tax fraud?" Charles laughs.

Raul doesn't laugh. "No," he says. "Not that."

"I knew a colleague who was nabbed for taxes, a sharp guy," says Charles. "But what a boring crime—such a dud criminal. He'd have to admit to that on the inside, I'm sure. He went in without a scar. Came out a year later, ashamed but meaner."

"I won't go back there," says Raul. "It's like dying in slow motion."

Charles stands up. He raises his hand, palm up, and inflates his chest, as if instructing pupils who are not there. He feels jolted and foolish, a bizarre sensation that preceded his earliest fighting in the trenches near Pyongyang. Deeper in this emotion Charles can sense dignity, rebellion. His open hand is shaking and he can't steady it. Neither fugitive pays much attention.

"I want to go with you," Charles says, equally to both men. "Farther than Tennessee—I'll get you to Mexico. We'll just keep going. We'll all go. I know a way through, via Dallas, a patrol-proof way," and behind Charles his wife sobs. He refills both cups, hands the second one back to Raul and leans over the chair. "Ah, doll," says Charles. "No need to weep. We've waited the last ten years for these boys."

Manny gasps near the window. "They're coming," he says. "Three cars—I see them," and he backs from the window into Raul. Whiskey leaps from their cups onto the carpet.

Raul runs to the window and rips open the curtains. Sunlight splashes in, blinds him. "I don't see," he says. "There's nothing. You're seeing a mirage. A winter mirage."

Raul squints. He makes out the far glimmer of two patrol cars and a sheriff's sport utility. Then he does not see.

"Out—out," says Raul, bending to grip Jean by the nape of her neck. She pulls a bed lamp to her and swings it at the man's open hand, batting his wrist and elbow. The hollow lamp thuds on bone. Charles, standing three feet away, is incensed by the sudden attack on his wife, by how diminutive she seems in the shadow of a charging man. Charles tosses his cup into the scuffle, dotting Raul's face with drops of brown.

"Come on," says Charles. "Let's go without her. I see lights."

Manny pulls Charles by his baggy blazer sleeve against a dresser. A cheap reprint of a barn at sunset nearly shakes off its nail. Manny puts the blade against Charles' clavicle but lowers it as he winces, opting for a slot between the folds of his starched collar. "Enough with the hostage bullshit," Charles says. "Open the door and we are *gone.*"

Raul, who had started to barricade the door with a padded chair, looks instead to Manny, and both men breathe audibly. Manny nods. He backs away from Charles as Raul pulls open the motel door.

A cold wind permeates the room. It startles Charles. He watches the wind lift and play with his wife's hair, which sticks to her wet face. He sees the damage this day has left upon her, and he feels gutted by that. He remembers her on their first date, the summer of a year he's mostly forgotten, a dusty county fair near Joliet. They shared a sack of popcorn, and she sang beside a broken Wurlitzer. She sang without music and she was good. They smoked cigarettes by a river; in the reflected moonlight she was incandescent and mysterious. She cried that night beside the river, said her parents would never allow her a military husband. Charles said she shouldn't fuss, that nothing so real could fall apart, that he'd never felt more confident about a girl, or anything else.

"I want to walk the beach with you," Charles says to his wife. "At night. Until the beach patrol kicks us off."

Raul kicks the old man in his chest. The force sends Charles onto the bed, shoulders first. Everyone pauses. Charles manages a fractured breath, two breaths, and heaves himself onto his feet. He is exasperated and nauseous. Standing, he realizes he's taller than his captors by a full head, but attacking them would only hasten the inevitable. He cracks his knuckles.

"File in behind me," says Charles. "Run quick to the passenger side."

Charles goes for his Lincoln in a lanky rhythmless gallop. The men fall in behind him but they suddenly halt. The cook, in the archway of a motel porch, has a rifle, and he discharges it in a single cracking boom. Charles falls across the sidewalk, into the gravel, a red mist and flailing limbs. He settles beside his car and comes to his knees. He pulls at his chest, gasping.

The cook curses loudly and ducks into a room. Manny and Raul nod to each other, then dart from Room 135 to the Lincoln. They pull Charles into their arms, patting him.

Tangled in the searching arms of both men, peaceful and dizzy and curious, Charles can see a passing coyote beyond the highway. He admires the clean animal coat, the roving eyes and fleeting paws. Charles can see it all. The coyote is determined and hungry, crossing so much emptiness in a clipped, careful gallop. It heads instinctually toward a farmhouse and the easy takings of domesticated men and women. The snout, thinks Charles, is the most beautiful part.

The sirens converge on the Dream Motel but only in murmurs. Before the coldness overtakes him, Charles digs into his pocket, distinguishes the right shape, and hands Manny his upturned ignition key. The old man hunkers to the ground, rolls onto his back, and laughs like a jester toward a fit of passing clouds.

DOWN AND OUT AT THE
BREASTFEEDING SCHOOL

———————

Through the smoke, Johnson Mathers could see Dickey at the forlorn end of the barroom, stationed where he always used to be. Back when Johnson was cool. Back when the world had opened before Johnson like a gaping candy store, resplendent with weekend benders, poolside chicks, and the occasional one-night stand. Back before Johnson married a cop and his penchant for the occasional doobie was forced into extinction. In Dickey's hipster sneer and peacock neck tattoo Johnson saw just what he'd been looking for: a scalawag who might double as a sounding board. Johnson toed up to the bar, the longest vessel of its kind in southeast Atlanta. When Dickey saw him, he whooped: "Well I'll be a cat's ass in a dog's mouth!"

Johnson cuffed his old-fashioned, wove through a huddle of dudes, and saddled up next to Dickey. They bumped knuckles. "Was afraid all the old regulars had moved on," Johnson said. "I hate coming to bars alone, even this one."

"Short leash still?"

"Very."

"How is she these days, your cop wife?" Dickey said.

Johnson peered into his tumbler. His temples ached after another week of auditing failing car dealerships. He used to catch tax cheats for a living, but with the recession his scrutiny turned to corporations, whose executives wanted excuses to axe half the staff. Johnson bowed to assholes all day and feigned self-respect.

"She's pregnant," he said. "Eight months."

"Brother, congratulations." Dickey set down his PBR and clapped.

"No," Johnson said. "Stop."

"But this is the Irish mazel tov—drunken clapping," Dickey said. "Why stop?"

"Because it's all over now," Johnson said. "I mean this is the absolute end of being young. She's allowing me this one last half-night out; I have a curfew. We're going to some place called 'Breastfeeding School' in the morning. We have to log three hours. And then shopping. All day. Saturday—poof, gone."

"Shopping?"

"For onesies. And specialized pacifiers. And this fucking space-age bottle that minimizes air intake, and thus the need for burping."

Dickey slapped a wiry hand on Johnson's arm and hollered: "Shots!"

Though thirty years old, Johnson had essentially been grounded for several months. And his wife, Gilder, was capable of stomping to Risky's Tavern and retrieving her wayward man like an inebriated burglary suspect. She'd dragged him home once before, last winter, at the twenty-week mark, the night before they learned the baby's gender. In the February chill she exaggerated her authority, issued empty threats about her Taser. Johnson kept thinking how pretty she was in cop-mode. And how, deep down, she was still the criminology major he'd met in college.

"Don't run away from this," Gilder had said that night, her hand in clockwise orbit around her abdomen. "We're going it together, from here until forever."

"You got it," Johnson told his wife. "You. Me. It. Forever."

Midnight descended. To Johnson, the barroom swayed like a kelp forest of buffoonery. In the crowd was an assortment of ascot types, undergrad slackers, older couples spilled from a nearby symphony, hip-hop kids with unlit cigarillos, and gold-digging saboteurs. He stared at his watch.

"It's the end of Johnson's last night, isn't it?" Dickey said, sucking a Parliament.

"I have to be coherent," Johnson said. "I have to learn something at the school."

"What's the point?" said Dickey. "Not your tits."

"The man, they say, plays a vital role."

"Men are predators, not nurturers."

"Not modern man," Johnson said. "Modern man is a bitch."

As Johnson settled his tab and stood up, Dickey leaned in: "Come out to the parking lot," he said. "I have something in the back of my Cavalier."

Johnson backed away. "I'm not smoking anything," he said. "They test at Alfred and Associates. Piss and hair."

"Just come," Dickey said. "You'll go home happier, and you'll learn more at school."

Streetlights cast a dirty yellow pall on Dickey's moribund Cavalier, a rust-bitten convertible. Johnson checked his watch—five minutes late already. Dickey opened the trunk and exhumed a pizza box. "I read somewhere, or maybe heard it on television, that all parenthood really boils down to is the ability to sacrifice," Dickey said. "It's a noble thing you're doing."

"Yeah, sure."

"You know," Dickey said, "I think I heard that line about sacrifice on 'Oprah.'"

"You dragged me out here for pizza?"

Dickey made the conniving hand gestures of a novice magician. "This is special pizza, boy," he said. "A mushroom recipe I've been working on. Fully organic with only the slightest hint of psychotropic backlash."

"You're out of your mind."

"This one's on me."

"I'm not eating anything from you."

"Quality cheese, a little prosciutto," Dickey said, poking Johnson's ribs, "and I'm pretty sure I found the right pasture."

"I never tried mushrooms."

"Then you don't know the cosmic answer."

"Whatever, Dickey."

"Hey, maybe it won't work," he shrugged, "but you can't say I sent you home hungry."

Johnson clasped the box and turned toward home. "I appreciate the thought. See you when I see you."

To Johnson's surprise, Gilder had slept through his tardiness. He poured a glass of water from the fridge and cracked a lite beer. Pale blue moonlight permeated the kitchen. Johnson took a seat and eyed the pizza box, its company logo blacked out with frenzied marker swipes, as if Dickey had feared being sued. He opened it and inhaled a surprisingly fresh aroma, a hint of basil and mozzarella. He dipped a finger in the sauce—smoky, oniony. He reconciled the risk: Dickey had always talked so much shit, surely this was his way of disguising a kind gesture for an expectant family. One way or another a single piece of good pizza wouldn't kill a man.

"Okay," Johnson said. "This better be groovy, or whatever."

Johnson washed the slice down with beer, licked his fingertips. Nothing really happened—no flying dragons, no glittery sorcerers. After ten minutes he tiptoed to the bedroom, curled beside his snoring Gilder, and let his mind fill with dreams.

Gastrointestinal tremors besieged Johnson an hour later. He raced clumsily to the master bathroom, bashing a steel wastebasket, slamming the door.

"I give you an inch," Gilder scolded from bed, "and you drink yourself sick."

"Not drunk," he pleaded, knees on tile. "Something I ate."

She harrumphed and went quiet again.

When the vomiting subsided, Johnson glimpsed himself in the massive bathroom mirror. He looked haggard and crazy, like the Mister Hyde interpretation in classic cartoons, his pupils like hazel poker chips. He was stricken with the feeling that his parents were coming over, Bob and Judy unannounced, and that they were angry with him. In his cheekbones and forehead he could see the blending of various European lineages, an Americanized stew in one berserk face. He questioned the vitality of his own name, wondering what those syllables would mean to excavators 5,000 years after the meteors. Johnson fully extended his tongue to examine the taste buds, which made him think of snakes, red pythons in the attic, so he turned off all the bathroom lights and cowered beside the toilet for hours. Chirping wrens and thrashers brought solace, but also conjured visions of carnivorous flying squirrels. He repeatedly flushed the toilet, thirty flushes in an hour, one cataclysmic purge after the next, a sound that cleansed his harried soul. His breathing stabilized. But then Gilder's alarm clock blared. She hit snooze once and rewrote modern history. Nine minutes later, she turned the alarm off.

Gilder rapped on the bathroom door with long, sharp fingernails. Trapped, Johnson budged open the bathroom window. He was contemplating an army crawl onto the roof when the door creaked open.

"Fresh air?" Gilder groggily said. "You slept in here?"

Johnson sat on the toilet, staring down at swirling ceramic tiles. "I'm so sick," he wheezed. "Can't go."

"Bullshit," his wife said, disrobing and stepping into the rainfall shower, her midsection a veiny beach ball.

The water danced down Gilder. Johnson recalled the great waterfalls of Hawaii, where they'd honeymooned, where she admitted, tongue loose on Mai Tais, that marrying an accountant felt like a letdown. She'd always fancied a veterinarian or cowboy, she said, but her compatibility with Johnson was too strong, too valuable, too funny to ignore. She had apologized a hundred times, but Johnson could never let those comments go.

"I'm not John Wayne," he said, on the toilet. "You know I'll never be John Wayne."

Gilder flung open the shower door. "You drunk prick," she said. "Splash your face, have coffee, and wait for me in the car. I paid $90 for these classes, and you're going to learn something. Stop acting like a baby yourself and start thinking about your son."

Johnson worked his jaw in circles and nodded. He exited the paranoiac shack the bathroom had become. One look at his sunlit bedroom and he felt better. He could sense the global retreat of night, the darkness dragging across Texas plateaus, bound for San Diego, pulling with it his nightmarish introspection. He almost felt like laughing, but he remembered his orders to wait in the car, and that wasn't funny. He meandered through the home, took one more huge bite for breakfast, and pushed the remaining pizza into the garbage disposal. He went outside. He felt light as bubbles.

Before long, Gilder plopped in the Honda's driver's seat. She was impatient and un-caffeinated, but Johnson felt buttressed by her spitfire energy. In the soft-lit morning she looked like the angel of fertility, her blouse glowing with clean frilly whiteness. He loved this woman with all the affection of his past partnerships combined, and he could see that now with arithmetical clarity. "Why that happy look on your face?" Gilder said. "Did you get blown by hookers last night?" He didn't answer. She shook her head and drove leafy summer streets toward the hospital. They slipped onto the freeway and melted into light weekend traffic. Midtown towers flicked by like backcountry telephone poles.

"**D**on't get a boner."

Gilder growled the order as they joined a torrent of human pairings loading into the Ronald Wichita Auditorium, an egg-shaped addition to Peachtree Hospital. Gilder clasped her husband's hand, which invited a return bout of paranoia. They hadn't held hands in years.

"Why would this give me a boner?" Johnson said, gulping. "Do you know what a directive like that can do to a man?"

"They're going to use real photos," she said. "I heard some women might even model, to show us technique. You can close your eyes during all that."

"Can I close my eyes all day?"

She yanked his arm. "What did you *do* last night?"

Johnson said nothing.

Inside, the auditorium was vast and awkward, a steep slope with worn cinema chairs. The stage was heavily shellacked and crowded with big-breasted mannequins. There was a podium and swan-neck microphone. Behind it all stretched a wide white screen. They found an aisle seat and Johnson watched the women pass. Against the screen they were wobbling silhouettes, penguins smuggling basketballs. The husbands bore facial expressions suggestive of lumbar pain.

"There could be a mutiny," Johnson said.

"What?"

"If they aren't satisfied with the show, don't you get a feeling these women might revolt?"

"This isn't a *show*, you dumbass."

Johnson grit his teeth and drew sanitized oxygen into his chest. "You know what Oprah says about parenthood?" he said. "You hear about this? She says children should be sacrificed."

"Look at me," Gilder said, squeezing his arm. "What's wrong with your pupils? Tell me what you took."

"Baby, look," he said, and then paused. He could hear a thousand areolas darkening. "Keep asking me this shit, in a place like this, and I'm liable to spontaneously combust."

185

"Just shut up," she said. "Okay? Not another word. Take notes."

Johnson focused on the virgin paper of his notebook, the blue lines waving like Maui swells. The auditorium had reached capacity. A video flashed on the screen, showing a petite but hard-stepping lady walking a hospital corridor, healing people. She stared into the camera, into the darkened auditorium, and smiled: "Welcome to the Breastfeeding School!"

Johnson whispered: "The Grand Empress cometh."

In the flesh, the Grand Empress arose from stage left, and the room's lights fell dim. This was really happening. She was dainty but direct, clad in a red business suit, her feet pounding in black heels. She tossed grandmotherly smiles to the crowd. Johnson was sure he could see through the façade, that she was really the wicked headmaster of a Third World orphanage. Behind her the screen transformed into a gargantuan breast diagram, a paisley flower of milk ducts and fatty tissue. She took the microphone and introduced herself, to Johnson's ears, as Doctor Carole Something.

"Babies are born suckers," Doctor Something said. "Let's get that straight, right off the bat."

Johnson leaned back into his seat, wishing he might evaporate, or fall into a secret corridor. He studied the other men and decided it best to not evaporate, but to be a damn man. The doctor spoke of nurturing bonds, skin-to-skin benefits, and—worst—Montgomery glands, the bumpy outposts around the nipple's hollow tower. This required an illustration, then a real breast photo, which consumed the entire screen. It was the least erotic thing Johnson had ever seen, a brown-eyed Cyclops lunging at the crowd.

Johnson leaned over: "She stole our money."

"Write down what she was saying," Gilder said. "The bit about bloody nipples."

"Jesus."

Next up was a sketch of twins suckling their mother, one breast each. Johnson thought of puppies. Then he thought he saw puppies in the aisles. "Okay," he said, "break time. I'll be in the hall."

186

Johnson exited the auditorium and bee-lined to the nearest window, for proof the hospital hadn't sunk to a lunatic netherworld. He wandered into the men's restroom, where two husbands near the sinks were discussing college football.

"I only ate one slice," Johnson told them.

The men looked at each other. The taller one, who wore a sport coat and leather driving shoes, smiled. The shorter one donned a pinkie ring. Johnson knew this was no time for men with pinkie rings.

"I think we all ate the slice," the tall man said. "Or else we wouldn't be here, listening to this mumbo jumbo about inverted nipples."

All three laughed. Johnson was convinced he'd found kindred voyagers on the psychedelic crazy train.

"You guys afraid of Oprah?"

The tall one tossed a wadded paper towel in a countertop hole. "She scares the hell out of me," he said.

Johnson extended his knuckles for bumping, first to the tall man and then the short one, but neither obliged. They didn't seem to know what Johnson wanted; his fist hung lonely in the air. Their cordial acceptance of him shifted to cold analysis.

"You doing okay, man?" the short guy said. "Look a little wound up."

"Oh," Johnson said, "peachy."

Said the tall one, "It'll be over soon."

"How do you know?"

"Program says so."

"Who's fucking program?" Johnson snapped. "Tell me what you mean."

The men gave up on Johnson and walked toward the door. As Johnson lifted his arms and gasped, the tall man turned around. "You know, you should get back in there," he said. "This isn't about you. It's about your kid."

Johnson broke into a drenching sweat. He knew what had to be done: retrieve his wife, take her to a park with a wide green field, and tell her everything. He calmly exited the bathroom but took a wrong turn; instead of auditorium doors he came to an art deco mezzanine. It was a vast, silent space. Beneath the entryway was a bench, upon which sat a figure Johnson mistook for a sculpture at first, but determined via her sniffling nose to be an actual woman, and a very pregnant one at that. She faced the exit, even leaned toward it, but she didn't stand, anchored by an unseen weight. Johnson wanted to confide in her, to cleanse his angst in her motherly aura.

"Do you know which way the Breastfeeding School is?"

"Back the way you came," she said, "then left."

Johnson tipped an invisible cap. "Is the program over?"

"No," she said. "I couldn't take the full three hours at once, you know."

The marble between them felt to Johnson like thin glass, but he wanted to examine the sunlight in her blond hair, the sincerity in her face. "Can I come closer?" he said. "That bench looks amazing."

She leaned against the wall, pointing to the vacancy beside her. "How far along is your wife?"

"Oh," he said, "there's no going back."

Johnson shuffled across the marble. Up close, the woman was morose, her abdomen a bulbous contradiction to her slim frame. She tried to hide her eyes because she had been crying, but blushless channels on her cheeks divulged her secret woes. Johnson sat down and said, bluntly, "Hormones?"

She snorted. She showed her puffy eyelids. She didn't care now. "Possibly."

Johnson flexed his toes, his hands flat on his thighs. In reverence of her and the unborn child he kept a weirdly perfect posture. "I've had a long day," he said.

"You look tired," she said. "No offense."

Johnson shrugged. "I'm recovering from food poisoning." He nodded at her belly, her hands. "Will your wedding ring not fit, either? My wife's won't."

"Don't have one," she said.

"Oh, why?"

She seemed offended, but she answered. "He wants to chip in from a distance. The father. A bartender I barely know. This wasn't exactly in his plans, or mine."

Johnson felt his face drop. "Is that why you're out here?"

Her face wilted. "I think I was the only one in there by myself."

"No."

"I was," she said. "Really think I was."

"It'll be okay."

She rubbed her eyes.

"Look," Johnson said, "I don't know what I'm talking about, and I don't know you, but I'm pretty tuned in to our cosmic energy, and I can tell you this…that baby is going to be a dancer."

She reached over the bench and clutched Johnson's hand. Her faint blue veins were like his mother's. He put his ear to her belly, rested his head on the bench, and pulled up his legs. Eyes closed, he told her he'd heard the baby pirouetting. He fell asleep as she whispered goodbye, patted his head, and vanished.

Hands on hips, Gilder stood over Johnson as he awoke. She knelt to his level and studied his face, as she might a gunshot victim. Behind her, the seminar attendees were leaving in droves, chatting about parking fees and maternity wards and the oncoming commitment of everything. Johnson focused on his wife's face. Before she could issue one stern word, he extended his hand, let it rest on her womb, and in the center of his palm he felt a tiny nudge, his son's first high five.

AXIS OF SYMMETRY

I could sense he was following me before I actually saw his truck. You don't need the rearview to tell you these things, not always, not when you're expecting it, when you deserve it. The headlights jerked onto Peachtree Road and barreled so intensely up behind my Volvo there was no mistaking the driver—he with chrome testicles hanging from his bumper, he with God-knows-what-caliber thing on his person, he on a death mission. The stoplight ahead burned red, red, red, and I coasted to avoid stopping. At ten miles per hour he whipped into the center lane, nearest my drivers-side door. We stopped. I stared ahead. He tossed a crushed Miller Lite can that struck my window, so I put the window down, one clenched hand on the wheel, one boot on the gas.

"Don't bother going there," he said.

That was Tony for you, a plainspoken directive spat from a pile of muscles. His thin upper lip twitched, his baldhead smooth as river rock. His truck's interior pulsed with blue-lit buttons and high-tech amenities, an LCD television crowning the dashboard. The pea-green truck itself was beefy, tricked-out, and race-ready, indicative of machismo and manic obsession to detail. Looked like it used to be a Ford.

"Don't go where?" I said, hunching my shoulders. "That you, Tony?"

"You didn't see me here." He rubbed a fancy bathroom towel over his face, his head, under his chin, and tossed it on the floorboard. He inspected himself in the rearview.

"Okay," I said. "Didn't see anything."

The light flicked green but neither of us moved. I looked down to the black street, dotted in the first dead leaves of autumn. I wondered if the details of our interaction would reemerge in some windowless interrogation room, the detectives grilling Tony, the subject being my corpse. The tension in his voice and body reminded me of Death Row inmates I had seen in prison documentaries. On the other hand, Tony was the king of empty threats. The other week he was going to poison my Labrador, Chipper, with antifreeze. And hunt down my sister in her Midtown law office to push her off the rooftop moon-garden. When Tony hated you, he said things of this nature, mainly because he had nothing else to say. The stuff was borderline hilarious and too easy to dismiss as hot air. Violent disillusionment. Poppycock.

"Not finalized," he said, cuffing his gearshift like a scepter. "Goddamn it, you knew it wasn't finalized."

I lifted both hands over my doorsill, exposing my weaponless palms. "Go easy, Tony." I slid my right hand into my pocket, just to touch the knife, to reassure myself a sharp Swiss piece had my back. "We got that taken care of, through the lawyers. You might not like it, but there's going to be restrictions, certain distances. We needed finality with this, because it isn't healthy, not for us, not for you, not for—"

"Finalized it myself," Tony said.

"Excuse me?"

"You didn't see me."

With that his truck pounced into the intersection, not so fast as to bark the tires, but fast enough to suggest the driver was unsatisfied with himself. The truck tore into the night, the empty street; the city welcomed it from afar like a bullet-riddled circus tent. I sat through another green light and watched the truck shrink with distance. Had Tony been waiting for my Volvo? Had he doubled back? I continued in the same direction for two more blocks and swung left down Melinda's lane, to the stately, diced-up Greek revival that housed her apartment and three others.

I parked on the street and stepped into her yard but halted beside a magnolia. Swear to God I could feel it then, the pull of a predetermined outcome. Something was ill, something about the light. It's different the way moonlight cradles old houses in autumn— beautiful, but you can't deny the wicked luster of imminent winter. Or was it something more abstract, something unseen? A clairvoyant in Daytona Beach once told me you can sense death through concrete walls. She was drunk, but she was right.

I teach English to half-baked high school dropouts at the Rebound Academy, a sort of prep school for lives spent in the service industry or prison. I gravitated to English when I realized that even simple math tied my brain in knots. The kids, then, are better with numbers than me. But at the risk of sounding immodest and crude, I tell my friends my pupils can't sniff the jock of my imagination. I use made-up stories to understand math and science, to make obscure bits of horseshit stick where I can mentally retrieve them—a trick I've been doing since fourth grade. Fractions, to my mind, involve a carton of eggs. Multiplication is rabbits, humping and birthing. Pretty ironic that I fell for a math teacher, and she for a dunce like me.

When Melinda told me what her estranged husband wanted, she used math terms, employing lingo from elementary arithmetic. "Fifty-fifty," she said over tacos that night at her apartment. "Tony won't listen to any other suggestions."

"Not fair," I said.

A few specs of renegade cilantro lay on the table. I angrily flicked them off.

"Behave," she said.

She was beautiful that night, her eyes like sad emeralds. We'd met in rehab, believe it or not, after prescription medication had thrust its fangs in both of us. My demons came after back surgery; hers after wedding Tony.

"He's been sitting on his ass for, what, three years?" I said. "You paid for *all* this stuff"—I pointed to her vintage record player, her framed acrylic painting by an artist of regional renown—"and you should rightfully keep it."

"I don't exactly have leverage."

"Hell with leverage," I said. "I'm talking about justice."

"I've got nothing, no leg to stand on, not with this, with us..."

Her eyes shot to me, to her hands, to me, then back to the tacos. That was Melinda. She could softly acknowledge life's ugly bits, like marital infidelity. "There's a concept that applies," she said. "I know it sounds nerdy, but it fits. It's called the 'axis of symmetry,' the idea that a line passes through something and makes the figures on both sides a mirror image of each other."

"Geometry," I said, smiling. "Disgusting."

Melinda reciprocated the smile. "Well he's disgusting, but that's what he wants," she said. "If I get market value for the house, we'll be okay. He'll take that stupid truck; I get the Toyota. The joint savings, if you can call it that, is what kills me. The dog is another issue."

She pointed to her shit-spewing Pomeranian, a puppy named Gizmo. The dog's ears perked at the false promise of tacos.

"He loves Gizmo," she said, "but he can't have him."

I was lost. "Axis of what?" I said. "How'd you say that again?"

I could see movement in the other street-facing apartments.

Melinda's neighbors were always such prissy little egotist shits. Transplants from the northeast, or maybe Nova Scotia, wherever custom holds that talking over people with dull updates about oneself is acceptable. They really liked soccer, all three of these chicks. They thought of my gray hair and old academic Volvo as evidence that I sucked, that I was well on my way to being the world's youngest curmudgeon. My perpetually aching back pointed, in their eyes, to premature decrepitude, a sitting man's dilemma. But they all had applauded Melinda on separate occasions, saying, basically, *Hey, Peter might be lame, but at least he won't backhand your face and threaten you with a piping-hot iron.* They called her brave for walking out on a mortgage with her name on it.

The neighbor girls were watching me in the yard. I stepped back into a walkway light so they could see me better. I lifted both hands and wiggled my fingers, as if saying hello to children. The one they called Princess lifted the screen and stuck out her blond head.

"Peter," she said in whisper-shout. "Thank freakin' God. Something's happened. Something at Melinda's."

"What?"

"We called 911," she said. "But go up there, go in. We can't wait for the cops. They said it'd be ten minutes, like, *ten minutes ago.*"

"Jesus."

I started jogging but froze when I heard Princess break down. That wasn't like her. I looked up and hunched my shoulders.

"It was so loud," she said.

"What the hell?" I said. "What are you saying?"

"I mean," and she clasped her temples, "I mean like a *chainsaw.*"

I remember dropping my car keys. I remember contemplating the act of hustling, of ripping open the lobby door. I remember nothing else until I slid on the slick hardwoods of the landing and went knees first into an antique side-table. By the time I stood up limping the Swiss piece was open in my hand.

Tony wasn't exactly irrational at first, just pissed like any dejected asshole deserves to be. The last five years with Melinda, he'd had the caveman complex that evokes jealously whenever his woman strolls the sidewalk, shops the fancy mall, grabs a coffee before teaching math—any exposure to the outside world that couldn't be moderated by his imposing watchfulness. When the pills bit and she started missing work, even Tony gave his blessing, nudging her through the doors of Twin Saints House of Forgiveness. It would be Melinda's lone haven.

The counselor had nearly succeeded in pulling me out of pill-depraved night sweats when Melinda first arrived, a thin Barbie doll in knee-high boots. Every guy in the room wanted to fix her, to mend her fractures, to win her adoration despite the wedding ring.

"I started pinching from my mother's pill bottles," she told us that first night. "I'm not happy. I can't really go into it, but I'm not. I teach school kids. I need to get a grip."

In two weeks she was staying after meetings to chat with me over coffee. She said my silliness and oddball stories made her laugh. Whether she gravitated to me because I was single, or because I had steady employment, or because I hadn't been smoking crack from car antennas, I don't know. All I know is that during those talks I could see something in her regenerate, and then wither when the time came to go home. She'd wrap herself in a double-breasted peacoat and brace for more than wind. The more we said goodbye the more it hurt me, too.

Two months in, she came over to my condo after session. A week later, we made love. She cried in my arms and inadvertently fell asleep until four a.m. That's the night when Tony became what you might call irrational.

She missed two weeks of sessions. Quiet panic gripped me. I had no phone number, no address, no lifeline to the vanished Melinda. "That asshole killed her," I told a port-wine fiend named Bradley. "I'm next."

Bradley rolled his eyes.

"I'm not kidding," I said. "I've been barricading my door. Went to the pawn shop, bought a quality little knife, man."

Then one night she was waiting at my condo gate. A Tuesday, I think. In the streetlight pall a handprint burned on her right cheek.

"Should we call the cops?"

"I'm leaving," she said, "getting an apartment. Doing the paperwork. Right now I need a refuge."

I tried to hold her but she pushed me away. I opened the iron gates and kept a good safe distance. Inside, she closed my blinds and propped a chair under my entryway doorknob. She made me flush my aspirin down the toilet. She curled on my loveseat and pressed an icepack to her face. "His father beat him senseless, in the backwoods, where they raised him," Melinda said. "This is how he vents."

My hands trembled, I was so angry. "He's no victim."

She moved the icepack to her forehead, closed her eyes, pursed her lips, and strained her face against tempestuous thoughts.

Melinda's door bore a muddy boot print, a few inches left of the knob. The air reeked of gasoline. On the threshold dripped three plum-colored splotches. Not a rational thought in my head, I just stood there a second, sensing a situation within her apartment I did not want to disturb, or to digest all at once. I took a deep breath, stared at my boots. That's when Melinda's acrylic painting, what was left of it, caught my eye, leaning against the wall opposite her door. It had been cut perfectly in half and, apparently, discarded. I turned to go in. The doorframe wore jagged cuts, like claw marks.

I pulled my sleeve over my hand and tapped the knob, as though it could be hot. Clutching the knife handle, I nudged open the door with my knuckles. A shattered mirror lay in her hallway, its frame chopped in two. Stepping delicately on glass I came to the spare bathroom and peeked in. Disheveled, but nothing horrific. I eyed myself in the bathroom mirror and mouthed the words: *You can do this.* That's when I heard the crying, coming through the overhead vents, a distress call linked by ductwork to the master bathroom.

"Melinda!" I yelled. "Hang on, Melinda."

I bolted through the kitchen, the living room, around her queen bed, and kicked open the bathroom door.

There's that famous scene in *Scarface*, the bathtub dismemberment scene, which always scared the bejesus out of my sister and me, having shown us the true underbelly of humanity. Suddenly I was living it, in my girlfriend's cutesy pink bathroom, the mirrors and framed photos and her beloved Turkish bath towels ablaze with red confetti. The air hung pungent with the coppery smell of butcher shops. In the tub sat Melinda, weeping so viciously she couldn't breathe, holding in both hands equal halves of her Pomeranian, the poor animal split nose to tail, its innards spilling in her lap.

"Melinda," I said, calmly enough to surprise myself.

She only wheezed.

"Baby," I said. "Is any of this blood yours?"

She dropped Gizmo's parts but left her wet hands open. She shook her head no and gave pitiful eyes. My blocking the door seemed to relieve her, to ensure her nothing would get her without first getting me. I pulled her from the tub into my arms, her neck jumping with shock and panicked breathing. In the scattered seconds of quietude I could hear sirens and the scurrying feet of the neighbor girls. I could hear true finality. I buried my face in Melinda's hair because it was soft, because it smelled like strawberries, because it masked the smell of gasoline.

HANGING ABDUL

I t's not easy to hang somebody in a pomegranate tree, especially a young insurgent with fire in his guts. He writhed around all those fruits and leaves, at times a buried and faceless commotion, a bat in a burlap sack. The skinny branches bent and I prayed they'd twist, snap, crash in a cloud of dust. Guess I could have asserted myself like I was raised, stepped in and saved a scumbag's life. Guess I just wanted it to be over.

Opium farmers trudged by, pulling goats with lead ropes. They pretended not to notice. Corporal Cantone from Yonkers pointed an M4 to intimidate the farmers, keep them quiet. I smacked him across his neck.

"Hey, idiot," I said. "That's going too far."

"Then what's *that?*" Cantone said, finger toward the pomegranate tree. "You backwoods piece of shit."

Stringing that fucktard up by his neck was bad judgment, a headline-caliber mistake, I kept telling the guys. But it's hard to talk

199

sense when they've got that jackal mentality: circle the prey, toy with it, slow-death it. Google "Jackals" sometime and you'll see they converge on a carcass in small groups, the hungriest of the pack getting first lick. Elder jackals are prone to observation, to patience. No matter the age, it's the kind of animal that doesn't like being kicked around. Best I can tell the species is damn loyal, too.

We'd ascertained through the translator that his name was Abdul, some renegade fighter from up north. A short, surly man with hardly any face beneath that condor's nest of a beard. "How fucking cliché," somebody had said, on top of him, beforehand. "Abdul."

Abdul was another in a long line of fucktards bent on pumping us full of 7.62 millimeter rounds. Those antiquated bullets that get in you and dance. He didn't care about our ambitions, our mothers, could give two fucks about my '71 Mustang back home in Macon. Still, I said, "Just rough him up, kick his beard, detain him. There's tons more like him." And that was the truth. The fucktards infest this swampy nether region—the diaper of Afghanistan, we call it—that's hardly mentioned on CNN, which pisses mom off but also kind of calms her.

His dying took several minutes. At one point I had my M203 in hand, the 40-millimeter grenade launcher, thinking about lobbing a couple rounds into the tree, showering the guys in Abdul.

Thonk, thonk…splash!

Corporal Griffin Douglas would have liked that—a grand, violent tribute to him. His killer busted in a billion pieces, crimson air and hot sun. You do those things for brothers when it doesn't matter anymore. You blow men apart, Call-Of-Duty style. Him or me, I choose him.

You especially do it for a guy like Douglas, a unifier, a brash Southern rascal who made big proclamations (like swearing one night he could jack off twenty times a day). Douglas was a complex man, don't get me wrong. He had this determined way of rising in the morning that made you forget home, forget hell. He made you feel purposeful. We'd watch him on patrol and structure our movements in anticipation of his. Gay as it sounds, the guy was beautiful.

"Rise and shine, you lazy bitches," he'd say at the base, slurping instant coffee and pocketing extra amo. "They're out there squirming in the dirt, training to kill our grandkids."

Maybe Douglas was too reckless to last here, a big Eagle, Globe and Anchor tat emblazoned on his forearm. He played all-in, like he didn't believe in promises. A tat like that was his evidence, a means to announce his loyalty to the Corp without saying shit.

There was also a sensitive side to Douglas, a thinking side. He roughhoused and chest-puffed around the FOB all day, but at night I could hear him cry. He had a little baby daughter. We only learned that pulling together his materials—the drawings and rough-drafts of homebound letters—for the casket flight. Funny he'd never mentioned the girl. Only grunt in our platoon with a kid, he kept her in that sacred, unspoken place.

"I believe in the tribal mindset," Douglas wrote in his final letter to Julie, his girl in Birmingham. "You can't take this stuff lightly, the pressures of heat and shitty MREs and goddamn death in the nooks of every village," he went on. "But there are laws and codes. NATO restrictions. We can't shoot them if they drop their guns. It's crazy…the rules of engagement. We're getting so frustrated, and angry men are triggered by all sorts of things."

There was one difference between Abdul and the others: They weren't such good shots. He had the accuracy to maim as well as kill, the face before the heart. I shudder to think he did it for some noble, for-hire need, like to feed his grubby kids. So I don't guess. I don't humanize. At least not on purpose.

Abdul must have been watching us for five clicks, wolfing the bamboo grass, waiting. We came to a canal that fed a wide green sea of pot. We didn't cross the creek line; we'd been warned the water was chockfull of mines and piranhas. Our purpose was to reinforce Sergeant Taylor's squad up the road, securing villages for another squad behind. Six firefights in four days and we were tired, our edge dulled. Douglas got ahead of the minesweeper, breaking the V-shaped formation, and Abdul drew a line in the dust, judging distance. He walked the rounds right to Douglas' feet, his groin, his blue eyes. My first thought was that Douglas would never cry again.

We dove in the grass. M16s hacked until Abdul came out waving his shirt, a dirty apparition. Then he charged us, knife in hand, but martyrdom isn't that easy.

Corporal Cantone, the New Yorker, wrested the knife away while four others punched Abdul's face and chest. Another guy drew a rifle at point-blank range. "Wait," someone said, and I'll testify under oath next week that I don't know who. "Don't shoot his ass. I have an idea."

Three months before, in a letter back to Georgia, I'd warned my wife I was seeing weird things among my fellow grunts. Animalistic traits, foreshadows of barbarity. A lance corporal from Iowa we called Sketch taught the guys to tie a slipknot, the key component in a slip noose. "Just tie it into an S," said Sketch, "scrunch it down and coil it around the middle like a boa constrictor...hold the loose end and pull like hell."

I yanked him aside.

"What the hell's that?" I said.

"Nothing," he said. "An old Boy Scout trick."

"I don't think that's useful knowledge."

"Kind of late now, Pops."

My platoon is chockfull of goddamn nickname experts. Like for the Taliban. They're pussies on the prowl, fucktards in our clutches. They call me Pops because of my last name, Van Poppel, and because they say I act like everyone's dad. I guess it's the older brother in me, the kid walking his sister to school while mom pulled doubles at Applebee's and Huddle House. Dad had left one summer to play guitar in Florida beach bars, gave up, and joined the Navy. He sent a photo of himself with some money each Christmas, from Istanbul or Sao Paulo or Nova Scotia, each a sloppier version of the previous man. The envelopes ceased when I was ten.

After high school I got hopped up on Gulf War movies, the classics like *Three Kings* and *Jarhead*, quit my job at the lumberyard and finally called the recruiter back. Climbing the ladder of some company felt like a path for suckers, for brain-dead morons. Besides, that recruiter was a persistent bastard. When I think of him I don't want to blame him but the urge to shake his hand isn't so strong either.

Four years as a Marine and they've stuck me with Operation Southern Independence, plunked down in godforsaken Helmand province in what looks like Hollywood Vietnam. No airy mountain ranges for us. At noon it hits 120 degrees, your canteen water so hot it blisters your tongue if you chug. We hump eighty-five pounds of gear—flak jacket, Kevlar mask, amo, chow, batteries, et cetera—and I've lost thirty pounds, enough to make my wife shit herself. "John," she wrote once, "you look damn *sick!*" So I've quit emailing photos. I don't open myself up in emails or letters, either. I just send courtesy words. I put the white pines and cool Georgia winters and my house with its two-car garage in an off-limits mental place. I lean on the guys to keep me sane, to fuck with me and make me laugh. To keep that little feeling alive that this is all an adventure, that my life and those of my brothers is part of a great movement of good, a benevolent force like daybreaks in January.

One minute we were playing volleyball at Camp Leatherneck with the Australians and the next we had our orders and were tiptoeing over IEDs when some pussy shot my friend in the face and we scrambled with medics to push his slippery blue eyeball back in its socket.

Ooh-rah!

"What are we *doing?*" Sketch asked about a month into the mission. "I mean, think about the difference in this and what my grandpa was doing on Saipan. They were kicking ass, saving the fucking world. All we do is wander."

The objective is a little more complicated. We started in the province at a ramshackle patrol base, grouped with some Brits. Big picture, we were told to be like politicians, except instead of votes we

203

had to win the trust of village elders. These wrinkled old wise men—most of them low-level poppy peddlers—run things, and for the most part they're sick of war. But they'll say jack shit, at least in public. So we host *suras*, these happy gatherings like barbecues, only with goat and chai tea. The elders spill their guts and we make proposals (never promises) in return. Sometimes a pussy ditches his telltale sash and his gun and sneaks into the meetings. When that happens, the elders shut the hell up. Blabbing to us means a surefire beheading in the night.

Corporal Douglas could pick out the pussies like nobody's business, a bona fide pussy sniper in social situations. "Look," he said once, pulling me to the corner of an awkward *sura*. "The one at the chow line, in the vest...he's high. His eyes got that slow, dumb look."

"Yeah?"

"Absolutely," Douglas said. "One had a vest like that last week. Fucker was hiding black-tar heroin. Two kilos."

"Good eye," I said. "Now stop staring."

But Douglas's curiosity in the man only intensified, his eyes squinted in mean thought. He hated having that element around, a lunge away from jabbing a knife in someone's kidney. "You think it'd spook the meeting if I shot him?" and he belted his loud, guttural laugh, which got me going, too.

"I think ISAF would be all sorts of pissed," I said. "You'll have your chance, cowboy."

Whoever had tied the noose was good. It was robust and perfect-looking, some Clint Eastwood shit. "Where the hell did that rope come from?" I remember asking, trying to break up the crowd. "A dead horse," someone barked. They were kicking Abdul and ripping at his beard, both his eyes swollen like gala apples, his nose bloodied and kicked to a zigzag. Before I could intervene, the rope was choking him, thwarting his panicked prayers to Allah. A couple of guys kept punching while a couple more monkeyed up the tree. Branches snapped and pomegranates thudded like dropped pop flies.

Took them ten minutes to find a suitable branch; they settled on the thick, crooked spine of that old tree.

In the background medics loaded Corporal Douglas into a Blackhawk, the yellow smoke they'd popped encircling them. I watched them put the morphine away. They pointed to the bamboo grass that had given us Abdul, and the bird climbed into the sky, rocking its M60 into the grass, a golden rain of spent shells falling.

"If Abdul wasn't alone," said Cantone, dissociating himself from the beating, "that bastard's alone now."

Two nights before Douglas died we lay awake on our cots, chewing the fat. He told me his uncle had flown 100 combat missions in Vietnam, that he was organizing a parade in Douglas' hometown, some one-stoplight hamlet outside Birmingham. We had two months left but this uncle was hammering out the logistics way in advance, down to the music they'd be playing on the courthouse lawn.

"My uncle keeps asking about our progress, in his emails," Douglas said. "Like it's something we can measure."

"What've you told him?" I said.

"Not a damn thing, really," he said. "I don't know how to quantify any of this."

I rolled over and clicked on a Maglite. It threw morbid shadows on the canvas walls. "Tell him we're winning," I said. "Tell him we're winning at something."

We both shut up for a minute.

"Eventually, they'll get tired of fighting us, or we'll lose," Douglas said. "One way or the other."

"Alright," I said. "Enough with the talk."

I clicked the flashlight off but couldn't sleep. Some sentiments are hard to stomach. For a moment I had visions of backyard campouts beneath the loblollies with my friends. I imagined my dad commandeering some warship in the Dead Sea, or off the Tasmanian Coast, which made me feel worse.

"What else do you talk about?" I said in the night. "You and your uncle."

"Mostly fishing."

"What kind of fishing?"

"Catfishing."

"What kind of catfish?"

"Bullheads, channel cats…down on the river."

"Okay," I said, rolling over. "Don't talk about that, either."

They cut the body from the tree. The khakis snagged on branches that tore his skin until at last the tree let go of Abdul. He landed feet-first, then dropped flimsy like a crash-test dummy in the dirt. For a moment we stood over him, dumb, expecting the chest to rise and fall. But the head was yanked good, permanently looking down. His eyes were frenzied and distant. The reality of his death fell over us like a cheap, steel cage. I've tried to forget what happened next, but it has a grip on me. Agreements have been made so that it won't be mentioned in court.

Sketch was the first to whip out his dick. Three or four others followed. They pissed all over Abdul, soaking his khakis and wetting his beard, surrounding his twisted body in filthy black mud. It was a disgraceful ceremony, but for too long I couldn't react.

"Enough," I finally said, and we all kind of drifted away.

Not sure why, but it makes me feel better to pretend Abdul was famous, like a diabolical warlord. Something more than a little puke who slept on dirt floors, the virgins dancing in his dreams. I wish he was Abdul, King Fucktard of the Nawzad district, or something like that. A trophy kill that made the news for all the right reasons.

I wish, at least, that he wasn't so easy to bully, that he didn't work alone, that we'd had to whip him and some lowlife insurgent posse of his. We're all human beings, first and foremost, and everyone likes a good, fair fight.

HANGING ABDUL

Since Douglas' death I've lain awake most nights and thought crazy shit. I think big-picture. I imagine that unseen forces are leading us along a vast grid, be it the hands of politics or history or God. Watching men kill each other only verifies for me that combat is the worst of all intersecting points. I guess making love would be the opposite, the best of humanity, but I don't care much for that. It's been six months since I screwed my wife and the urge barely bites at me anymore. At this point in life I think I'd rather fight than fuck, finish this war while I've got the health.

DIRTYVILLE RHAPSODIES

The Mad Bear Cub, as we call him, went out and got his face smacked again last night, his swollen cheek a gift from Atlanta police, he says, but we know it's more likely his own doing, a kiss from some tree he didn't see coming, or the work of another tourist he pestered too much. He drops his face and white-man Afro in his hands, swears he's cursed, and not five minutes into his morning nap, pisses his dirty corduroys.

There's nothing so dangerous as the Mad Bear Cub on potent liquor. This is how he earned the nickname. Usually an amiable jokester, the Cub on liquor becomes this frothing woodland creature with no patience for human companionship or personal hygiene. He hacks through crowds and goes scratching and growling along shelter floors until he finds the most inappropriate thing to bite. His name is otherwise Leonard.

He lives under a bridge downtown. He has a tent made of woolen Army blankets and fishing line. He talks of his girlfriends, his conquests, women he never had and never will. He's figured out that I'm a journalist in sheep's clothing, researching an exposé about failed homeless shelters subsidized by the city, living the subterranean life for two weeks and letting my beard go wild, but he's glad to have the company. His big fat eyebrows hop with delight.

"I'll tell you about the Dirtyville Rhapsodies," the Cub said one night, over cheap malbec he'd thieved from the Edgewood Grocery. "That's the songs the hobos played when I rode trains, back through Indiana, across the West and into the South, back in the dust."

I gave him an incredulous eyeball-roll, which seemed to provoke him. "You're not old enough to remember the Depression," I said. "Don't even try that shit."

"But I'm depressed, and that means qualified."

"You're aimless, not depressed," I said. "You and your clan wouldn't work jobs if your lives depended on it."

"We need to get drunk again."

From beneath our bridge we have a highway and partial skyline view. At night I watch the tops of corporate skyscrapers, these American Gaudi spires. I'm beginning to love it here, or the thrill of nonconformity this place affords; I'm a computer slave no longer. I scribble little bits of poetry to pass the time, to keep my senses sharp. My editor has high hopes for this story, a national community service prize from the Journalism Society of American Letters. That's what you call pressure when you haven't written one coherent sentence.

"Participatory journalism gets the judges every time—hits them right in the heart," the editor, Tom Dunwoody, told me last month. That was back in the brainstorming stage, both of us seated with page designers around a boardroom table of Japanese driftwood. "Get out there and get dirty, Fiasco."

That's my pseudonym on this assignment: Fiasco Verde. We thought it best to keep me incognito, especially in the trenches where I could get arrested. No need to have my real name volleyed among cops. Incarceration is good for story but not career.

The bums don't know it but I'm doing them a favor. The reading public will see they are true people, not scavenging animals. I feel like Batman, sent to rectify the injustices that befall our city's shadow people, these lazy can-shaking bastards.

I take that back. Some are actually more crazy than lazy. The narcotic dragon has its claws in others, its tongue licking their desperate, withered necks.

These guys, it must be said, are skilled aggressors—not felonious criminals, per se, but persuasive, persistent money zombies. They have adapted to this life. They don't mind their grimy fingernails, their body odor like rotten pumpkins. Many millions in tax dollars have funded gleaming, tucked-away new shelters, but the homeless loathe them because they too closely resemble homes.

Imagine that.

"You like paying for empty shelters, being raped by the city like that?" editor Tom asked me. That's where the story idea was born—my rankled, frugal editor's distaste for ballooning property taxes. The camping under bridges was my call.

"No, sir."

"Then keep that feeling close to heart when you're in the field."

I stopped taking notes, slugged some espresso. "No disrespect," I said, "but shouldn't I go in with an open mind?"

Editor Tom folded his hands, rested his chin on the tangle of knuckles. "This isn't a feature story on frilly cupcakes. This is purpose-driven. This type of stuff can legitimize a start-up magazine."

"Okay," I said. "Got it."

So now I tolerate the Mad Bear Cub's piss. Wafts of it creep like sick ghosts across my pile of blankets; the stench meanders through the streets and literally turns tourists in the opposite direction.

In many ways the Cub is a child. In many other ways he is the truth. He has nicknames for his friends, these wayside stragglers caught in our underground filthpool. I'll get to them in a minute. No hurry. Bums under bridges aren't going anywhere. A ship of fools hath few pressing appointments.

I left my wallet and all other belongings above ground, where my baby son waits and my wife worries about me. Don't own my house but I pay all the rent, so everything in there's logically mine, in theory. Here I own a K-Mart sleeping bag, blankets, five-pounds of trail mix and the gallon jug I fill with water-fountain filthdrink. The Mad Bear Cub is my family now, my surrogate filthfather, my fascinating lab creature, my guide. I'm absolutely getting to the bottom of this shit.

About the friends:

They drift and flow like plastic on the ocean. No daily objectives but sleep, shade, and wine. The one they call Bowlman is hilarious. He earned the name by drinking—constantly and awkwardly—from this prized little bowl, which he called "The Chalice of Champions." When he's high on wine, a sad distance overtakes his blue eyes: the thousand-yard stare. He spins the type of stories that would get him institutionalized in most corporate settings. "I *mean* it," Bowlman said the other night, "the mayor is a bona fide pimp."

In cahoots with Bowlman is a friendly but temperamental cat they call Rocks. There's another one I've personally nicknamed the Blond Asher, because he constantly smokes his long street butts and, in the most perplexing of underground miracles, keeps his hair fluffy and clean. All three of them drifted here from St. Louis in various other decades, attracted by mild winters and rumors of lax enforcement when it comes to panhandling ordinances.

Bingo.

The Mad Bear Cub is convinced he's the shadow oracle, the ringleader, although he physically takes us nowhere and is more useful as comic relief. He keeps up with baseball standings by way of discarded newspapers. He was ribbing Rocks yesterday about the Cardinals' shitty season, about the seven-game lead the Braves hold over the Phillies. Rocks snatched him by his throat and lifted him off the ground, Darth Vader-style, immediately the stuff of underground legend.

"I said to hell with the goddamn Braves," Rocks shouted, rush-hour traffic bending the bridgework overhead. "You want me to put your body where they won't find it? You *want* me to?"

I worry what might happen should Rocks discover my true identity, how I'm gainfully employed by *Big Peach Magazine*, how I'm documenting the ramblings of Bowlman and others in secret notebooks. The Cub was perceptive enough to catch me writing, to coax the truth from me when I was tattered on rum that first night. I'd brought one bottle of Pirate Joe's—a last-minute buy at the Costa Rican duty free shop on my honeymoon last year—to break the ice. The rum made me a celebrity with these guys, and they fascinated me from the get-go. The ripped Union Bay jeans and dirty flannel I've worn for *twelve* days now squelched their suspicions, right off the bat. The clothing was an uninformed guess on my part, but I fit in perfectly. Amazing how you can just waltz right into depravity; amazing how hard it is to climb out.

I've started talking bum, too. A lot of ain't no and wasn't none and absolutely no mention of current television programs.

"No damn way you'll drink that old-ass wine," I might say.

"Think I might could," the Cub returns, and he might does.

The one nobody trusts is called Nasty. In a rage last summer, he actually broke Bowlman's bowl, smashed it on the interstate for no reason. I can't begin to guess where the "Nasty" moniker came from, and he won't divulge its origins. His narratives rival the Cub's, which earns him points, but I can't shake the feeling that Nasty could thrust a blade into my guts He's capable of thieving my trail mix and tossing my carcass on the interstate. We keep our eyes on Nasty, which isn't difficult because he's goddamn six feet eight inches tall.

The editor demands daily updates. So I have to sneak off and risk blowing my cover to use the last active payphone in northern Georgia. The secret quarters I keep stashed in my boots are swiftly dwindling.

"It's coming together," I told editor Tom yesterday. "You don't get this kind of dirt from spokespeople."

"Have you infiltrated a shelter yet?"

"I don't know," I said, "I'm not convinced that's the real story here."

"You know the assignment," editor Tom huffed.

"Yeah," I said. "I do."

The last bum of consequence is Captain Smooth, an adherent to the Cub but chief rival of Nasty. Rumor has it the Captain holds a law degree and once advised the children of civil rights leaders. His calculative walk and articulate retellings of history have scored him the most complimentary of monikers, but he's a background player. He never takes his sunglasses off. He breaks a basic tenet of bumming—Steal For Thy Self—when he filches wine and feeds it to the Cub.

"Fuel for comedy," Captain Smooth explained to me Tuesday. "We need that here."

By the second Thursday I don't know what I've gotten myself into, what these journal scribbles mean: "City of gaps, city of maddening vehicle rivers, city of craftsman porches, city of scabby wildlife." Everybody's expecting me to reemerge from the experiment on Sunday. I have brunch reservations.

I use two of my remaining ten quarters to call my wife on Friday, to hear the chirpy babblings of my boy. I miss the kid something awful.

"He said his first word," she scolded me, none too happy with my participatory journalism ambitions. "You missed it. It'll never happen again."

"No!"

"Yeah, really."

"What was the word?"

"'Stupid,'" she said. "I swear to God he said 'stupid' yesterday."

"No!"

214

By Friday I've got a boy with dumb tendencies and a homeless, middle-aged role model who pisses his pants. I have a journal half-full of crap and just one more pound of trail mix. My favorite pen was stolen and now I'm writing in pencil, which I hate doing. Pencil feels so uncommitted, so tepid.

Friday nights under the bridge are festive. No one pays attention to calendars but there's something in the Friday air you can taste, the sweet sugar of workaday liberation. The guys reserve a bottle for the ritualistic discussions of Friday nights, these rhapsodies beside hard-charging interstate traffic. Midtown revelers jam the streets on Friday, get inebriated, and drop everything from menthol cigarettes to marijuana joints to good old paper money. Plus the weekend brings tourist hordes and their loose pockets. The Cub gets liquored up and basically attacks them, but it works sometimes. Nothing parts a tourist from his dollar like genuine fear for his life.

The Cub ignites a Coleman lantern, thieved from the back of a mini-van, the closest possible thing to a fire that won't get us tossed in the pokey. We pass a mag of acrid vodka. Its container is plastic and its label says vodka. I ask the group how they've gotten away with this life so long, being that living under bridges is technically illegal. Nasty's mean eyes squint at the probing question.

"A great line of mayors has been sympathetic to us, to our predecessors," Captain Smooth says. "Look around you. You've got drifters here from all over the States, from all over the *world*. There aren't many hazards. I knew a guy in Chicago who snuggled with a boiler beneath a factory, woke up with half his face burned off. Too damn cold outside. Up in D.C., they catch you bumming, they just starting whipping your ass, no questions asked. Long as you don't get stupid, start grabbing tits like the Cub here, you're going to be just fine."

The Cub chokes on a mouthful of vodka, spits what he can't swallow onto the lantern, as if trying to breathe a fireball. "I brush my teeth," he says. "I floss. I do everything society tells me but sleep in a bed and obey some mortgage." We all toast to that. "I'm the freest motherfucker in this country, and everyone up there, on the streets, in those towers, is jealous," the Cub continues. "I'm telling you the Depression, with the pioneers of bumming, isn't no different than the Recession. It's all about the underground kings and the dumb monkeys chasing fancy shit up above. Now tell me—who's happier?"

We high-five like schoolboys. All of us do, that is, but Nasty. He keeps looking at me. Bowlman and Rocks hug each other and have a quick, impromptu vodka-chugging contest. A tractor-trailer groans by on the interstate, a zippy Porsche Boxster swims the truck's wake, and the cars never end.

"What kind of name is 'Fiasco?'" says Nasty. "How'd you ever get a job with a bullshit name like that?"

The big guy has me on edge now. I analyze everything he said, wondering how much he knows. He looks downright ravenous, and there's no way a guy like me, five-foot nothing with an old golfer's body, could keep a charging Nasty at bay. I don't need him outing me on my second last night.

"You a Mexican?" Nasty probes further. "Name sounds pretty damn Mexican, and best I can tell, you're a skinny little white man."

"It's a code name," I smile. "I'm with the CIA...all you motherfuckers are under arrest."

The guys break out laughing, Nasty notwithstanding.

"I don't believe you," he says. "I don't believe a damn thing from your mouth."

My heart pounds and I'm desperate to change the subject. "Nasty, I can't help you then," I say, motioning for another vodka swig. Rocks scoots the bottle toward me and I clutch the neck. I pull a long, fiery mouthful before Bowlman wrenches the bottle from my hands and squirrels it away beside him. "My name's Fiasco and always has been," I say, grimacing. "What can I do to convince you?"

Nasty gets on all fours, pushes himself to his feet, his white curly hair nearly touching the ribs of our bridge. "Piss your pants," he says, his huge raunchy mouth bending into a smile. "Go on. Right now. Any guy named Fiasco is crazy enough to piss his pants, right in public."

"Hey, man," I say. "Let's be adults about this."

"We all do it," he says. "The Cub has a chronic problem doing it. I want you to piss your fucking pants, man."

"Now *that* would be a story," the Cub laughs.

"Story?" I say, winking discretely. "I'll do it—but I ain't *telling* nobody."

I have a flashback. Not to childhood like you might think, though I did piss my pants tons then, enough that my psychologist mom interviewed me three times—no, I flash back to college, to a night I reportedly spent at the Ballyhooed, the greatest defunct bar in the history of Athens, Georgia. It was the heart of football season, maybe November, and I'd been given an ultimatum by stadium security: leave or jail. I was aiming toward Broad Street but halftime tailgate parties got in the way; by the time I finally made the Bally I'd lost all enunciation capabilities and my chin dripped with chicken-wing gristle. I met my future wife in that condition. She offered to wipe my chin and I told her I loved her. Like the born nurturer she is, she found my pathetic state adorable, offered me a place to crash after I'd fallen asleep at the bar and nearly fought some Auburn fans who dropped ice down the ass of my pants. So back at my future wife's apartment her roommates had twenty people in town, which meant I had nowhere to sleep but my future wife's bed, which of course I soiled with hot piss at 3 a.m. She didn't wake up until daylight. She took a shower. When I woke up, I could hardly think, I was so embarrassed. I rolled the sheets into a damp ball and stuffed them under the bed, like that would solve things, and when I got home there was a note in the pocket of my jeans: DON'T WORRY. HAPPENS TO THE BEST. CALL ME SOMETIME (SOBER). JILL. The number was blurred with piss, unreadable, but I knew a friend of hers, who got us together the next weekend. I told her over dinner that pissing myself was *not* a chronic problem, just a freak childhood relapse. Jill had put it behind her. She thought it was neat that I studied journalism.

"Right here, Nasty, for you..." and I point to my thigh, pushing. A dark-blue trapezoid expands and festers to my knee, becomes this warm lagoon of bodily waste. It's the first time I've seen Nasty smile, and I like him better this way. The Captain falls off a bucket he's laughing so hard.

The Cub jumps up and down. "My God, I haven't seen that since San Francisco, some hippy trying to keep warm in '75," and he walks up next to my pants, pointing out the coves and tributaries of the shameful purge. I just sit there, awkward, as if exhibiting a new tattoo, or a scar. "This here's the craziest man under the bridge," the Cub says. "Can't say I *ever* pissed myself on purpose. This's one to tell the grandbabies."

In a few minutes the wetness cools but starts to itch and stink. "Give me the vodka, you bastards," I say. "Go make some money. I'm starving."

By Saturday evening the trail mix is gone and my hangover won't subside. It's worse than the unproductive sleeping day that followed the port-wine night. I've gotten what I came for here. All I can think about is the apple muffins and cheese grits and chorizo and cappuccino I'll be shoveling in my mouth at Java Café come morning. I wait for all the guys to gather and I tell them the lie.

"I'm walking to Decatur. Got a cousin over there. He'll hook me up with some food and drink, and I'll bring it back down here," I fib to them all. "You won't see me for a couple days, at least."

They hardly budge, lying instead like salted slugs. They drink from dirty water bottles and I see how selfish they are, how intensely they live for themselves. How in all six of their cases this is the consequence of giving up—not neurosis, not affliction, not hard-drug addiction. The bridge is a quitter's paradise. But I guess they're onto something. Sooner or later their livers will fail or their esophagi will wear away but until then they are drivers on their own midnight highways. They have no bosses. They take chances for a living, while, until this assignment, I can't say I'd really stuck my neck out for a decade. I got comfortable standing at the onramp, the cubicle, waiting for a ride that never came, writing features about frilly cupcakes. My jeans are filthy and the dust has finally collected in the corners of my mouth. I've never felt more acrid in my life, but I'm going to miss

218

them. Only the Mad Bear Cub gets off his blankets to walk me out from the bridge, to bid adieu on Baker Street.

We emerge to a sunny, hot day. I cram my blankets and the plastic trail-mix jug in a city trash barrel, journals in my back pocket. I shake the Cub's hand.

"When's your deadline?" he says. "Or are deadlines just in the movies?"

I laugh and look around, still paranoid of cops in the daylight. "Deadlines are absolutely real. Mine's coming up...Wednesday."

"You good to go? You get what you needed?"

"I'll be honest, Leonard," I say, "I don't know what the hell I'm going to do. I feel pretty good about having done it, having made it. I've got a boy at home, a few months old. One day I'll have to explain pissing my pants on purpose."

"Blame it on me."

"I will," I say. "Believe me, I will."

We shake hands once more, and I turn toward home. A few steps later I worry that he's following me, but I'm reticent to check. I'm wracked with guilt for thinking like that, but I don't want him knowing where I'm headed, not even the general direction of my neighborhood, because word could spread and the bums could hurl a rock in my window and make off with my food, my oil paintings, my kid. I clutch my face, rub my eyes, and turn around.

The Mad Bear Cub is gone.

Also by Parkgate Press (Dionysus Books)

www.mattfullerty.com

THE KNIGHT OF NEW ORLEANS
The Pride and the Sorrow of Paul Morphy

A quiet boy is born in New Orleans with a spellbinding gift: he can beat anyone at chess. But what happens when love, desire and ambition intervene?

THE MURDERESS AND THE HANGMAN
A Novel of Criminal Minds

The story of female killer Kate Webster, the man who hanged her and the missing head found 132 years later in Sir David Attenborough's garden.

Author's Note

A debt to: my family, every one of them; my mother, specifically; my wife, certainly; my lunatic friends, every one of them, too; my impeccable mentors; the rambunctious juvenile metropolis; my wonderful little girl; the bastards who called me a fool.

About the Author

Josh Green's work has appeared in The Los Angeles Review, The Baltimore Review, Atlanta magazine, Creative Loafing (Atlanta), Indianapolis Monthly, Ascent, New South, Lake Effect, and many other venues. By day, he's a freelance magazine writer and award-winning crime reporter with a metro Atlanta newspaper. He lives in the city, with his wife and daughter, and is at work on his first novel.

This title is coming soon as an ebook from Parkgate Digital.